"I HAVE TO WORK SOLO BECAUSE FOR ME THERE HAS TO BE A RISK. THIS ISN'T BECAUSE I LIKE CHEAP THRILLS BUT BECAUSE I NEED THE STIMULATION OF CONSTANT HAZARD TO WHIP UP THE NERVES AND GALVANIZE THE ORGANISM TO THE PITCH WHERE I CAN DO THINGS I COULDN'T DO OTHERWISE. IF I HAD TO RELY ON OTHER PEOPLE TO KEEP ME ALIVE I'D GET SLOPPY AND MAKE MISTAKES AND THAT CAN BE FATAL. . . ."

That's Quiller talking—but now Quiller was more alone than even he wanted to be . . . unable to tell friend from enemy . . . unable to believe his superiors any more than his quarry . . . and knowing only that he was trapped in an assignment where dead men refused to stay in the grave, and live killers were everywhere. . . .

"Fast-paced, hard-hitting and surprising . . . in the tradition of such other Quiller classics as *The Quiller Memorandum* and *The Striker Portfolio*."
—*Chattanooga Free Press*

The Mandarin Cypher

ADAM HALL

A DELL BOOK

For Joan and John Terry

Published by
DELL PUBLISHING CO., INC.
1 Dag Hammarskjold Plaza
New York, N.Y. 10017

Dell ® 681510, Dell Publishing Co., Inc.
Reprinted by arrangement with
Doubleday & Company, Inc.
Printed in the United States of America
First Dell Printing—December 1976

Contents

1

Mandarin

It was three in the morning when she phoned me and I went straight round there through the pelting rain and found North slumped in a chair looking like death.

"What happened?"

He didn't answer. I don't think he heard.

Connie said: "Thank God you're here," and got some brandy and put it into tumblers, shivering, only a thin dressing gown round her shoulders, hair all over the place and her big eyes frightened. The rain hit the windowsills in sharp taps, like someone typing.

"It's okay now," I told North, but he sat staring up at me with his face appalled, as if I'd told him Big Ben had just fallen over; but his pupils looked normal, he didn't look doped and he certainly wasn't drunk. Connie brought one of the tumblers for me, chipped round the rim, and I held it for him. "Come on, slosh this stuff down, you're ten drinks short." But he wouldn't take it, didn't seem to catch on to anything I was saying.

I didn't know him very well: he was one of the new ones, said to be brilliant, specialized in the documentation snatch, knew his Kremlin, had a lot of Slav languages. The one obvious thing about him at the moment was that he was recently back from a mission.

"When did he get here?"

"About an hour ago."

He was still fully dressed, his wet mac thrown over a chair near the door. People came to this place to have a drink and go to bed with Connie and he hadn't done either. He just sat there looking totally blank, his tie pulled loose and blood on his knuckles.

"What happened?" I asked her again.

"Nothing, really."

"Well how did he get like this? Was anyone else here?"

"No. He was hitting things," she said irrelevantly, "punching the wall and—"

"What's he been talking about?" I put it as just another quick question so that she wouldn't think it was significant. The thing was that when a man came back from a mission a bit broken up he was liable to talk too much and blow the whole works.

"He said something about 'nearly crashing,' and 'ten-tenths shit across the airport,' things like that, nothing that made any sense."

I remembered she thought he was an airline pilot: we always have to make something up. It doesn't matter which girl we're with, they never know who we are. Nobody does.

"Did anything in particular start him off?"

"Not that I can remember. He came in looking sort of done up, and wouldn't have a drink, and wouldn't say what was the matter. Then he slowly went wild." She drank some more brandy and choked on it a little. "I've got to be up at six, you know—can you take him away so I can get some sleep?"

I watched North for a bit. He was looking more settled now, with a strange half-smile on his face as if he'd quietly come round to thinking that the only thing to do was laugh the whole thing off. The smile didn't look very good because he was still white to the gills.

"You'll be okay now," I told him, and looked round for the phone.

"Can I use this?"

She nodded and I picked up the receiver while North pulled himself out of the chair and said "Excuse me," and went quietly off to the bathroom and shut the door and blew his brains out, by the sound of it.

Connie screamed just once and I got across the room very fast and tried the bathroom door and found it locked and took three paces back and then went at it, going in with a lot of momentum left, with the door stopping halfway because he was on the floor. Then I came back and told her not to go in there, and picked up the receiver from where it had dropped, and dialled the number.

"North has just killed himself and there's been a lot of noise, so we'll need smoke out."

I gave them the address.

Connie was hunched on the floor, shivering badly, couldn't take any more. "Christ, what a night," I said. "D'you think you could get us some nice hot coffee?" Give her something to do.

Five minutes later I saw a black sedan pulling in to the kerb three floors below and I thought that was pretty fast, even for the Bureau, but they were people in uniform getting out, so I supposed one of the neighbours had called emergency when they'd heard the gun go off: if he'd been punching the wall there wouldn't have been much sleep for anyone, and the bang in the bathroom had been the last straw.

"In there," I told the sergeant. He must have come up the stairs two at a time, quicker than the lift, because he just nodded and blew out a lot of breath and went over and pushed the door open. Then he came back and asked if he could make a phone call and I said yes.

There was a nice smell of coffee now and I could hear Connie getting through a lot of Kleenex in the kitchen. She'd called out once—"Why did he have to come and do it *here?*"—which I suppose was a healthy sign.

Johnson got here next, looking very compact and noncommittal, taking a look in the bathroom. The sergeant had his notebook out, and started with me.

"Will you give me your name and address?"

"No," Johnson said as he came back from the bathroom, and pulled out his wallet and showed the sergeant his identity and then told me to clear out.

Connie was in the kitchen doorway holding a green plastic tray with two cups on it, looking at Johnson and wondering who he was. I called out good night to her and opened the door as Johnson said: "Look, Sergeant, I'm going to call my chief, then we'll work out the best way to handle this. There's no immediate need for an amb—" then I shut the door and went down the three flights slowly, pressing the time button to put the lights on, nearly walking into someone.

"What's the trouble?" A man in pyjamas, red-eyed from sleep.

"Just a family row."

The September rain was soft and fresh-smelling as I crossed the pavement and got into the car. Connie wasn't one of my girls, though I'd met her once or twice and I

was on the list of names she had to call if any kind of
trouble came up. Of course we can make what friends we
like, unless there's an actual directive warning us off, and
that only happens if by sheer chance we've taken a fancy
to someone with a job in a foreign embassy or with their
name on the books as a security risk. All the same, the
Bureau tries to steer a few girls our way, clerks and secre-
taries working somewhere along Whitehall or across at the
Foreign Office, civil servants with a known background.
One of our people—I think it was Carslake—said it was
the best-run call-girl system in the whole of London, and a
director heard him and got him hauled up on high, because the Bureau is terribly sensitive about things like that.

I went along there now, turning through Hyde Park
with the rain hitting the windscreen and slowing the
wipers. Except for the fact that we worked for the same
outfit, I had nothing to do with North and he had nothing
to do with me, but some of his misery had rubbed off and
I knew I wouldn't sleep if I went back to the flat, and anyway we all seem to gravitate to that dreary bloody building whenever there's trouble. Comfort in numbers, I suppose, when the nerves start playing up.

There wasn't anyone in Field Briefing or the canteen at
this time of night. Signals was in full operation because of
the Irish thing but I couldn't talk to anyone in there,
they'd throw me out. I found Dewhurst wandering about
morosely on the first floor.

"When did North get back?" I asked him.

"Who?"

"North."

I took off my trench coat and shook some of the rain
off it.

"Two days ago." He looked at me in the bleak electric
light, trying to see if I'd heard the news.

"I was there," I said.

"Where?"

"In Connie's place."

"Oh my God, were you?" He dug his hands into his
pockets and stood with his shoulders hunched. "All I know
is he got out of Lubyanka about a week ago and came in
by plane through Antwerp. Next thing I heard he was
picked up in St. George's psychiatric department. How the
hell did he manage to fetch up round at Connie's?"

We were standing outside Monitoring, and there was some stuff coming through on the short wave, something about street fighting breaking out again in Cyprus, and Dewhurst wandered off and I went with him, wanting to hear more about North, if he knew anything, like scratching a sore. Since last week I'd been on a ten-day call, which meant two things: they had a mission lined up for me and at any next minute they were going to shove it in my hands and tell me to get on with it. And when you're on a ten-day call your nerves are quite tender enough without some poor bastard like North blowing his head off right in front of you.

It was like scratching a sore because there wasn't any need for me to know any more about North. On the shadow-executive level we work in totally separate fields and there's just no connection.

"How long had he been there?" I asked Dewhurst.

"Where?"

"Lubyanka."

"Oh, I dunno, really."

Lubyanka is the place you're sent to if you're picked up on the wrong side of the Curtain and they specialize in implemented interrogation and if you can ever get out of there alive then you'll finish up like North. There wasn't anything more I wanted to know about him—the whole thing had suddenly turned my stomach sour. We were standing by the stairhead now, with the open space between the flights running from the top of the building to the bottom like a vertical tunnel, the low-wattage bulbs throwing a depressing yellow light through the rows of bannisters, Dewhurst quietly watching me.

"You're on call, aren't you?"

"Yes," I said.

"Well, I wouldn't let a little thing like this put you off your stroke. He simply didn't have what it takes, that's all."

He wandered off to see if there were any more signals for him, and I stayed where I was for a minute, looking into the shadows of the stairwell and thinking it wasn't the sort of epitaph we'd ever want to be landed with ... *he simply didn't have what it takes.* ... We'll fight like hell to go out respectably when the crunch comes and the last gate slams, *then tell us who your contacts are*, the bright lamp burning into your eyes and the bruises throbbing, *I've told you already I haven't got any contacts on this operation*, the nightstick again on flesh already aching for peace, *but you were seen using a letter drop*, the big white light coming through your eyelids and into your head and burning there, *you mistook me for someone else*, the stick or the flame or the jerk of the current or whatever it was they were using, *tell us*, using so expertly, *there's nothing*, their foul breath heavy and excited, *tell!* the light in your head, *screw yourself!* and reason beginning to go, *tell us!* the jerk of their hands, *no!* Always the answer, the same answer, for as long as you can—*No! No! No!* Till it's over.

Not because of any loyalty to the Bureau, nothing like that, because by this time you're quite beyond any thoughts of alma mater and the team spirit and whatnot, all you're trying to do is get yourself a half-decent epitaph out of sheer stinking pride, *deceased during mission*, nothing spectacular, *found with security intact*, just something we can live with in the last few minutes before we die. Unlike that poor little bastard we hope to prove to the clerks and the accountants and the operations staff and the whole bloody bunch in this building that when the crunch came and the last gate slammed we'd got ... after all ... what it took.

I went down the stairs—this place gave you the creeps at night—shrugging my wet mac on, passing one of the briefing staff in a lower corridor.

"Hello Quiller, what are you doing here?"

"None of your bloody business."

It occurred to me, driving back to Knightsbridge through the rain, that I could be entirely wrong about this: maybe North *hadn't* told them anything in Lubyanka, maybe he'd stood up to it and got out clean and then just couldn't stand the reaction, gone a bit too far. There must have been something still left in him even in the last few minutes of his life, because he'd made an attempt to explain his misery to Connie in terms of his cover: "nearly crashed," and something about fog across the airport. That hadn't been easy to do and he'd done it so maybe they'd chalk up something decent for him as an official epitaph, better than the one Dewhurst had given him.

Not that we'd ever hear of him again. Outside the hermetically sealed circle of his immediate contacts—his briefing officer, mission controller and director in the field—there wouldn't be any enquiry. After tonight, along those warrenlike corridors of that anonymous building in Whitehall where no one officially exists even when they're alive, there'd be no questions asked, and the name of North would never be mentioned again. In the Bureau, death is a disease with no complications.

The call came through over the weekend and I ducked down the steps below the leaky guttering and got into the car, every bloody window misted up, had to find the cloth and even then it wasn't much better, the rain drumming on the metal roof and the street lamps just coming on as I drove through the park. Well over the limit and one eye on the mirror, no real hurry but this was the sixth day of the ten-day call and that meant they'd set it up for me in record time: someone had been on the blower or there'd been a bunch of signals in and Parkis or Mildmay or Kinloch had looked at the picture again and said all right, tell him to come in.

No real hurry but it'd been nearly two months since I'd done a mission and I'd forgotten how it affected the nerves when the call came through, nothing to show, just an eyelid flickering, a tendency to keep the foot down through the park, that sort of thing, because we'd made it the last time and the time before that and it had brought us closer to the time when for one reason or another a wheel was going to come off and our name, along those quiet and echoless corridors, would never be spoken again. Nothing to show, just an eyelid flickering and the sudden awareness of a composite personality—"we," "us," "our," because the shadow executive, creeping alone through the maze where his work has led him, cat-nerved and ferret-quick, sniffing the damp and the dark and ready to run, ready to kill, comes inevitably to know the plurality of the creature that lives alone and close to death, the mind busy with logic, talking to itself and reasoning the way ahead while the flesh chills and the body pleads for life, go back, go back while there's time, and the psyche calls for courage, go on, go on while we can, calling sometimes for more than that, for everything, banners raised and bugles sounding, *forward my friend* to a fool's death and cheap at the price, out of pride.

Lights flashing, hemming me in. Black plastic waterproof over his uniform.

"Can I see your licence, please?"

"All right."

A temptation to flash the worn leather holder with the card framed in it, the one that would get me through almost any door, 10 Downing Street or New Scotland Yard or Chequers, but you had to justify it later in debriefing and the Bureau was fussy about it, take your head off at the neck while you weren't even looking.

"D'you know what speed you were doing over the last mile?"

"Flying too low, was I?"

Worse for him than for me, he was getting soaked out there, serve him bloody well right, he should've joined the Navy.

There was a parking slot open for me in the yard behind the Bureau: they always see to little things like that when you're on call and in a way it's infuriating because you're always trying to catch them out and you never can. I slopped up the worn steps, one shoe leaking, and pushed the door open, nothing on it, no name or number or brass plate or even *Keep Out*—nothing at all and therefore perfectly appropriate to the business this building housed. At this hour there were quite a few people about but the corridors were almost as quiet as they'd been the other night when I'd talked to Dewhurst by the stairs. The Bureau is a government department but officially it doesn't exist, and this nihilistic status has long ago cast a sort of creeping blight over the people who work here. Most of us don't even know each other even by our code names because we're a shifting population of rootless souls and our business is our own business and we're not interested in anyone else's.

Sometimes one of the directors will put a team together, an active unit with field discretion on explosives, and drop them into whatever banana republic or emergent nation is playing with the matches; but most of the active staff are shadow executives, single-objective people with very specific orders: *Peking has appointed a new military attaché in Sumatra, go and vet him; Cuba has just put a unit of*

*combat troops under secret training, go and get pictures;
there's a member of the Secretariat on his way to the border in Berlin, go and help him across.*

Exchange of vital information takes place between missions behind closed doors. Friendships aren't discouraged:
there isn't any need, because we're dedicated professionals
and all we'd want to talk about is our work and that'd
bore the bejesus out of us because a lot of the work is a
strain and all we want to do between missions is try to forget it.

"He's along at the Lab," Tilson said.

"Who is?"

"Egerton." He watched me with his pink and amiable
face, tapping his fingertips lightly together.

Not Parkis, then, or Mildmay or Kinloch. Egerton. It's
like pulling a name from a hat: you never know who
you're going to get the next time out.

"Where is it?"

"Where's what, old horse?"

The little bastard watched me amiably. He knew what I
meant but he was playing hard to get, so I took a shoe off,
the one that was leaking, and let the water out all over his
nice parquet floor.

"Where's he sending me?"

I was showing my nerves, because Egerton would tell
me quick enough where he was sending me, but I wanted
to know *now*. The minute you're called in for a mission
you become desperate to know everything—whether
you're going to freeze to death in Moscow or fry in Casa-
blanca, whether it's a penetration job or a snatch or a radio tap, who's to direct you in the field and who's going to
try getting you out if you come a mucker—you want to
know *everything* and you want to know it as soon as you
come in, because, I suppose, the more you know about
something the less you're afraid of it.

"No earthly idea, old horse."

So I put my shoe back on and did up the soggy lace
and told Tilson he could screw himself and he said thank
you very much and I went along to the stairs and down
two flights and right to the end of the corridor. The red
lamp over the door went out before I reached it: that
would be Tilson, told them I was on my way. I went in.

Shaded lights and a workbench and radio gear and a

screen and some chairs and a long table where Egerton
was sitting, one thin leg dangling. He didn't look up. One
of the other people switched the red lamp on again and
the man with the headphones adjusted the volume.

You'd have to give me longer than that.

How much longer?

I don't know. I'd have to think.

Egerton looked up.

"Is this the third cycle?"

"Fourth, sir."

"Can we have isolations?"

The man with the headphones put the tape on fast-for-
ward and stopped and corrected, I assumed the thing was
a voice spectrograph.

I ...I ...I ...I ...

Am . . . Am . . . Am . . . Am . . .

Afraid . . . Afraid . . . Afraid . . . Afraid . . .

So . . . So . . . So . . . So . . .

Idiom all right but an Englishman wouldn't say "I am
afraid," he'd say "I'm afraid," it didn't sound like a
speech, more like an intimate conversation.

"How many have we done?" Egerton asked.

"Seventy-four, sir."

"You mean altogether?"

"Well, the whole series of matching spectrograms, and
then the fixed contexts. We did the randoms yesterday."

Egerton sat like a quiet thin-legged bird on the edge of
the table, looking at nothing, saying nothing, until after
half a minute the man behind me gave a little embarrassed
cough and in the silence I heard the cloth of his sleeve
rustling as he moved his arm, fingering his hair back,
probably not used to Egerton's holy silences.

"What?"

"I didn't say anything, sir."

"Ah yes." He got off the table. "Yes, well, that's fine.
Do those again, will you, and double-check?"

The man with the headphones took them off slowly.
"The whole seventy-four?"

"Yes. And let me have the report from Williams."

Somebody whispered oh Jesus and flipped a switch
rather sharply but Egerton didn't seem to notice anything
because he wanted the whole seventy-four comparisons
done again so they were going to have to do the whole

seventy-four comparisons again and that was the only thing that had the slightest interest for him.

"Did you want to see me, Quiller?"

"I'm called in."

He'd taken to wearing glasses recently and his dull brown eyes wandered around the edge of my face as if he were trying to find the middle.

"Oh yes. Why don't we go upstairs?"

In the corridor I asked: "What were the voice prints?"

"Ah. Well, they'll be working on those."

So I shut up and we took the main stairs because the lift in this building gets jammed between floors twice a week and we just can't afford the time.

Egerton had possibly been an owl in a previous life because he'd picked a room on the top floor and turned it into a sort of nest, lined comfortably with maps and books and posters of Edwardian bicycle advertisements, furnishing the rest of it with cherished objects—a skull, an abacus, a bulb horn, that kind of thing—possibly flying through the small high dormer window with them in the dead of night.

"Make yourself at home," he said, and draped his body behind the desk like a pile of bones. "When did you get back?"

"Where from?"

"Cyprus, wasn't it?"

"I haven't been out," I said slowly, "for close on two months."

He reached over and dropped a folder onto his desk and said absolutely nothing for three minutes. I threw my trench coat across the fireguard he used in winter and sat down on the Louis Quinze chair that years ago had been filled with stuffing. The phone rang and Egerton answered it.

"Well?"

There were streaks of rain on the window and the glow from the street sent their shadows trickling on Egerton's face as if he were quietly crying, and it suited him, I thought. They said his wife had committed suicide at some boardinghouse on the south coast not so long ago; but nobody knew if he was miserable because she'd done it or if she'd done it because he was miserable.

"Has Mildmay seen him yet?"

I could hear Tilson's voice from the receiver, so they were talking about Styles, just in from Ankara, a sticky debriefing session because we all knew that Styles was in it for the money and one fine day the Rusks or the Turks or the Arabs were going to make him an offer he couldn't refuse and he'd blow the whole network if they didn't watch out.

"Not in my opinion."

Or he'd be found floating.

"I can't see him at the moment, I'm sorry."

He put the phone down and looked at the stuff in the folder again and sat back and said: "There's nothing concrete yet." He expected me to say something, so I didn't. "Things are a little confused over there."

"Over—"

"In Peking." He folded his thin raw hands, studying the scars of the winter's chilblains for a moment. "Have you been briefed on China?"

I got off the Louis Quinze chair and he looked up in surprise and I said: "I haven't had a mission for two months and they put me on a ten-day call and brought me in after six days and nobody's told me a bloody thing except that Tilson says you're my Control."

He gave me a bleak smile.

"I know how you feel." He didn't.

"Look," I said, "have you got a mission for me?"

"Oh yes."

I hadn't expected that. I sat down again, and a thought came at a tangent: the second voice on that tape, the one with the right idiom and the wrong tone, *I am afraid so*, could possibly be an educated Chinese.

"The problem," Egerton said apologetically, "is that they got the timing wrong. It wasn't their fault." He checked a sheet in the folder, looking down through the lower lenses of his glasses and trying to get used to the focus. "We were all ready to send you in, and now we're not." He shut the folder and slid it to one side.

"Oh for Christ's sake."

I got up again and squished around in my leaky shoe.

"Not, anyway," he said, "for a few days."

"A few *days?*"

He looked surprised.

"Yes."

The thing is that after two months you get the feeling you'll never be able to do it again unless you can do it soon, and it brings the nerves to the boil. I thought he'd meant weeks, not days.

"Look, if it's Peking—*is* it Peking?"

"Yes."

"If it's Peking, why don't you put me into Hong Kong, so I can wait for the signal?"

He looked up sharply. "Why Hong Kong?"

"Well, I'd be right on the doorstep." Even to get out of London would be something, I'd at least be on my way. He was thinking it over so I sat down again and caught a spring of that bloody Louis Quinze right on the buttock.

"Bring me the blue file," he told someone on the phone, and put it down and looked at me and said: "Frankly I'd rather you waited here. We're expecting signals."

He could switch them to Hong Kong, it was a Crown Colony, but it wasn't my job to remind him of that. A woman came in, brogues and a bun and a whiff of carbolic, typical Bureau staff, and left a blue file on Egerton's desk, and then of course I realized why he'd popped a tuck when I'd suggested Hong Kong: it looked as though they had something running there and he was wondering how I knew.

NIAVONVW.

He brooded over the folder, slipping one sheet out at a time and craning his neck instead of moving it nearer, he ought to have those things changed, the tears running down his long thin face while the rain pattered at the window. I wouldn't mind, once I could get him off the pot. Once I'd elbowed him into putting me out there I wouldn't mind having him as my London Control. He was a miserable sod and overcautious (he'd brought Walsh back from Beirut a month ago just because they'd busted a cypher), but he wouldn't ever make the kind of mistake that would leave you without a chance.

NIBVCNVW?

You don't see with your eyes, you see with your brain, and while I was thinking about Egerton there was peripheral cerebration going on, trying to read the name on the folder, typed in capitals and upside down from where I was sitting. I gave it my full attention.

MANDARIN.

His thin raw hands moved softly, shifting the papers, the hands of a priest performing the last rites.

"No," he said slowly. "We could use you there for a day or two, but I don't want to take the risk." He put the last sheet back into the folder and closed it and pushed it to the end of his desk. "As soon as the signals come in, you can take the first plane after all."

I drew a steady breath. "What risk?"

"Well, communications, really. I don't care to switch signals. The risk of *delay*, really."

I took another slow breath and let a couple of seconds go by, because if you try jumping Egerton he shuts like a clam.

"Be a delay anyway, wouldn't there? What's Hong Kong—twenty-four hours?"

"A little more than that, I rather think."

He phoned again and put the receiver back and took his glasses off and pinched the bridge of his nose.

"We'd save that much," I said.

She came in again and he gave her the file.

"Did you want to see Colonel Fraser, Mr. Egerton?"

"Not particularly."

"He's waiting."

"Oh is he?" He put his glasses on again. "All right, I'll be along in a moment."

She went out and I didn't say anything because he might still be thinking over what I'd said, about saving at least twenty-four hours if I went right away.

"It would mean helping us out a little," he said, looking into the middle distance.

"I wouldn't mind that," I said.

Like trying to get a bird to eat out of your hand.

"It's just a routine investigation." A bleak smile. "Not quite your field."

"That'd be okay. Just for a few days."

He got his long thin legs together and stood up and wandered about for a bit, finally stopping and gazing quietly at a young lady in knickerbockers holding her very own new bicycle.

"Well perhaps we could, yes, fit you in."

Gotcha.

2

Cypher

I was still hanging around at midnight waiting for someone to take me in Field Briefing, bangers and mash in the
canteen when I finally got fed up, then back to square
one, thinking I might have been a bloody lemon after all
if this was the way they were going to play it.

There was a lot on, of course, and not all of it overseas.
Those bastards had put one in St. Paul's, nobody hurt, a
small one or not very efficient, but that wasn't their fault,
then one of the staff at the Palace had found something
rigged up in the kitchens, God knows how they'd got it in
there through doubled security. Lawson was in charge of
the main counter-terrorist unit and somebody had heard
him say if he actually caught one of them at it he'd spear
the bastard bodily on the railings outside the Tower and
the thing we all knew about Lawson was that he'd probably do it.

Signals was hard at it and all you could see were trays
of tea going in, but then Signals was always manned, even
when most of the other sections were shut down. There
must be a whole unit going out, for Field Briefing to keep
me hanging around like this. I didn't check with the upstairs people to see if Egerton had changed his mind, because he would have got a message to me: he had good
manners, whatever else.

"Quiller?"

"Don't tell me."

"Macklin's ready for you."

I was in Monitoring, military communiqué from Cyprus
Radio, air attacks increasing around Nicosia while the Security Council issued further appeals for a cease-fire, the
old 1974 lark all over again, couldn't care less. Field
Briefing was the next floor up and I began hurrying and
then remembered this wasn't really the outset of a mission,

I was going to have to piddle about in Hong Kong for a while, looking at all the postcards. Well I'd asked for it.

Macklin was buried in a filing cabinet and poked his head out and told me to sit down. Tilson had gone off hours ago and we were alone, with the bright fluorescent light tubes buzzing in the ceiling and Macklin's ashtray thick with dog ends. He came over, giving the metal drawer exactly the correct amount of push so that as he sat down opposite me it rolled shut behind him with a click.

"Not really your kind of operation."

"It's just something to do out there while I'm waiting."

"Yes, Egerton mentioned."

He was sorting out the material, one glass eye gazing slightly off centre, the hard fluorescent light discolouring the scar so that it looked even deeper than it was. He'd been running an escape chain and got his minefields mixed up on the chart near Helligenstadt, three months of plastic surgery so he wouldn't frighten the children any more, then he'd opted for an office job, lucky to get it.

"There's not much," he said, and slid the file across the desk to me, never handed things to people if he could avoid it, still had the shakes. "You'd better curl up with it and give me a prod when you're ready."

One of his phones was ringing and he answered it and I opened the folder and went through the stuff: George Henry Tewson, 43, five foot so forth, several pictures, last seen alive July 22, Tai Tam Bay, Hong Kong. Three local fishermen (named: see Coroner's Report) saw him lose his balance in the boat and go overboard, "a big fish tugging at his line." According to several other witnesses, disturbance in water indicative of shark attack. Remains never found, but wallet and some papers washed up on Turtle Cove Beach, unmistakably identified, confirmed by wife.

"I can't help that," Macklin was saying on the phone, "the whole unit has to get airborne at the same time. Do without the navigator if you have to, and find a pilot who knows his maps."

It occurred to me that it was a bit odd giving me a briefing officer like Macklin to spell out this little job I was going to do for Egerton, strictly a gumshoe number. Maybe he was just filling in for someone, as I was.

Nora Millicent Tewson, née Harmer, now legally desig-

nated widow, still in Hong Kong, now resident. Present
address—

"Listen," I said, "I can read the rest of this stuff on the
plane."

"What plane?"

"That's what I mean, there could be an early flight."

His glass eye looked at me dully, slightly off centre. I
remembered it was the left one you had to look at.

"What's the rush?"

"I can't stand this interminable bloody rain."

He gave a sudden lopsided laugh and the scar went
pink.

"Can't ever wait, can you—"

"Listen, I've been out for two months—"

"Shagging yourself to a standstill—"

"Oh balls, listen, fill me in, will you, give me the main
outline."

He flipped a switch and said: "How soon can you put a
man in Hong Kong?"

They said they'd call him back.

He looked at me again. "We just want to know a bit
more about what happened to Tewson. On the face of it
everything seems to be quite okay: he and his wife were
on a package-tour holiday, the third time they'd been to
Hong Kong in three years, and he went in for sport fishing. It's shark water and that kind of accident sometimes
happens if they don't lash themselves to the boat. All the
same, we've had a request to check on it and make quite
sure it *was* an accident."

I didn't ask who'd requested it. After a few years at the
Bureau you learn the language, and in Field Briefing their
job is to tell you everything you ought to know and if they
seem to be leaving a few things out you don't ask questions because it'd just be a waste of time. The mission con-
trollers work on the principle that if you know too much
it'll get in your way. Some of the crudest operations, like
busting an opposition cell or getting a man across a fron-
tier, can carry the most complex political significance: you
can be quietly picking the lock of a dispatch case in an
embassy in Zagreb without the slightest knowledge that the
imminent East-West summit depends on whether you get it
open or not; and the people who structure policy feel that

if you realized your responsibility you'd probably break the hairpin.

We don't argue. At times this sort of built-in reticence can be a bloody nuisance but in the long run they're probably right.

"What did Tewson do?"

"Isn't it in the file?" Macklin asked.

"No." I'd read that far.

He gave a shrug, spreading his hands. So there it was again, and I shut up.

"Mrs. Tewson is under—" Then a buzzer went and he opened the circuit. "Yes?"

"Travel."

"Right."

"Depart Heathrow 04:10 by BEA, arrive Rome 06:35. Depart Rome 08:22 by BOAC, arrive Bangkok 05:27 following day. Depart Bangkok 06:15 by China Airlines, arrive Hong Kong 10:18 London time, 18:18 local time."

Macklin said all right and cut the switch and I looked at my watch. It wouldn't exactly be cutting it fine but I didn't have to stroll.

"Can I do it that way?"

"If you can get cleared in time."

I spun the file around so it faced his way and he opened it and started flipping through the stuff but I could see he wasn't having to read any of it and I noted this.

"Mrs. Tewson is still very cut up, started drinking now and then—"

"Has our lot talked to her?"

"No. But we've had her under surveillance, just routine—name of our man is Flower. Specific—"

"Who?"

"Flower. Specific instructions: share the surveillance, advise and control Flower. Report at discretion, treat as highest priority, preserve all cover, utmost care in approaching Hong Kong Police Department or Special Branch: certain officers suspected of links with Communist China. You can use—"

"Are they satisfied it was an accident?"

"The enquiries are closed. Coroner's verdict misadventure."

"Any valid suspicions of foul play?"

"None whatsoever."

Of course I could have read all this for myself on the plane but he knew what I wanted: the bare bones of the thing so that I could put any relevant questions on the spot. You can't get cleared satisfactorily until you know what you're going into.

He still wasn't having to read anything, just the odd heading to jog his memory: he knew this material pretty thoroughly and I thought again about that. An executive of Macklin's status and experience shouldn't be handling a minor operation like this one, wouldn't have enough time to give to it. The top briefing officers at the Bureau don't work regular hours: they won't even show up unless there's a big mission breaking, but once they show up they won't go home again till the whole show's ready to run. To look at him I would have said Macklin had been working twenty-four hours at a stretch and he could have gone home and left a second-stringer to brief me on this squib-sized assignment. He hadn't.

With Egerton it was different: he was a top controller but would handle anything that came along, up to half a dozen operations unless there was something really critical on the board.

"You can use a safe house," Macklin said, "if you need one."

I didn't ask him where. It would be in the material.

"There's a local contact?"

"At the safe house."

"What's his rating?"

"Total reliability but not well informed. He's all right on topography, of course—he's been there fifteen years."

"Can I have something again, Macklin? Something in specific instructions."

He went back to page two, the paper making a soft scuffing tattoo until he pressed his hand against the desk.

"Report at discretion, treat as highest priority, preserve all cover"—but his eyes weren't moving quite as fast as he was meant to be reading—"utmost care in approaching—"

"Fine, that's what I thought you said."

What the bloody hell did they mean, highest priority?

"Signals through the Admiralty, and you'd better pick up a cypher."

"Fair enough."

It was no good asking him. And no good asking Egerton—who'd probably gone home by this time, past midnight. Macklin was a top briefer and shouldn't be handling this one and they'd used the very circumspect phrase "highest priority" for a distinctly low-key operation but there was a plane for me, take off in four hours from now, get out of London and head for Hong Kong and stand by for Egerton's signal, the real one that'd trigger the mission he'd got lined up for me, so don't start asking silly questions or they'd say we thought you were keen on going, well you don't *have* to, be doing it on my own doorstep.

"Fair enough," I said again and got up.

"You'll be briefed on Mandarin when you get out there."

"That's the big one?"

"Yes."

"Who's going to be my director in the field?"

"We don't know."

"Oh come on, Macklin—"

"Really," he said. "We'll probably fly someone in from Peking."

Oh will you, I thought. There was only one place in Peking where they could get me a director and that was the Embassy, so they must have a man in place, narrowed it down a bit, I could even find out for myself if I got my phone numbers right. It was very important and normally it's one of the first things you're told, because you can refuse any given director if you don't feel you can work with him: your life's usually involved and you can get someone like Loman, brilliant but desperate for personal kudos, talk you into a suicide bid if it'll get him a medal, it wasn't his fault I'd come out of Tunis alive; or someone like Thornton, totally dependable, pull you out of the gates of hell if he can get there in time, but short on Rusk-think patterns and mission sense and therefore dangerous; you can refuse anyone they want to give you and you don't even have to say why. Otherwise I suppose the insurance company would never stand for it.

Macklin was stifling a yawn, getting another cigarette. I said:

"Been pushing you, have they?"

"I've done my bit today, old boy."

"Off home now?"

"You bet."

I said give my love to Marcia; that was his wife.

The security guard used his key and took me in.

"All right Sam," she told him.

The guard went out, snap-locking the door.

"Long time," she said.

"Too long."

She spun the combination, her back to me, touching a hand to her greying hair, waiting for the timer to stop. The auto-destruct warning buzzed and she threw the tumblers, starting on the second combination.

"What was your last one?"

"Third series, seventh."

The door of the safe swung open and she brought a single sheet across to the table, a Xerox copy in a plastic cover. There were only three cyphers currently available, which explained why Macklin had been working the clock round: there must be some special units overseas, probably Cyprus.

"What's this one?"

"Just come up."

"Gor blimey."

It was replacing a whole series. The Bureau hang on to their pet numbers till they're too dog-eared to use, so it could only mean this series had been busted somewhere out there where the signals were hot, and I just hoped it hadn't blown anyone through the roof.

"Fancy," I said.

The thing was built up with extended-phase digits, sometimes three or four to a numeral, with reverse transfers and the alert provided by omissions in the blanks: you just left out the space between any two phrases and "forgot" to reverse.

"Have they got someone new?"

"It's Mr. Hanbury," she said rather sharply. We're never terribly impressed with the stuff they give us and it makes them touchy.

I said I'd take it and she picked out a box, small, flat, waterproof, fireproof, neutral grey.

"Any acid," she said, "but it takes thirty seconds."

"All right." If I worked at it I could probably wipe it out in Rome.

There wasn't anyone in Accounts till someone shot in

from next door: it's common knowledge that anyone holding up a shadow executive on his way through clearance
gets taken to bits and sold as Meccano.

"Sorry, sir."

"Hell d'you think this place is—M.I.5?"

I filled in the form: *Nothing of value, no next of kin,
no messages.* T.C.'s for five hundred pounds, a Barclay-
card, two hundred in cash, it seemed a lot for the Hong
Kong end but maybe it'd have to finance Mandarin as
well.

"You can obtain local currency anywhere, sir, day or
night."

"Fair enough. Can I have the rates?"

He gave me the booklet and I put it into the briefcase
with the rest of the stuff.

In Firearms they were well on the ball: there'd been a
rush on from the mob Macklin had sent out, pack enough
submachine guns on board and you have to leave the navigator behind.

Weapons drawn: none. I'm rather a disappointment to
them: they're always wanting people to try out the latest
models for them.

Capsules drawn: none.

He'd got them ready in his hand but put them away
again in the locked drawer when he saw what I'd entered.
They never know what we're going to do and sometimes
we don't know ourselves: it depends on so many things:
what field you're going into, who your director is, what
degree of risk, what info memorized, so forth. Also it's a
peculiarly personal thing and involves much more than
just life and death: it raises issues like motivation, the will,
the threshold of pain, the question of identity itself, what
is this thing that's screaming like this and can it remain
whole, can it retain command of whatever it is? I used to
take capsules with me in the early days but after they'd
roughed me up in Leningrad and again in Cairo I realized
cyanide wasn't the answer because pain carries its own
anaesthetic if you can hold on for the first few stages and
they can't get anything out of you if you're unconscious or
a gibbering idiot and they know that—or at least the professionals do, and they're the people we're usually up
against.

Another thing is that if they find a capsule on you they

assume you must have some pretty interesting stories to tell, so they go to work intensively.

All I needed from Travel was the air ticket.

"Are you the one for Hong Kong?"

"Yes." I put it into my wallet. "What about China?"

"Taiwan?"

"The mainland."

He went over to the files and checked and came back.

"Are you detailed for Mandarin?"

"Yes."

"They'll fix you up in H.K. There's no regular visa—you'll be processed by the Secretary for Chinese Affairs."

Even if Field Briefing could have taken me earlier I would have had to hang around for Credentials because they'd produced the complete works, covering me for Mandarin as well as the Hong Kong thing.

"Never thought we'd get through in time."

Marge was the only one at the Bureau who could make you look round, not that it was saying a lot, china-blue eyes and a big blond wig and so much eye shadow it looked like sunglasses, but the thing about Marge was that if you came back after a year's absence she'd say hello you've changed your parting. She's gone now, seduced by the totally counterfeit charisma of M.I.5.

She had everything laid in a row along the counter, and I began on the left while she perched on her high stool like a life-size doll and watched me. Passport: Clive Wing, border frankings mostly European but two for Bangkok and one for Japan. General cover: coin dealer, member of the British Numismatic Association, agents in Holland and Switzerland, specializing in Mexican and Austrian gold pieces, centennial medallions and high-value government proof sets, sole representative for Mendoza S.A. of Buenos Aires, investment brokers. A name like Wing was to be expected: perfectly acceptable English surname but could also be Chinese on a written document in the absence of other identification.

Driving licence, membership card of the B.N.A., letter of introduction to three leading coin and bullion brokers in Victoria and Kowloon from Mendoza S.A., latest issue of *Coin Quarterly*.

"When did you lose the other one?" asked Marge.

"Other what?" I signed for receipt of documents and started shuffling the stuff into my briefcase.

"You had a beautiful blue Parker."

"Behave yourself, Marge, you don't have to advertise."

She swung her legs and giggled and I went out and that was the last I ever saw of her; there's a typical number in there now, lisle stockings and a slight moustache.

It was still pouring with rain and the wipers had a hard job coping with it on the way back to the flat. I changed my wet sock and put some clothes in a bag and looked at my watch and thought no and then yes, picking up the phone and taking the risk that she'd mind being woken up at this hour, *burr-burr,* there wouldn't be time to go round there even if she were alone, *burr-burr,* she wouldn't be at the Connaught or anywhere because she had to be on the set at seven tomorrow, *burr-burr,* unless she'd been *hello?* Sleep still in her voice, a soft laugh, of course she didn't mind, long eyes and copper hair and the way she turned her head, my God are you off again? The whole of London suddenly full of Moira and not far away, no, I said, there's only just time to get the plane, New York, she hated quickies, she wanted everything and champagne afterwards, when will you be back, not long, I told her, not long. Goodbye.

Or maybe never, which of course was why I'd had to ring her, taking out insurance on the risk that one day soon I might get in so deep that I couldn't get out, or cross their sights and not have time to hear the hum, and go down wishing, in the confusion of rage and fright and refusal to believe, wishing I'd at least picked up a phone and said goodbye. They say you always think of your mother but I don't remember mine, but my God, I know when it comes I'm going to remember Moira.

At two-thirty the phone rang.

"Yes?"

"D'you want some transport, old horse?"

Tilson was back: he was admin. and worked shifts.

"I'll take the Jag."

"Want it picked up?"

"If you will."

"Okay. Take care."

The line clicked, severing the last connection, and I went downstairs and threw the bag in the car.

The place was like a morgue, only seven flights on the board and one man with a mop trying to get some of the floor dry before the next coach came in: there was a blocked drain outside and the pavement was flooded.

"Rome."

"Yes, sir."

There was no delay on the screen printout.

"What time was this booked, can you tell me?"

He tore the perforation and used a stapler. "You mean when was the reservation actually made?"

"Right."

He checked his books. "Five P.M. yesterday, sir."

"Thank you."

Oh that bastard Egerton.

On the way to the waiting area I saw a man who reminded me of someone, pale face and a kind of lost expression, couldn't think who, then I remembered: North, getting up so quietly like that, excuse me. They do it so often in bathrooms, I suppose because it's messy. I put a cheque into the Interflora box and a message, twelve red roses, *Cheer up, Connie, life goes on.*

A high faint whistling from beyond the roof and a sudden rush of lights. An entire Italian family in the waiting area, electing their next president, their hands presenting inarguable arguments in the air.

Taxiing to the end of the runway I got out my homework, committing the thing to memory: the extended-phase digits were in groups of vowels, labial consonants, labial and dental, so forth, and I ran off *cheer ... up ... connie ...* and *eger-ton ... you ... bas-tard ...* and reversed the transfers, forgetting the alert mechanism and having to look. This one wasn't going to be too easy, old Hanbury had done his nut.

Getting the green from the tower: the brakes came off and my spine began pressing into the seat. Reverse transfer and regroup, try again. But I couldn't concentrate because a top man like Macklin doesn't normally handle a low-key operation and they'd used "highest priority" in terms of cover security in a routine enquiry into an accidental death and now I'd got him: Egerton had booked me out to Hong Kong a full hour before I'd bust a gut persuading him to send me there.

Jets roaring, the shoulders pressed hard to the seat.

So I wasn't just helping them out and I wasn't going to hang around looking at the postcards till they switched the signals from Peking and triggered the real one for me, the big one. It was already running: Mandarin.

3

Contact

"*Fettuccine.*"

"*Si, signore.*"

While I was eating it I reversed ten transfers, switched all groups at random and dropped the alert in every time without making a mistake, running off *rome air-port 07:45 who the hell is tew-son and why wont they tell me*. Then I reached for the vinegar and leaked some into the little flat box and watched the plastic card slowly dissolve. She was dead right: it took a good thirty seconds, not exactly the kind of trick you'd want to leave till the last minute if you found yourself in a shut-ended situation. Most people keep the key on them throughout the whole mission unless they run into problems: it's as tough as a credit card and you can take it through fire and water and it won't break unless you actually stand it on edge at a bus stop but I like to get rid of it early—it gives me the creeps because if they *do* happen to get to you before you can stop them, they can begin reading your signals and sending stuff back and you won't necessarily live to know you've blown the whole operation.

Si pregano i passeggieri per Bangkok di recarsi all'entrata d'imbarco numero uno.

Final check for messages. Negative.

Bangkok and the heat of a humid noon burnishing the gilded cupolas; palms and tamarinds and somewhere in the reek of kerosene a hint of sandalwood. Inside the building a bunch of people, mainly Japanese, were crowding the Royal Bank of Thailand counter: that would be the *devaluazione monetaria* featured in *La Strada*.

Nothing on the message board for Clive Wing.

There was a twenty-minute delay on the screen at China Airlines and I asked about it and they said the plane had come in late from Tokyo avoiding a typhoon that was now moving northeastwards towards Korea, so I had time to walk around, stiff as a board after twenty-one hours up there and already feeling the disorientation as the metabolism struggled to adjust, the windows full of jade and teak and silk, the smell of incense and a display of gold pieces on black velvet and a board showing the world market: *Mexico 50 Pesos 1.21 tr. oz. US$242 Bid, $249 Asked, Austria 100 Corona .980 tr. oz. US$190 Bid, $197 Asked*, the only two that interested me, the prices much lower than in London or New York.

Will passengers for Hong Kong please go to Gate No. 1.

12:25 and the air steamy across the tarmac, *tso sun, tso sun*, music tinkling from the speakers, no smoking, seat belts, so forth, the thing was he probably thought I'd blow up in his face if all they'd had for me was a routine investigation into Tewson's death and he was absolutely right, I would have. So he'd had to catch me softlee, softlee, and not the first time, it was Egerton's speciality, and I would have walked out on him flat at London Airport the minute I knew about the reservation, except for two possibilities: either George Henry Tewson was a topkick in some kind of specialized field or this operation was just too sticky or tricky or hair-trigger sensitive for anyone else to want to take on. He could have gone right through the list without getting a bite—because we can refuse a mission and there's nothing they can do about it—so he'd come down to the one man who might conceivably be persuaded, the one who'd been out of ops for nearly two months and was ready to take anything, *anything*, so long as they wrapped it up to look fancy.

Silk and small hands, a cherry-red mouth.

"Would you like some tea?"

18:40 and a cloth of gold flung across the window where I sat, the humped green hills of two hundred islands growing night-black before their time as the day lingered along the Tropic of Cancer, *we hope that you enjoyed your flight*, a rhythmic vibration setting in and the weight coming off the seat, *and will fly with us again on China Airlines*, fishing junks below on the flat gold water, sam-

pans and a submarine and the chalk-white wake of a hy-
drofoil as it settled to the surface, in from Macao.

"Will you be staying long in Hong Kong?"

"It depends on what business I find."

"Oh yes, you told me—you deal in coins."

"Coins and bullion, they're the best hedge against infla-
tion."

"Ah yes." He unclipped his seat belt, smiling. "In Tokyo
we put our faith in transistors."

The white Tiger Balm pagoda across the window, and
Victoria Peak, then boats coming past in a swinging blur
as we flattened along the approach path, tankers,
freighters, two destroyers of the U.S. Seventh Fleet and a
group of junks from Canton with the Chinese Communist
yellow-starred flag and then the sub again, "S" class with
the Union Jack, *belts until the plane has come to a stop*,
the hollow roar as the jets reversed and then the unaccus-
tomed silence as the power came off, leaving conversations
suddenly exposed.

*... but heroin's their worst problem, even the school
kids have started using it. ...*

*... they're not really poor, darling, I think they just like
living on boats. ...*

*... the prettiest girls in Asia, Joe, and I'm not kid-
ding. ...*

Warmth underfoot across the tarmac and the air
clammy against the face, the end of a long day's heat, the
sinuous flicker of her cheongsam ahead of us as she led
the way against the frieze of ponderously moving shapes,
Swissair, Lufthansa, TWA, and beyond them a curtain of
jewels across the harbour as the island began burning in
the dusk.

"Taxi?"

"Cathay Hotel."

"Take ferry?"

"No, tunnel."

The Cathay because in the dossier of Nora Millicent
Tewson her present address was given as 403 Jade Imperial Mansion, ten minutes' walk away. Besides, if I
chose anything more than seventy dollars a day those ar-
thritic old tarts in Accounts would bust a corset.

The place was near Cat Street and there was a boy outside roasting a duck over charcoal, with a woman already waiting. The clatter of a mahjong game sounded from a doorway farther along, where a letter writer sat with an upturned keg for her table.

I passed the shop twice, wanting to familiarize myself with its environs, and then went in. The place was full of snakes, a hundred of them; I can't stand the bloody things.

"Mr. Kwan?"

"No, Younger Born. I am Mr. Chiang."

He came out from behind his jars of snakes and stood with his hands together, short and at first glance fat, then if you looked again, muscular.

"Will it rain, Mr. Chiang?"

"It has rained."

"Will the typhoon come?"

"It has gone."

"How many brothers have you?"

"Seven."

"And sisters?"

"Seven thousand."

"What is the goose?"

"It is gold."

I showed him the scar under my wrist and he nodded, going to the door of the shop and closing it and coming back. The sizzling of the duck was no longer audible but the clack of the mahjong pieces came faintly through the walls.

"Don't these bloody things ever get out?"

"They have no wish. They are fat now, and ready soon to hibernate. That is when the price will be high."

"I'm happy for you."

He led me through the bead curtain and up some pitch-dark stairs to a room under the roof, the air heady with herbs. There was dust everywhere from the sacks filling the shelves, except on the radio, which was as clean as if he polished it every day.

"What are your main stations, Mr. Chiang?"

"Peking and of course Taipei."

"The Embassies?"

"Your Embassy in Peking, your Consulate in Taipei." He went over to the set, soft-footed and eager to please. "You wish to make contact?"

"Not now."

He was disappointed, stepping back but still looking at the set as if it had suddenly stopped working.

"When did you come to Hong Kong?"

He swung his large head to look at me. "A long time ago."

"From the mainland?"

He looked away, and in a moment went down the steep flight of stairs ahead of me, his stubby hand on the rail. "Yes, from the mainland. We swam across Deep Bay one night. But I reached the shore alone."

"Who was with you?"

"My wife."

One of the snakes rose heavily as our shadows passed over it, and spiralled round the big glass jar; I could hear the dry scuffing sound of its skin as it moved. Mr. Chiang stood with his short black shoes neatly together.

"That is all?"

"Yes, Elder Born."

He unbolted the door and I left him. The duck was done but the boy and the woman were arguing about the price. On the other side from where the letter writer sat there was a jeweller's and I went in and asked if I could use the phone. Mr. Chiang's number was among those I'd memorized from the briefing material and I dialled it.

"*Wai?*"

"*Lee seen-saang hai-shue ma?*"

"*Nee-shue mo yan sing Lee.*"

"*Doei m-jue. Ngaw daap chaw seen.*"

I hung up and put a dollar on the counter but the girl shook her head so I circumspectly picked it up and thanked her and turned left outside the jeweller's so as not to pass the snake shop again. When London sets up a safe house abroad it doesn't fool around, because the whole mission can sometimes be thrown in jeopardy by an unreliable contact and of course blown up if he's a double and they know that, they've known it for so long that a lot of us still survive. It was just a reflex that made me do it and anyway it wasn't conclusive because if he'd wanted to phone anyone to say that Wing had arrived in Hong Kong he needn't have done it within three minutes of my leaving the place: but that was when he'd be most *likely* to do it. I'd lowered my voice and all he knew was that one of the thirty thousand foreign devils in Hong Kong speaking atrocious Cantonese had got the wrong number.

And all I knew was that for a period of ten seconds during the critical three minutes when he'd been most likely to inform a contact that Clive Wing had arrived on the island his phone had been innocently disengaged. Most of us work on the principle that if you've got the time and the chance to check every step of the way, it's worth doing. It's a bore checking the ignition wires for tampering every time you get back into your car after you've had to leave it in a suspect area and I must have done it a couple of hundred times, including the time in Calcutta when I found they'd rigged a bomb.

I picked up a dark-blue Capri from Fleetway Rent-a-Car in Watson Road and took it past the Cathay and found some shadow where the trees in the park hid some of the light from the lamps. Jade Imperial Mansion was one block distant and I went there on foot and saw him sitting in a Hillman with the visor down but I didn't stop because this was completely unknown territory and I needed to feel my way in.

I didn't stop at the board in the lobby either because there were people about and I noted them. There was enough light on the board to confirm in passing that 403 was on the fourth floor and I took the lift to the top and went down seven floors by the emergency-exit stairs, finding the back entrance and going through the service complex and coming out by the park and getting into the Capri, putting the window up to leave a reflection and checking the time, 8:44. The parking slot for 403 was on the far side of the building but there was only one exit and at 9:21 I heard the Hillman start up and a minute later the Jensen came through the gates and turned west and then north and then west again into Gloucester Road and we were in business, the traffic fairly thin because most people were in the theatres and restaurants and supper clubs at this hour and the only one I didn't like was the Taiwan-registered Toyota and I took a right and a left and a left and came up on the lights at red and watched him go past, no reaction whatsoever, too far behind the Hillman to be tagging that, but it had been worth the risk of losing the Jensen and having to find it again because the opposition-in-place in whatever city are very watchful and you can pick up ticks just by stopping to tie your shoelace.

In six blocks I came up on the Hillman again and this time overtook it, slotting in behind the Jensen and noting the ash-blond Peter Pan head that never turned to look sideways, the occasional glint of emerald below her ear, the way her eyes flicked obliquely upwards at the mirror and down again, once the flash of a gold lighter, her movements deft and her driving calculated as we ran into Harcourt Road and bore left along Cotton Tree Drive. At the next set of lights I went past her and got a clear visual impression in profile, thin, bony, rat-faced attractive, her head not turning, the flash of an emerald ring as she used the ashtray, then I was past and put three private cars and a taxi between us before I peeled off and made a U turn and came back to wait.

Flower should have been on to me by now but he was looking straight ahead as he cleared the lights and I made the turn and fell in two cars behind, beginning to worry because he'd looked so young: the top security departments were taking them straight out of school these days and letting them loose too soon.

A right into Garden Road and past the Hilton and left again and slowing, taking the smaller streets: she knew her way and didn't hesitate, any more than Nora Millicent Tewson ever hesitated, I was beginning to think, about anything.

The Hillman tried to stop in time to pull in somewhere behind her when she began slowing but there wasn't enough room so he went on past and left her looking for a slot. I backed up and couldn't find one and put the Capri under a *Strictly No Parking* sign and found cover and waited. There were a few people about and Flower wasn't far behind her when she came into view and crossed the road and went into the Orient Club. I gave it ten minutes and followed.

"You are a member, sir?"

All smiles but standing right in my path.

"No."

"Would you care to take out a membership?"

"Please."

He went on talking while I signed the form, nothing

more than a formality of course, police regulations, licenced as a private club, many apologies for the necessity, so forth, one hundred Hong Kong dollars.

Imperceptibly he had moved out of my path as I reached for my wallet, and I was ushered between heavy curtains into the traditional ambience of incense and candlelight, not a large place but pretty full, the tables mostly in alcoves, the waitresses Eurasian and topless, the men mostly in white suits and D.J.'s, the women discreetly glittering, some of them wives. Imported floor show, Edwardian vaudeville, half a dozen long-legged girls kicking their net stockings out, those were the days and all that.

They got me a table and I began working, picked her out over there near the band, still alone at a table for three, watching the floor show, smoking, smoking rather hard and sometimes looking around, the earrings catching the light, not looking for anyone, but at them. Flower was nowhere near her but perched at the far end of the bar looking bored. When I was sure I asked for a telephone and a girl came and plugged one in.

"Directory Enquiry—can I help you?"

"Please. I'd like the Orient Club."

"Which club?"

"The Orient."

"Just a moment."

Across in the alcove she was lighting another cigarette, looking up, looking around, but not at people coming in through the curtains: she wasn't waiting for anyone. They were bringing her first drink, no cherries or anything fancy for Nora Tewson: it looked like straight scotch.

Enquiry gave me the number and I dialled.

She began on the drink straightaway. She's still very cut up, Macklin had told me.

"Orient Club."

"I'd like to speak to Mr. Flower."

Had to repeat it, then had to spell it.

"He is a member?"

"Yes." He'd come straight in.

It wasn't the kind of place where you went up to lonely-looking women and asked them for a dance but someone was doing it, an elderly and elegant Chinese. She was shaking her head a little too emphatically and he took a step back, bowing quickly, dissembling. I suppose he'd

thought that by her looks she had more breeding, not a
very good judge.

"Mister Fowler not here, sir."

So I spelt it again and said he should be there because
he'd asked me to telephone him. There were probably a
hundred people here, a lot of them on the small dance
floor now the girls were taking a break, and they didn't
want to go and look; I quite saw their point. In five
minutes they got him, and the bartender showed him the
phone in the corner, just inside the curtains.

"Hello?"

"I'm from London," I said. "I came in on Flight fifty-
three."

The code introduction for the first to the fifteenth was
to throw in a random number and listen for two below
and four above, world-wide, all missions, it saved trouble.

"That's how we missed each other," he said. "I was on
three seven."

He was turning round slightly, just enough to keep his
eye on Nora Tewson. I asked him:

"When did they start the tag?"

He turned his back on the room again, blocking his free
ear because of the band.

"When did they what?"

I suppose he wanted it straight from the book: maybe
he was college-trained, Norfolk. "When did the subject
come under opposition surveillance?"

He didn't say anything for a bit and I began getting
worried because it wasn't possible for me to tell whether
he couldn't hear properly or whether he was having to
think something out. There wasn't anything for him to
think out: I'd asked him a perfectly simple question.

"D'you mean," he said, "she's being—"

"Don't look round."

I said it sharply because he'd begun turning his head the
other way and for a second I didn't believe it. He turned
back to face the wall and I hoped he'd begun sweating as
hard as I was. In a minute I said:

"You mean you didn't know?"

There was a short silence, then he said: "Oh shit . . ."

It was about all he could say because he was obviously
straight out of training so they'd given him the simplest
job on the list and London had sent him a top-ranking

shadow executive all the way to Hong Kong to tell him he'd mucked it up. I felt for the poor little bastard but that wasn't the point, he was dangerous.

I looked for a waitress and let my eyes pass across the table for two on the far side from the bar. The man hadn't moved. He glanced at the Tewson woman every five seconds, away to the dance floor, back to the woman, every five seconds, police-trained, possibly Special Branch, but Macklin had told me the enquiry into Tewson's death had been closed. I was waiting for him to look across, just once, at Flower. He was the thin tubercular Chinese with glasses I'd noted in the lobby of Jade Imperial Mansion and again in the four-door Honda that had been three cars behind Flower when we'd turned into Gloucester Road and again when I'd been waiting in cover across the street from here.

"Shut up," I told Flower. He was trying to talk.

I gave it another full minute. The man was like a robot, every five seconds and never varying, never interested in anyone else, *never looking at Flower,* a professional amateur with precise instructions—*don't let her out of your sight*—and doing his job to the letter.

"Flower."

"Yes, sir?"

"You're off the hook. They haven't seen you."

He said bitterly: "That isn't my fault."

Give him credit at least for knowing what he'd done. But he'd been lucky and that was what made it potentially dangerous: if that little police-trained robot had got on to him he wouldn't have stood a chance—they could have roped him in and put him under intensive questioning and blown his cover, *finis.* Worse, they could have tagged him to any rendezvous that he and I might have made, putting surveillance on me and forcing me to show my hand by throwing them off. Of course there were built-in fail-safe factors and even if they'd caught him and put him under the lamp he couldn't have exposed the Bureau or anything to do with it because he'd never been there; they don't let a raw recruit go anywhere near the place till he's proved he's safe. And I hadn't on principle gone near him myself when I'd seen him stationed outside Jade Imperial, any more than I'd gone near him when I'd come in here. But it doesn't matter how hard you try to keep the safety mecha-

nism operative: you can make a mistake or have some bad
luck and then all you need is someone like Flower and the
whole thing's going to blow.

"Are you here in the club?" Flower was asking me.
He'd asked me before and I'd told him to shut up.

"Just keep on looking at the wall."

But I was ready to drop the receiver and put the phone
onto the banquette below the table level in case he took it
into his head to look round anyway, because with his lack
of experience I didn't want him to be able to recognize me
at any time or in any place until I was ready.

"All right Flower, I want a quick breakdown on her
travel pattern."

A couple of seconds went by and I wondered if he was
normally as slow as this or whether it was nerves. "She
goes quite a lot to jewellers and places like—"

"Which ones?"

"Erm—the House of Shen, that was this morning. And
a place called Constellation '144'—that's in—"

"Where else?"

"Kaiser's, and—I think that's all. She—"

"Does she always buy something?"

"You mean jewellery?"

"Yes—come on, Flower—"

"Well I can't be sure whether she—"

"Then you bloody well ought to be, they've got windows
haven't they? Where else does she go?"

He didn't get any faster but it was no good my taking
the pressure off because I wanted to know things, a whole
lot of things. This wasn't really my kind of operation,
Macklin had told me; he must have known I'd have
Flower to deal with.

"She's been to the Bayside Club, the Danshaku and
Gaddi's." He was speeding up a little now and by the way
he was standing I thought he'd got a notebook. "She's had
dinner twice at the Eagle's Nest—that's at the top of—"

"Hilton, right. Companions? Contacts?"

"You mean—"

"Who does she meet?"

"Oh. Nobody."

"Nobody at all?"

"Not that I've seen."

I was looking across at her. They had a can-can number

warming up on the floor and she was leaning back, one arm lying along the top of the banquette, her bare shoulders pale and luminous in the low-key light and her small head poised as she watched the dancers. I wasn't surprised the elegant Chinese had risked a snub by going over to speak to her, and not surprised he'd got it. From Flower's observations she was avoiding men, avoiding people altogether, still upset by Tewson's death two months ago but not wanting to wilt in her apartment. Maybe this was where they used to come together, here and the other places.

"What's her usual time pattern?"

"She never leaves her pad before ten or eleven A.M. and she's usually back before midnight, unless—"

"Away all day? Lunches out, dines out?"

"Yes, she never goes home before eleven or twelve, once she's left there in the morning. She—"

"You'd say she drifts around, spending money or window shopping, killing time, that kind of thing?"

"Yes sir, I'd say that. I—"

"Never takes a trip—"

"Only Kowloon—"

"Shopping again? Drifting?"

"Yes. Once she stayed overnight at—"

"Overnight?"

"Yes, last Sunday, at the Golden Sands Hotel."

A break in the pattern and I pressed him on this, did she stay there alone, meet anyone, talk to anyone in the lobby, in the bar? Not that he saw.

"What was her room number?"

"192." A notebook, yes.

Went on pressing him, time did she get there, time did she leave, got him to think up a few of the questions for himself before I had to ask, finally drained him dry on the routine stuff like where she bought her petrol, what hairdresser, she go to theatres, walk alone in the streets at night, ever take a taxi instead of the car, watching her from where I sat and trying to learn the things I couldn't see, the things I'd have to know to reduce the risk of losing her when I took over the tag for a stretch. Then I let him go.

"All right Flower, where are you based?"

"The Wanchai."

"Hotel?"

"More of a boardinghouse really."

He gave me the address and I said: "Listen, you're off duty from now on till I contact you, but you're on stand-by so don't leave your base at any time except between 15:00 and 16:00 hours on any day, repeat, fifteen and sixteen hundred *and at no other time*. Understood?"

"Understood, sir."

"Leave here now and don't look around."

"Where can I contact you if I have to?"

"You won't have to."

I hung up and put the phone onto the banquette and watched him pay his bill at the bar and go through the curtains. The thin Chinese with the glasses was watching Nora Tewson and nobody else and I relaxed.

"Change this for me will you? There's gin in it."

"I'm sorry, sir, I thought you asked for gin and tonic."

"No, Indian tonic."

"I'll fix it right away."

Eurasian with a United States accent out of Taiwan, they all ought to be like that instead of the ones we've got in Accounts. In three minutes she was back and in fifteen minutes I saw the Tewson woman ordering her third drink and I began working out what to do.

The George Henry Tewson dossier gave me quite a lot, from his schooldays on, through Cambridge but missing out his job, filling in relations, contacts, interests, addresses, vacation movements, the marriage of course, everything I'd need if I wanted to go across there and say well well well, long time no see, you're looking marvellous and tell me, how's old George these days; there was nothing she could do about it because I even knew his golf scores.

But it wasn't the way in, for a lot of reasons. London said they'd closed the enquiry into Tewson's death so the thin man over there shouldn't be Special Branch, and the police-trained thing didn't add up to a lot because most of the Asian cells used people from official departments and he could be anyone, anyone distinctly dangerous if I didn't wipe my feet.

Her waitress had reached the bar.

Of course he could be insurance because a couple of years ago Tewson had been overdue with his fees at the golf club and his Austin was three years old and they'd come out here on a package trip and by the way she was enjoying her widowhood he'd either carried heavy life assurance in the U.K. or had known how to use a piggy bank or had taken out a short-term big-figure policy here in Hong Kong, which might explain why the thin man was Chinese.

I didn't think he was insurance.

Her waitress was leaving the bar.

The long way in was to keep up the tag till I found out enough to signal London and ask for further briefing but that would take time and if Nora Tewson was the key figure in Mandarin they wouldn't want me to sit back: they'd pulled me in halfway through a ten-day call and pushed me onto a plane and that could have been partly because they couldn't get anyone else to take this one on but it could have been totally because they wanted me to go very fast now they'd lit the fuse.

The thin Chinese could be on the tag to see if she made any contact with anyone who knew George Henry Tewson or knew anything about his death or who *wanted* to know something about it: so the only foolproof way in that would be fast, effective and noncommittal was to make first contact as a complete stranger and in public, going in deliberately under the opposition surveillance and making it quite clear that I knew nothing at all about Tewson, Tewson's death or Tewson's wife.

I got up, timing it so that as her waitress reached the table I was there too, pressing my way through the people towards the dance floor and catching my foot on a chair leg. The whole tray went down with a crash, not just the glass, better than I'd expected.

4
Ming

I took it off the windscreen and got into the Capri, starting
up and moving off past the club, looking for the Jensen as
soon as I was round the corner. She'd put it neatly in between some railings and a sand bin alongside the garden
of someone's consulate: the flag over the building hung
like a rag in the humid air. There wasn't a parking slot
anywhere so I took one end of the chain off the post in
the side entrance to the consulate and ran the Capri in
there, a dozen yards or so from the Jensen and facing the
right way in case I couldn't make final contact with her
before she left the club.

Then I walked back round the corner and through the
ornate doors.

"The gentleman forgot something?"

"What? No, I was double-parked, that's all."

I went to the bar and took a stool at the end near the
heavy curtains: in this area there was no backwash of

light from the floor show and I could watch the Tewson woman and the Chinese couldn't watch me because the ceiling-high papier-mâché dragon was in the way.

"Indian tonic."

"Gin and tonic? Yes, sir—"

"No. Listen. In-di-an tonic."

"Excuse me."

"You're perfectly welcome."

From here I could see the magnum of Veuve Clicquot and the dozen gardenias on her table but couldn't at this distance tell whether she was pleased with them or not. The flying-tray trick hadn't gone down too well.

"Christ," she'd said, "did you have to do that?"

"I'm terribly sorry—"

"That's not the point—look at this!" Indicating her model lamé sheath, patches of scotch all over it, the waitress on all fours between us looking for the glass, Nora Tewson with her hands on the edge of the table as if she were going to make a speech because the banquette was behind her knees and she couldn't stand up straight without support, did I know how much this dress cost, couldn't I see where I was going, so forth. Really am very sorry, such an exquisite dress, be delighted to pay damages, so on, till she went off to "clean up," the waitress on her feet again, excited because it had broken the monotony and this called for a suitable tip, yes, fifty Hong Kong dollars and this hundred is for a magnum of champagne, look, let's go to the bar, I want it done before she comes back to her table.

The magnum hadn't been opened and she wasn't smelling the gardenias but I suppose she *could* have thrown the whole lot at the band.

"I s-say, d'you know those—those gairls have got holes in those—those net stockin's of theirs? Wha'?"

I looked at him.

"How can you tell?"

He gazed back at me, perched dead straight on his stool, knees gripping the sides, perfectly aware that in his present circumstances the C. of G. was critical. Expression of glazed outrage at my stupidity, white cavalry moustache bridling.

"Wha'—what erzackly does *that* mean—how can you *tell?*"

He turned his back on me and raised his pearl-finish opera glasses again after wiping the steam off the lenses. Half an hour later a Chinese chauffeur in white uniform came through the curtains and got him off the stool without a struggle and carried him out so cleverly that it looked as if he was walking.

An hour after that I saw her signing the bill and five minutes later as she came past the bar I was going across to the phone in the corner, my back to her.

"I must say you know how to apologize."

I swung round.

"Apolo—? Oh. The least I could do."

"It was handsome."

Tone much less sharp after four doubles: I'd been counting them. Now the brittleness had gone she looked defenceless but would obviously bite off the first hand that moved too quickly.

"I thought it best not to present it personally." Tone rueful, rueful smile: doormat, please wipe.

Her face went still and her eyes became fixed on me, the pupils big in the near-dark here by the curtains. She couldn't have looked like this at me, or any man, sober.

"Pity you didn't," she said.

Fair enough.

"May I see you home?"

Eyes thinking hard, still fixed on me, and I knew now why she'd bite if anyone got too near: for the same reason that any animal bites—because it's frightened.

"Yes."

"Thank you. I'm Clive Wing."

Her dark eyes stayed on me for another few seconds and then she turned her head away with a little jerk and I supposed that whatever the problem had been she'd made up her mind about it. It could have been the simple, the obvious: Tewson had died over two months ago and there'd had to come a time when she was ready to speak to men again and maybe it had come tonight.

Outside in the warmth of the night air she tried to light a cigarette and I said let me have that and took the magnum.

"I'm Nora Tewson," she said, and flicked the lighter shut as if making a point of it. We'd only moved a few paces from the doors and the Chinese came out too fast and saw us and tried to go back and realized he couldn't and went on past us, turning his head away to look up at the light across the acacia leaves, walking briskly towards the corner.

"The name rings a bell," I said.

"Does it? My car's down that way." We began walking. "How did you come here?"

"In a cab."

Because she wouldn't want to leave a brand-new Jensen lying around and I didn't want her to see the Capri. The only thing was that if I'd been driving I could have got rid of the tag, not overtly, just playing the lights and the traffic. But it might not be worth risking: of the half-dozen theories in my mind the one I liked best was that Tewson had been an agent in one of the London departments and he'd been knocked off by the opposition and his wife had been talked into a decoy operation, in which case the thin man might not be a tag but a bodyguard. That would explain her nerves.

"Beautiful job," I said.

"It was expensive," she said, and swung out past the sand bin, clearing it by a couple of inches. Her anxiety state was promoting a steady release of adrenaline, combatting the alcohol: the psyche was relaxed enough to let her forget her widowhood for the first time but her physical reactions were still good enough to drive this thing through the eye of a needle.

"Tewson," I said. "That's Tee-ee-double-yew, ess-oh-en?"

"How long have you been in Hong Kong?"

"I flew in this evening."

"Then you won't have heard the name."

"I was here a couple of months ago."

She gave a slight resigned shrug. "Then you've heard it."

The Honda swung into the chrome frame of the near-side wing mirror and stayed there until she turned off Gloucester Road and headed south. I counted five and the configuration moved into position again.

She drove as she'd driven before, her movements rhythmic and calculating, her eyes always straight ahead as if she had to stare something down, something in the future

that would rush on her into the present if she looked away
and dropped her guard.

When there'd been enough time for me to think back
and call it to mind I said: "There was some kind of fishing
accident, wasn't there?"

Pause.

"Yes."

"And you don't want to talk about it."

Pause.

"No."

The magnum was half empty.

"Why aren't you drinking any, Clive?"

"Too acid."

We were sitting on the thick Hangchow carpet and she
looked at me over her clasped knees.

"Are you trying to get me pissed?"

"You've been helping yourself."

She looked steadily at the magnum. "That's perfectly
true. God, this stuff goes right through you, doesn't it?"
she said, and went out for the third time. "Fix yourself
some scotch or whatever you want."

I looked around again. The overall picture was inconsis-
tent: Ming to the tune of ten or fifteen thousand pounds
and then a lacquer table you could pick up in Cat Street
for a song, and in between them a brand-new cocktail
cabinet with chrome bamboo-style legs imported from Bir-
mingham. A nouveau riche with condescending friends
who'd told her where to buy the Ming and hadn't been
looking when she'd done some shopping on her own. But
the total contents of this apartment would still pull in
close on fifty thousand even at an auction and the Tewson
dossier said they'd come here for the last two years on a
package tour.

No books, no pictures. No picture of George Henry
Tewson, even in the bedroom when she'd shown me
proudly round. The whole apartment was just an expensive waiting room.

"To tell you the truth," she said, coming back and
smoothing her *lamé* skirt, "I do want to talk about it."

"About what?"

" 'Member you said I didn't want to talk about it?"

"Oh yes."

"Well—" She tried to lift the magnum and I went to help her but she put it down again, shaking her head. "I'd better not, had I?"

"If you feel like it."

"Why shouldn't I?"

"I'll put you to bed."

"I bet you would!"

She giggled and looked away and that was when the shivering began, but I didn't think it was anything to do with sex, at least not directly. Freedom or something.

"I've just realized," she said with a gusty little laugh, "it wouldn't've been funny if this bloody great bottle had been on that tray, would it!"

She lit another cigarette, gold lighter, Dunhill. That would have been a present. This was where I could say well, go on, tell me what happened to him, and just conceivably blow the whole thing.

"How old are you, Nora?"

"Little me? Thirty-two. Why?"

"I'm a bad judge of people's ages."

"I wouldn't have thought," she said with the frank stare starting again, "you'd be a bad judge of anything."

No extramarital affairs, the dossier said, *so far as is ascertainable*. This explained her little Victorian innuendoes and frank stares and so forth. It could explain the shivering too.

"It's time you threw me out," I said, and got up reluctantly, and quickly she said:

"I was going to talk about it, wasn't I?"

"Oh yes."

"He was in the Ministry of Defence."

Oh was he.

There must have been a good reason why London had kept this one out of the briefing and out of the dossier and maybe it was on the principle of never telling the ferrets what they don't have to know or maybe it had been part of the softlee softlee catchee monkee approach by that devious bastard Egerton because he knows if he tried to sell me a conventional intelligence operation I'd only tell him to tuck it up his truss.

"Pretty important job," I told her and knew instantly I was right on the nail. It had been the only thing she'd ever

been able to say about George Henry Tewson: the Ministry of Defence, you know.

"Pretty important," she said, liking the phrase. "Well I
mean it was important that he *worked* there"—she un-
curled off the carpet and stood with her hands clasping her
bare arms, not quite sure where to go—"actually his *work*
wasn't important, to tell you the truth."

"As long as it was to him."

"Oh Christ," she said with a sour laugh, "it was all he
ever thought about."

Then she knew where she wanted to go and it took ten
minutes for the whole trip, back to England and then to
Hong Kong for the first time, "all he could think about,
worked half the night sometimes, I don't believe he knew I
was there except when he wanted his meals," still with her
small ivory-pale hands clasping her arms as she trod
circles in the silk pile, not looking at me once, "he
wouldn't have gone across his own doorstep if I hadn't
dragged him, it was like getting a baby away from its
bottle, him and his slide rule," dropping the cigarette end
into the neck of the magnum, she was going to regret that,
"it was Spain at first, the Costa Brava, then I saw this ad
about the Exotic East and it"—she stopped moving and
stood dead still and looked at me—"it really turned me
on, you know? Perfumes and jade and jewellery and all
that sort of thing, I suppose you think I'm childish."

Said no.

"He liked it, in a way. It was the fishing." From this
point she lost touch and most of the time forgot I was
here. "It quite brought him out, the first time we came," a
curl of her light hair falling loose as she talked, her small
stockinged feet silent as she moved across the carpet, the
nervous giggles more frequent and the memories more
random, "though to tell you the truth it might have been
the Isle of Wight as far as he was concerned, everywhere
was the same once he'd got over the shock of leaving England for a couple of weeks," gesturing now and saying
suddenly and bitterly, "he never thought much about sex,"
stopping just this once to listen to what she'd said and then
going on, giving me the impression that she didn't really
want to tell me about George Henry Tewson but about
something much more urgent that she daren't even men-

tion, so this would have to do, giving her some kind of release.

I could have looked around at the Ming and the Cat Street Contemporary while I was listening because that was all I'd come here for, to listen, but she was using her body a lot, couldn't keep still, and I looked at that, and the movements it made, the way she shivered sometimes as she went on; she'd only meant to go in as far as her knees and it was up to her stomach now, the tense trembling fear of going too far, the thrill of not going back, talking to me all the time, and none of the time, about Tewson, "then of course I found he'd been putting it away in Saving Certificates and buying insurance and that kind of thing, poor lamb," her cigarette tracing smoke in the air as her feet did a pirouette. "That's how I can live like this, and quite honestly it makes a change. My God, I can go on once I get started—you must be bored stiff!"

Said of course not.

"Then I thought no, I'll stay here, and never go back at all. I don't want to leave him, you see? The psychiatrist said I was right, the one I went to. He said I'd get over it quicker if I stayed here, where George was."

Then she just stood perfectly still in the middle of the room looking at nothing, a girl with ivory skin and stockinged feet and a lock of hair and a sheath dress with stains where the scotch had soaked in, her head turning slowly as she remembered me, her dark eyes deepening.

"You don't have to go, do you?"

"No."

The shivering began again.

"I'm so bloody frightened," she said.

I walked north, away from the Cathay Hotel, going along Kingston Street and up as far as Gloucester Road without seeing any traffic, not really expecting to at this hour, three in the morning. A patrol car slowed a little to check me, going west, and turned down Cannon Street. The smell of the harbour came on the wind, and a ship was hooting, some way off, three slows, farewell.

It had been as if she hadn't slept with anyone for years, or as if she knew it was for the last time, an act of desperation, and afterwards depression of course, tugging the cigarette out with small sharp nails, tearing the packet, I don't even know who you are, Clive, who are you, so forth. Essential to ask her why she was frightened, two reasons: I wanted to know and she'd expect me to ask. No go. Did I say that, I must've been stoned, furious with herself for having said it and with me for reminding her.

There was a taxi outside the Excelsior and I got in.

"Mauritius Hotel."

The streets swung past and I shut my eyes, lingering flight disorientation and nothing to have to watch, everything under control. One certainty: she wasn't an agent, either ours or theirs. One probability: Tewson had been. But there were inconsistencies because everything fitted so well and then came apart: he'd presented a classic cover in his dossier, lowly work for a government department, three-year-old Austin and a few small debts and never travelling until Spain (to establish the new image) and then suddenly Hong Kong, three trips in a row and then careless, leaving a widow, no children. All right, started off in D.I.6, ferreting around Portsmouth and places, then seconded or transferred to M.I.5. for missions abroad, a feint in Spain and then the Far East theatre, something strictly specific and confined to Hong Kong as a base for the South China seaboard area. Then the classic sequence: approach from Peking, temptation, defection, exposure, elimination, but not before he'd been paid enough for his widow to blow it on Ming. Chief inconsistency: M.I.5 are a grotty lot but they wouldn't have given him the terminal handshake, they'd have sent him back to London for the full fourteen-year stretch, justice seen to be done, so forth.

I'm so bloody frightened.

Because she'd known about it and couldn't stop it running. But Tewson had stopped running and she was *still* frightened so what was running *now?*

South and then west again into Hennessy Road, a dark bundle of clothes on the pavement and some police around it, the end of the opium trail. We began slowing.

"Mauritius Hotel," the driver said.

I got out and paid and undertipped to provoke an argument because the lights weren't too bright here and I wanted to make it easy, oh all right then, here you are, but you people are bloody robbers, and he went away happy as anything with a Hong Kong dollar.

I went into the hotel and nodded to the night clerk

when he woke up, taking the stairs. The first-floor passage was conveniently long and I walked nearly to the end, thinking it could of course have been Nora Tewson herself who'd pushed the poor bastard into it, like Mrs. Tuckman: she was hooked on money and there might have been quite a lot of it from Mao if Tewson had something they particularly wanted.

I got my keys and pushed one of them against the door of the cleaner's closet and then opened it, going in and shutting it, nothing but bloody brooms everywhere, pitch-dark, don't tread on anything, there may be a bucket. Standing against the wall I thought the only thing she'd said that was really interesting was about his work, and even that had been clumsy: *Pretty important, well I mean it was important that he* worked *there, actually his* work *wasn't important, to tell you the truth.*

Most of what she'd told me was in his dossier and the rest I could check on. His cover had been something in technical or engineering, design or research or development, *him and his slide rule*, she wasn't bright enough to make that up or deliver it without overacting. Some kind of cleaning fluid stinking to high heaven, ammonia in it, eyes accommodating now, faint light from a ventilator above me. I couldn't hear him but I didn't expect to: there was carpet in the passage and he'd walk quietly, coming just far enough to note the number of the room next to the closet, then going away.

The watch was probably changed at midnight: this one was shorter and quite a bit older, no glasses, quite good, turning away when I'd come down from her apartment and through the lobby, nearly missed him. And a Morris, not the Honda, keeping such a big gap that I thought I'd better stand there arguing with my cab driver to give him a bit of time. *I don't even know who you are, Clive, who are you,* got quite excited when I'd mentioned bullion, I'd better pick up a tag tomorrow and take him to one of the dealers they'd given me in Credentials and then lose him afterwards, somewhere near the Mauritius.

Check: I'd given him enough time to reach the top of the stairs before I was halfway along the passage and there hadn't been any cover because the doors weren't recessed so he'd have had to wait there in case I turned round, and from that distance and from that fine angle of view, almost zero degrees, he couldn't see if I were going into the closet or the room next door. Satisfactory: given him five minutes to clear.

Proposition: she was still frightened so something was still running and she knew it and she knew what it was and London had given me the key to Mandarin at the outset: Nora Tewson. But I didn't know if Mandarin was their name for an opposition project they wanted me to penetrate or survey or destroy, or the name of my own mission on the files, and it was beginning to look a bit like a counter-intelligence thing. I didn't mind that: it could be a legitimate penetration job either way and that was in my field, somewhere to go into and go into alone, a prescribed target and access availability and a safe house for signals and refuge. So far there hadn't been any problem: since touchdown at Kai Tak I'd checked the safe house, made the contact with Nora Tewson, noted the opposition surveillance, gone in under it to develop the contact and established a false base, Room 12, Mauritius Hotel. The sole hazard potential was Flower and as soon as possible I'd have him recalled to London.

I turned the handle of the door and it took ten seconds to push it open one millimetre, the diameter of the human pupil in artificial light. Field clear. Stairs, lobby, street, check, recheck, clear. I had to walk as far as the Luk Kwok before I found a taxi.

"Orient Club."

"You want nice Chinese girl?"

"No, just the Orient Club."

Got out and paid him and watched him away. Recheck: clear. The street very quiet in the pre-dawn hour, no lights anywhere on this side of the consulate, a haze of gnats floating below the lamp near the sand bin. *Notice of Opportunity to pay Fixed Penalty,* so forth, put it with the other one, some people collect absolutely anything these days, check ignition wires and start up. Final check: clear.

There were no messages for me at the Hong Kong Cathay and I went straight up to my room and opened the door and froze.

It's not only dogs.

The room was at the rear of the hotel and on the top floor. It faced northeast and at this moment the first light was coming into the sky above the theatre and the trees in the park. The shutters were half open, the way I'd left them, making a silhouette against the ashy light. My cases were on the stand, the way I'd left them.

It's not only dogs that have a sense of smell, the ability to sense alien presence in the environment, or its recent presence. All animals have it, but in varying degrees of refinement. In humans it has been atrophying over the decades since they began living with machines and relying on lights, locks and mechanical systems, but in creatures of the wild it remains highly developed. In creatures of the wild and in those few of us who express and incur mortal enmity in pursuit of our complex purposes.

There was no actual smell that worried me. In the short time I'd spent in this room I had become familiar with the subtle blend of sandalwood, jute, linen, polish, Jeye's Fluid and the ingrained odours of the human body. Nothing was different about the smell. There was no particular sound. From somewhere in the hotel I could hear the clack of mahjong pieces and the far faint jangle of an alarm clock, but they weren't loud enough to prevent my detecting human breathing in the room here, if there were any human near me. There was nothing to be seen but faint light, shadows, areas of near-darkness, and various objects occupying positions familiar to me. The shutters, the cases, shoes, hotel literature, doors, lamps, bathrobe, everything I could see in the dim light was as I had seen it last.

The only cover in the room itself was under the bed and if a man were there he would be facing this way, towards the door, so I moved very fast, using the bed itself as a springboard and spinning as I hit the floor on the other side and checked the space underneath against the light from the open doorway. No. I opened the bathroom door and threw the bathrobe in and waited two seconds and dropped and went in and looked behind the door. No. Check wardrobe, check window, no point in checking the main door lock for signs of tampering because in a small hotel you don't have to force a lock, you get the concierge to turn his back on the keyboard for the required five seconds.

So everything was perfectly all right and I put the light on and shut the door and began checking small details: I'd left the bottom corner of the hotel literature precisely lined up with the pattern on the table and the three drawers had been left pulled open a quarter-inch at the right-hand, left-hand, right-hand ends from top downwards and the cases had been set with their top corners exactly touching, the left rivet an inch lower than the right, so forth, it wasn't anything special, we always do it and we do it with the speed of habit and we can check just as fast. It's absolutely foolproof providing the opposition isn't too professional but if it's professional enough then you don't have a chance unless you go into the more refined mechanisms: a hair across the wardrobe doors, tautened between notches; a dead match on the floor with the ash still intact; a pin balanced across the gap in the bathroom doorway.

I hadn't used these traps because no one had tagged me since I'd landed except for the two men surveying Nora Tewson and I'd made sure neither of them had tagged me to this hotel. When I'd picked up the Capri just now I'd been absolutely clear and I'd come into the hotel with security intact. Except for one factor: if they'd wanted to they could have got my address, the Hong Kong Cathay. I didn't think they'd want to, because I'd gone in overtly to make the contact in the Orient Club and I'd let them tag me to Jade Imperial and later from there to the Mauritius Hotel. There was no reason why they should suspect my cover: no reason at all.

Disregard.

Discount the animal instinct, ignore the slight raising of the hairs along the arms under their sleeves, the prickling of the scalp, the micro-watt surge of galvanic force along the nerves of the spine. Dismiss and rationalize: fatigue, flight disorientation, unfamiliarity with the environment, imaginative fears, so forth.

Very well. Because it was so very unlikely they would have taken any real interest in me so early, so fast. The young thin tubercular Chinese had been police-trained and predictable: he hadn't even noted Flower in the surveillance area. The older man had been much better and I'd nearly missed him in the lobby of Jade Imperial, but he'd been so cautious on the run to the Mauritius Hotel that I'd had to give him a full minute outside the place so he could keep me in sight.

The access to the Mandarin target was prescribed and

orderly: it wasn't a night drop or a crash drive or anything panicky like the Tunis thing. Egerton and Macklin
and the administration in London had roped me in but
they hadn't *thrown* me in: they'd given me time to contact
the key figure—Nora Tewson—and develop a relationship
and the thing I had to do now was give her total attention
until she showed me the way in and I sent for a director
and set the action up and got moving.

So there was *no* reason for me to stand here in Room
39 of the Hong Kong Cathay Hotel with the instinctive
feeling that someone had been here in my absence. *No*
reason. Because Mandarin wasn't as big as that yet: this
was still the preliminary phase and I'd have to make a
mistake or provoke them or get in their way before they'd
extend their own routine surveillance of the Tewson
woman and move into my field on covert combat level. If
they'd been here this early and this fast it would mean that
the initiative had already passed from the local cell or unit
to the major directive: not Hong Kong but Peking. And I
just didn't believe that had happened. I wasn't prepared to
credit the idea that within twelve hours of landing at Kai
Tak Airport I was faced with a mission that had started
blowing right open in the primary phase.

Sleep.

Normal precautions, pull the shutters and swing the
catch, throw the security bolt, put a coin on the door
handle and the two glass ashtrays on the carpet below, a
gesture to the needs of survival now that I'd rejected instinct. Last thoughts as I took off my things: call her later
today and listen to see if they've got her phone bugged, go
and ask Fleetway Rent-a-Car if anyone's been trying to
find out who hired the Capri, tell them about the carbure-
tion, difficult to start and that could be critical on a tagging run.

There was a mosquito whining in the bathroom and I
wondered what the humidity was in this place in September, felt somewhere near eighty. Then I forgot about it because when I squeezed some toothpaste on the brush an
air bubble popped and the stuff was too runny and I felt
suddenly cold and thought I don't mind London offering
me capsules but I don't like people putting the bloody stuff
in my toothpaste.

5

Flower

"Where the hell have you been?"

The light in the room was dim, because I hadn't opened the shutters. Earlier, bars of gold had appeared on the carpet as the angle of the planet, relative to its local star, had changed progressively. Now the beams of sunlight through the shutter slats were thinning again as I watched. Motes of dust drifted through them, suddenly bright and then vanishing, and I saw them with great clarity, as I saw everything in the room. I've noticed before that to miss death narrowly leaves you with your senses heightened: these bright hallucinatory images were always there before but you were too busy to see them.

"Nowhere," he said.

"Yes you bloody well have. I phoned you fifteen minutes ago and you weren't there."

"Oh—I had to go and move the car." He sounded surprised and aggrieved. "They wanted to unload a—"

"You could've given them the keys couldn't you, for Christ sake?"

Bit of a pause, then rather quietly: "Yes sir."

I let it go. I'd told the little fool to stay at his base at all times except between 15:00 and 16:00 hours and just now I'd phoned him at 10:25 and there'd been no answer from his room and they'd failed to locate him by page, said he'd gone out. Moving his car, all right, three minutes, but three minutes could make a critical gap at a time when there had to be instant liaison. The opposition believed I was dead and fifteen minutes ago they could have come in here to search the body and I might not have had time to do anything about it—except to phone Flower with a last signal so that Control would know what had happened. But he would have been moving his car. I needed him today but tomorrow I'd have him on a plane for London before he could do any damage.

"Flower," I said.

"Yes sir."

"Have you been on an active mission before?"

"No."

There was a click and I stopped to listen, but it was one of the cleaners in the passage outside, nothing on the line. I'd checked it for bugs when I'd made the connection and we were clear.

"Listen," I told him. "This operation has become extremely dangerous in the last few hours. You'll now have to follow my instructions with absolute precision, for your own sake as well as mine."

Someone knocked and I heard a key jangling and I called out for them to go away.

"In ten minutes, go and take up station at Jade Imperial and continue surveillance. Stay with the subject regardless of her movements, but break off the moment you think you've been exposed. Break off at once and get right out of the field and leave a message here for me, to the effect that Mr. Jones has telephoned and will call again."

I made him repeat it and he got it word-perfect and I hung up and listened again to the sounds in the passage: a trolley was squeaking, one wheel off centre, and a girl was laughing with a high silvery sound. They wouldn't have laughed like that if they'd come in here and found me on the bathroom floor with a blue cyanosed face.

I picked up the phone again and dialled.

"Good morning—Fleetway Rent-a-Car."

"I'll need something this evening. What time d'you close?"

"Eight o'clock, sir. May we reserve a particular vehicle for you?"

"No, I'll be along."

I hung up and put the whole thing into the computer again and the answers came out the same. Unless there'd been some kind of a break-in there must be a police link: the field had been absolutely clear last night when I'd picked up the Capri—they'd tagged me from Jade Imperial to the Mauritius Hotel because I'd let them but they hadn't tagged me from the Orient Club to the Cathay because I'd made sure they didn't. I'd got here clean: but they'd been here *already*, got here *before* me and rigged the toothpaste thing, just as they could have rigged a bomb.

Sole possible link: Fleetway Rent-a-Car.

I checked the time at 10:50 and went into the bathroom and put the tube into my pocket and spent five minutes throwing a whole web of traps around the room. Then I went out and put the notice on the door, *Don't Disturb*. I'd know if any of the staff went in there because they'd make the bed and everything.

Then I was standing for a moment on the hotel steps, looking around in the sunshine and catching the faint brackish tang of the harbour on the humid air.

"Lover-lee morniang," the boy said.

"Yes."

I didn't go down the steps. It was a lovely morning and the sunshine was casting soft shadows in the street where cars were parked. I looked particularly at the shadows, and the cars. The sensation of mortal vulnerability was intense for these few seconds, even though I knew that the odds were in my favour. If this hotel had been in the States or the U.K. or France I wouldn't have gone down the front steps at all: I'd have used the service exit or a fire escape and got to the car very fast in the hope of disturbing their aim or at least dodging the shot. Countries vary and there are characteristic national and even regional tendencies towards the use of the rifle, the knife, the bomb, the rope or the bare hands. There are other aspects involved: the need for speed, silence, accuracy, anonymity, so forth—for instance in Antwerp they blew Hodgson apart with the slot-metre massage boy the instant he got into bed and exactly an hour after he'd landed on a night flight from Paris, because he was an experienced operator in a highly sensitive field and they wanted him out early and would have prepared back-up techniques in case he didn't use the massage thing. But in Tunisia they'd hounded Fyson for three days with a telescopic rifle *and let him know it*, till his nerve went and he was taken out of the mission and found floating in Tunis harbour.

It depends who you are, what you're doing and how soon they want you out of the way. They'd let Fyson run because they'd wanted to know what he was doing before they went in and broke him up as a warning to the next man in. A lot of factors are involved but the first consideration is the locality. In the Middle East they like the knife and the garotte, but the farther you come into the Orient the more personal things tend to be, because they can use their bare hands with more effect than a bomb and they can do it in almost dead silence. They are subtle in other ways, and sometimes exotic, and in a place where they burn incense and eat birds' nests and adulterate the wine with snake venom as an aphrodisiac you can expect to find KCN in your toothpaste the moment your name comes up.

"Want taxi?"

"No."

I walked down the steps and the skin reacted, gooseflesh, the nerves already feeling the impact and the penetration, the ripping away of the bone. Then I was in the street and the sunshine was still bright and the soft air innocent. They might be relying on the stuff they'd put in the bathroom: it nearly always works because when you're cleaning your teeth you're usually thinking about something else. It had worked with Harris in Mexico City and the police had blamed the tart he was with, said she must have put it in his sangria.

I was checking the whole time as I walked along to where the Capri was parked, every car, every window, every angle of the rooftops, because they'd got on to me so diabolically fast that I couldn't rely too much on the Oriental preference for the bare hands: they could be in so much of a hurry that their orders were to throw the lot at me, whichever way I turned. I knew when they'd got on to me: right at the start of the tag last night when I'd taken up station behind Flower and the Tewson woman. It had been the Taiwan-registered Toyota, the one I hadn't liked, the one I'd actually checked on and ignored, like a bloody amateur. They'd seen me hanging around Jade Imperial and they'd seen me take up the tag when Flower moved off and from that minute they were on to me. Two months out of active operations and you lose the fine-tuned alertness that comes back to you as soon as you're in business again, unless you've left it too late.

Note: there were three of them watching Nora, at least three. The thin tubercular, the shorter one and the man in the Taiwan Toyota. The shorter one hadn't been in the

Toyota because he was working shifts with the thin man and they'd changed somewhere about midnight. At least three, logically four: a lead tag and a back-up for each of the working shifts. It seemed a lot of attention for a poor little widow consoling herself on Ming after her hubby had been drowned in that dreadful fishing accident.

There was a monsoon drain near the dark-blue Capri and I got the tube and squeezed the stuff out, holding it below the level of the roadway. It hung and dangled like a thin venomous snake, then fell away as I flattened the tube and dropped that in too.

I hadn't left any traps on the Capri so I had to go in cold, not liking it, starting with the front end and rocking it on the springs in case they'd put something in there with a pendulum detonator, not liking it at all, taking a look downwards through the driver's window with my hand screening out the reflections, using the key and getting in and checking under the dash, nervy and furious because I should have left routine traps around, bloody carelessness: I'd known Mandarin was already running when I'd taken off from London. Wires okay but it wasn't nice, turning the key and hearing the starter kick: I'd seen what was left of the vice-consul's Chevrolet in Saigon, bits everywhere and his scalp plastered against a tree.

Got moving and turned west into Leighton Road. Flower would be leaving the Wan Chai district about now and ideally it would have been safer if I'd driven straight to Jade Imperial and got there before him, cover the field and warn him if too many had moved in there this morning: one tag and a back-up were all right but things had changed since last evening—they knew I'd joined the operation. But I had to find out how they'd got on to me so fast: it was important because it would tell me a lot of other things as well—their capabilities, techniques and something about their local contacts.

Percival Street, going north. So they'd picked me up in the Toyota and when they'd seen me comfortably settled in the Orient Club they'd used a stock key off the bunch or put a wire coat hanger through the moulding and got into the Capri and poked around, finding the papers in the glove pocket: Fleetway Rent-a-Car. They could have rigged a bang for me on the spot, but maybe there hadn't been time to fetch the necessary equipment, or they hadn't felt a hundred percent certain I was in opposition or they thought I was Hong Kong Special Branch and weren't too worried, didn't want to do anything terminal. Obviously they'd been on to Flower just as fast and they'd been letting him run, possibly to see what he was going to do, possibly because they thought he was also Special Branch.

Now they knew I wasn't. They'd checked on me during the night and found out I was London Intelligence and gone for me straightaway, working for quick elimination. They were professionals out of Peking and they'd know the international networks: we all did, we all knew each other, you can't go through ten or twenty first-line missions in ten or twenty geographical areas without the opposition sometimes getting a look at your face, sometimes even getting a picture—telescopic and fuzzy with grain but still your picture, recognizable enough to go into the files.

Last night they'd seen me operating a tag and they'd seen my face and they'd made signals and looked me up. They might not know my name and they might not have a dossier on me but they knew I was London.

West into Hennessy Road and in four minutes I came upon the Fleetway Rent-a-Car office with its two windows, one of them smashed, that's right, and patched up with cardboard and sticky tape till they could get it replaced. I didn't even slow down, no need, just kept on going, south along Tin Lok Lane and then east again, heading north after a while towards the Excelsior. No police link, then: they'd raided the Capri outside the Orient Club and found the Fleetway documents but they didn't have anyone in the police who could ask Fleetway the name of the man who'd rented the car. They could have gone there first thing this morning and said a Ford Capri with this number had clouted their wing and not stopped, who was the renter and what was his address, so forth, but they were moving too fast and they didn't want to wait for the morning and the office had closed at eight so they'd just broken in and looked at the books: Clive Wing, nationality British, Hong Kong Cathay Hotel.

Final phase: they'd returned to their base, the impressive building with the big brass doors at the corner of Statue Square, overtly the Bank of China, covertly the party and diplomatic headquarters of the Communist Chinese Republic in Hong Kong, Peking's listening post and window on the West. They wouldn't have bothered to look up Clive Wing because cover names are only used once, and they wouldn't find Quiller on their books because it's a code name and never used for cover or signals, never used at all outside the doors of the Bureau in Whitehall. They'd looked up the mug shots in the Western Intelligence section and found this particular scarred and bitten-eared alley-cat face with the cynical mouth and the watchful eyes, the picture that some bright spark had managed to take when I was crossing the road or going through customs or feeding the ducks in Bangkok or Tokyo or Seoul—because they're everywhere, the Chinese, everywhere in Asia, a cell in every city and a plant in every consulate; and they'll follow anything that moves, they'll survey and observe and monitor every intelligence operation they can smell out, whether it involves Peking or not. They'd looked at the pictures and the man who'd observed me outside the Orient Club and outside Jade Imperial Mansions had identified me.

Very well, they'd said, this man is London. Eliminate him.

I left the Capri outside the Excelsior and went in and used a phone and the ringing tone began.

Flower had said she never left her pad before ten or eleven in the morning and it was now 11:21 and I could have missed her and that would mean driving through her travel pattern in the hope of seeing either the Hillman or the Jensen and taking it from there. But it had been near dawn when I'd left her this morning and she might want to catch up on her sleep, so I let it ring eight times, nine.

It didn't matter too much if her schedule was different today because part of my object was to meet Flower, get a complete report on every aspect of his surveillance, take his notebook and then tell him to get on the first plane to London and don't come back. I could make contact with him anywhere and at any time. But the other part of my object was to ease myself into the tag: watch her travel pattern and note the busy areas and shortcuts and cover availability, taking loops and coming back while Flower manned the tag.

Eleven rings, twelve.

If I found more than two of the opposition in the field

at Jade Imperial I'd warn Flower off and order him to London straightaway because there wouldn't be room for two of us if they were going to move into an actual guard action around Nora Tewson. The mission had already gone into active phase and it could keep on changing as fast as an automatic gearbox, all the way up through the range.

Fourteen, fifteen.

I'd left it too late. I'd have to take the risk and—

"Hello?"

"This is Clive," I said.

Slight pause and then a soft easy laugh. "Oh. And how do *you* feel this morning?"

"I'm only just coming down."

There was another soft little laugh, and she said sleepily, "Let's do it again."

"That's why I rang."

I was having to think what to say, because the bug was already there when she'd opened the line: they had a permanent three-way station operating. There'd been the slight *ker-lunk* as the circuit had tripped in, and now the line was hollow.

"Hoping you would," she said.

"Would you like to go somewhere tonight? The El Caliph—"

"Not tonight," she said quickly, and didn't say why. I tried to catch the tone, to imagine what she would have added in explanation, *I've got to do my homework,* or *my mother's coming round,* it was on that wavelength.

"Tomorrow?"

"Yes."

"What time shall I come?"

"Don't come here. I'll meet you there at eight."

"The El Caliph Room?"

"Yes."

I tried every time to listen between the words and get the message. Her voice wasn't sleepy any more: it was a little breathless, secretive, excited, guilty, not quite any of those things but all of them. In her inexperienced way she was conducting an intrigue.

"All right," I said.

"Clive."

"Yes?"

It came in an arch little rush. "I've never known anything like it. You know?"

"Nor have I."

"My God, I bet you have."

I said I'd never met anyone like her, been searching all my life, so forth, repeated the time and place and let her ring off first. An instant of regret as I put the phone down, because if I ever met her again it'd have to be without the ticks in tow and that was unlikely. Painfully inexperienced, arch, gauche, coy, but hungry and demanding, like a half-starved waif, wanting to learn and then going for it hard the moment she got the message, *God, I've seen them do this in a film,* wanting to do everything and do it now, as if it was going to be for the last time, *Clive, I didn't know it could be like this,* some of the dialogue, presumably, from the same film, though she meant it, and finally *you bastard,* for some reason, *oh you bastard,* meaning this too and leaving blood on me with her nails. It seemed fairly clear that she'd made the mistake of marrying a slide rule and couldn't think of anything to do about it except play about with a flickering projector in a girl friend's cellar.

Slight progress made: I'd confirmed they had a bug on her phone and there would obviously be others here and there among the Ming. She didn't know about it, or with her Victorian attitudes she wouldn't have said what she did on the phone just now, and she certainly wouldn't have done what she did last night. Another point of interest was that she couldn't meet me tonight because she had to do something she didn't particularly want to do, and conceivably she had to do it in Room 192 at the Golden Sands Hotel, because Flower had told me that the only time she'd made a definite movement was when she'd gone expressly to that hotel and stayed the night.

If they picked me up today and I shook them off they'd know where to find me again if I checked out of the Cathay, or at least they'd think they knew. I suppose I'd have to send another magnum and a dozen gardenias or something to the El Caliph Room tomorrow night; that snivelling old crone in Accounts was going to fracture a whalebone at this rate.

The sunshine bright as I went down the steps, the smell of the sea much stronger here, the ragged banners of the sails in the typhoon shelter and the throbbing of power-boats.

"Want taxi, sir?"

"Yes."

Because they knew the dark-blue Capri. I left it where it was and got into the cab. "This is for you." I gave him ten dollars. "You drive the way I tell you and there'll be another ten when you've finished. What's your name?"

"Kwan."

Not much more than a kid, a bit scared of me, eyes very wide, didn't know who I was, knew I wasn't the police or I'd have just flashed my I.D.

"All right Kwan, get down into Yee Wo Street and head for Causeway Road, quick as you can but don't break the speed limit unless I tell you."

"If I break speed limit I lose licence and they—"

"Shut up and start driving."

I began checking for tags the moment he turned left into Cannon Street. The odds against a tag at this point were a thousand to one and that's one of the ways you can get pushed right off your perch, by thinking what the hell, it's a thousand to one we're all right.

I told him to take Sugar Street and turn left and make one slow pass through the operational field and I saw the Toyota parked under the trees by the park entrance and the Hillman a hundred yards farther north.

"Kingston Street," I told him quickly and he did rather well: most people would have overshot and we'd have had to traipse all the way round the block and come back and risk losing the action and showing our hand by blinding along to catch up. "Very good, Kwan. Now go to the end and turn round and stop."

It was an hour's wait. I wondered if she was changing her schedule like this because she'd spent a sleepless night and was tired or because it had some bearing on the fact that she was going to break her routine again tonight.

This man is London, yes, eliminate him. They'd done it before, of course. If this man had been Hong Kong police or Hong Kong Special Branch they'd have let him run for as long as he wanted to: there'd been an official enquiry into Tewson's death and either of those departments could have decided to reopen it unofficially by watching his widow for a bit, see what they could pick up. I was damn sure this Peking cell was confident they'd never pick anything up even if they went on looking forever, so why make a fuss and get in their way. If this man had been Washington or Moscow or Paris or Bonn they would have shot out a foot and asked him what the hell did he think he was doing. But this man was London, and he had to die with his teeth clean, just as the other man who was London—George Henry Tewson—had died with his feet wet.

Jensen.

"Kwan."

Hillman.

"Please?"

Toyota.

"Follow that Toyota."

He nodded and stood on it and I nearly got whiplash. Going down through the park I said: "Notice that it's dark grey and rather dirty, and that it's registered in Taiwan. Remember it has that aerial on the roof. Try and keep two or three cars between you and the Toyota, because I don't want him to see that we're following him all the time. If there's anything you don't understand, ask me."

"Is okay, all okay."

"Good."

Down Leighton Road and heading southwest, Jensen, Hillman, Toyota, taxi—Christ, all you wanted were the flowers. I didn't tell him to keep an eye on his wing mirrors as well because he'd have quite enough to do in the lunch-hour traffic. His off-side mirror was too high from where I sat, but the righthand end of the interior mirror gave me a couple of inches if I sat well in the corner and the chrome on the pillar beading was nice and clean and picked up primary colours.

I wasn't really expecting an easy ride. They knew I was London, they knew my face and they knew I was interested in Nora Tewson. Wherever she went, they'd look for me: and you can calculate fairly precisely—all other things being equal—just how long you can keep up a tag in a taxi before they get the vibrations and close in. It isn't very long.

The knife flashed and the pineapple came open like a flower unfolding. His hands were so quick that I was reminded of a stopped-action film, the fruit seeming to peel itself in a series of jerks without anyone there. One of the Americans was crouched on his knee, squinting and turning the focus ring of his camera; and three small Chinese children stood porcelain-still and hand in hand, watching the fruit seller with their luminous black eyes unblinking.

The Jensen was parked a hundred yards away near Queen's Road Central, and I could see most of its windscreen from here. It was pointing this way and couldn't go anywhere without passing me: a U turn was impossible on this stretch and there weren't any side streets available. Her bright head moved in the sunshine and she stopped again: they were mostly jewellery shops in this area.

I couldn't see the Hillman because Flower hadn't been able to find a slot when she'd pulled in, so he'd come past and left it somewhere out of sight, passing me on his way back to look for her. He didn't see me, or know I was there. It was much brighter than it had been in the Orient Club last night and I saw him clearly for the first time: a rather intense-looking boy with a Tudor haircut and very pale skin, a lot of pens clipped inside his breast pocket, one of them probably full of tear gas: they go in for gadgets at that age.

I couldn't see the Toyota either but I knew where it was. We'd all been here a good thirty minutes and I'd taken a loop on foot to see if there were any shortcuts available in the travel pattern Flower had given me: along Hillier Street and down Jervois—nothing but bloody snake shops, they give me the creeps—and back into Queen's Road, finding the Toyota and passing it and coming up far enough to see the Jensen. It was the thin one, with glasses, and he was standing over there at the entrance to the silk emporium.

I still wasn't quite sure, but it had looked very like a sudden pincer movement. We'd been tooling along Des Voeux Road in line astern when a bus had pulled out and three or four cars had bunched, two of them quite unnecessarily because they could have got past without any trouble. I just left ten dollars on the seat and was inside the dry cleaners' and out through the back before anyone had time to ask any questions, picking up a taxi in Wing Kut

Street and telling the driver to wait, because I'd been quicker than the traffic. The jam was just clearing and I saw the Jensen coming past and told him to slot in there. No harm done, and I had in fact seen the doors of those two cars coming open when they'd bunched behind the bus, though of course they might have just decided to get out and walk, such a lovely lot of windows here to look at, so forth.

The smell of pineapple was in the air and the man was telling me I ought to buy one, it was pure and delicious and quenching, so I moved on, he was quite right: static surveillance from obtrusive cover was asking for it, if that really had been a pincer attempt in Des Voeux Street.

A rickshaw man went padding past, the wickerwork creaking, a pair of girls on the seat laughing delightedly.

"C'est mieux que le Métro!"

"Mais un peu plus cher!"

The sunshine of the early afternoon was slanting across the rooftops, lighting the windows on the other side of the street, where it was reflected across the two lines of traffic. I saw her bright head moving again as she turned away from me and began going towards the Jensen. The lights had changed and a No. 5 double-decker was leading the pack from the Wellington Street intersection, and for a couple of seconds I couldn't see the thin Chinese; then the traffic strung out a little and I had him in sight again. He hadn't moved.

She hadn't stopped anywhere for lunch yet: we'd been kept on the move the whole time since we'd left Jade Imperial, and I needed a chance to break off and get close to Flower and make a rendezvous for whenever she holed up somewhere; then I could get his report and take his notes and tell him to book a flight. She was nearing the Jensen now and the next phase was ready to open: the Chinese would wait till she was in the car and then he'd turn suddenly and come down this way on the other side with that gangling head-forward walk of his and be in the Toyota with the engine running by the time she came past.

I'd have time to make a brush contact with Flower and give him the rendezvous and let him get to the Hillman.

But it didn't work out that way, because when she reached the Jensen I looked at Flower to make sure he'd seen. He obviously had: he was turning and making his way down on the other side, hurrying a little and trying not to show it. The pavement was a bit crowded and as far as I could see he stepped off the curb at the wrong time and someone shouted and there was the fling of an arm and then a long red smear where the wheel of the bus went dragging.

6

Breakthrough

"Wai?"

"What is the goose?"

"It is gold."

"This is for London, immediate."

"Wait."

I listened carefully, thinking he was warning me.

"Yes?"

He'd just been getting a pencil.

"Mandarin. They picked the flower. Wing."

I could hear his breathing as he wrote it down: he'd been in the shop below when the phone had rung.

"Yes."

"Please repeat."

"Wait. *Mandarin. They pick the flower. Wing.* Yes?"

"Picked." I spelt it.

"Yes. *Picked.*"

"Thank you."

Then I got Fleetway and said I'd left the Capri outside the Excelsior and they could pick it up there and I'd see them as soon as I could to sign the papers and they said they'd prefer me to bring the car in personally and complete the formalities and I said they wouldn't be in business long if they didn't learn to cooperate, feeling savage, wanting to curse everybody just as one does when it's been one's own fault.

I can't stand a messy death. I don't mean the smear bit, I mean a death that doesn't do anything, doesn't mean anything. Thornton did it the right way, Thornton above all people, hit the Caucasus Mountains head on with a twin-engined Petrov X-7 trying to dodge the missiles they were sending up from the base at Krasnodar, one big bang and no heel taps, the whole of the Bureau laughing all the way to Codes and Cyphers with the stuff he'd given the Queen's Messenger in Odessa, complete blueprints of the submarine complex and defence installations with blown-up photographs; if you've got to go, do it like that.

Bobbie? Oh, he's fine, I think. He's off abroad again, you know, some sort of government work, to do with the consular staff welfare scheme. I believe that's what he told us. Yes, we do miss him, of course—we were hoping he'd go into Arthur's bank, but there you are, so long as he's happy, that's the main thing, isn't it?

A long red smear down the street and my fault because I should have kicked him out of Hong Kong last night when I'd seen he was low-calibre and dangerous and too young to be out alone; they'd let him run because they'd thought he must be Special Branch and then they'd picked me up and seen it was intelligence and finished him off. The thing they were running was so big and they were so determined to push it through that they weren't even interested in asking questions when the opposition turned up: they just moved straight in for the kill.

I left the phone box and went out to the street again. There was a case for asking London for a director because the pressure was coming on hard, but there wasn't anything to report yet, there was no breakthrough. The key to the breakthrough was Nora Tewson, and she'd gone.

I'd had to cross the road and go up there to make sure they'd been thorough, and she was already coming past in the Jensen before the traffic began jamming up around the "accident." There wasn't a taxi in sight and I'd been tempted to wave to her, well well well, fancy seeing you here, take her to lunch, get everything I could out of her. But that would have been expedience, not design. The Jensen was a death trap and I left it alone, edging back from the knot of people and finding an alley and getting clear, checking with every step because they were still here somewhere in the area.

The alley led onto Kwong Yuen Street and I turned right and hurried but couldn't see her car. There was a taxi near the intersection and I got in and we did the whole travel pattern, starting with the House of Shen, Constellation "144," Kaiser's and the places she'd stopped at earlier in the day, in case she was looking for something specific and trying to make up her mind, doubling back.

No go.

At four o'clock I picked up a Taunus from Self Drive and went to the *Standard* office, back-numbers department, giving them the date I needed. The report took some finding because the tourist trade is a major industry in Hong Kong and they like to feel that everything looks just as it does in the brochure.

Tragic Death of British Visitor, page 10, one small photograph of George Henry Tewson, the same as the one I had in my briefing file and obviously from the same source, undistinguished, glasses, indefinite age. There wasn't anything I hadn't been told already. I asked if I could use their phone before I left but she wasn't in. The self-disgust about letting that poor little devil get caught in the machinery like that had so far kept my mind off the present situation. The present situation was that the key figure was changing her routine tonight for the second time and it could be critically significant and I wasn't going to be there unless I tried everything in the book and had some luck as well.

On my way back to the Cathay I stopped to buy a pair of Bushnell 7×50's with a $7° \ 30'$ field and ultraviolet filters because Jade Imperial Mansion was a quarter of a mile from the hotel and I might risk holing up there for another few hours if the binoculars could give me a reasonable view of the entrance gates the Jensen normally used. There was a chemist's next door to the optical place and I went in and bought some more toothpaste, *Neodens Safeguards Your Health*, more than you could say for the last lot.

I parked the Taunus at St. Paul's Hospital and walked down Cotton Path into Tung Lo Wan Road, crossing it and keeping on, going round past the theatre into Causeway Road, checking the windows of Room 39, shutters still closed.

A gentleman had telephoned three times, they told me at the desk, a Mr. Chou. He hadn't left his number. It hadn't been Flower and it hadn't been Chiang and no one else knew me in the whole of Hong Kong. I said I was going out again this evening but I'd let them know when I left, so they wouldn't have to page me if Mr. Chou called again. Then I went upstairs.

They must have been very quiet or the management would have heard about it by now. Every drawer was upside down and the carpet was off the floor and draped across the bed. They'd pried several boards up and stripped some of the wallpaper and turned off the pipe tap in the bathroom and dragged the tank away from the wall, taking down the air-conditioner grilles, unscrewing the wall plugs and turning the wardrobe on its side to get at the bottom. The lamp brackets were on the floor with the wires pulled out of the swan-necks and the bathroom door handles were off and lying on the windowsill. The base was off the phone but it worked and I dialled and waited for ten rings but she didn't answer.

It took an hour to check for booby traps, even though I didn't need to move more than a few things: clothes, shaver, toilet bag, so forth; the shoes weren't any good because they'd taken the heels off. I was sweating a lot by the time I'd finished (someone had slammed a door when I was picking up the shaver), but I'd decided to do it instead of just walking out and re-kitting at Lane Crawford's because I wanted to know if they thought I was green enough to blow myself up in here, and to know if they'd rigged something for me anyway: if they hadn't, it could conceivably mean they were going to let me run till they could bring me down and interrogate. As a general rule, you don't ferret your way into their operation by picking their locks, you do it by picking their minds.

I tried again twice during the hour, ten rings each time, the cover line being I missed her and was she sure she couldn't make it tonight, oh well, have fun. If she answered, I was going to take the Taunus along Caroline Hill Road and work north and find somewhere convenient for starting the tag when the Jensen showed at the gates. She didn't answer.

I was still drawing blank at 18:00 hours. Now that they'd been here again and Mr. Chou had started breathing down my neck I didn't feel like opening the shutters wide enough to take the 7×50's because they might have put a man on the peep down there or in a building nearby, and just the glint on the glasses could be fatal.

The maids could come in any time now to turn down the bed and things wouldn't be easy for them so I took one of the suitcases and went down and checked out at the desk, very pleasant, yes, and what a wonderful view, but my office had called me back, another strike, yes, wouldn't it be excellent if they could only run things in England as they ran them in Hong Kong.

Crossing the road to the hospital car park I felt the nape of my neck tingling. It was normal but uncomfortable and there was nothing I could do about it. They hadn't rigged anything for me but it didn't mean they might not use some other method when they were ready. The thing is, as soon as you start working in a sensitive field you're going to attract attention and as often as not you're going to be put on the opposition list, right at the top, if they think you look like getting in their way. The deeper you go into the tunnel, the more difficult it's going to be to come out again alive. It's no good digging a hole and waiting till they've gone because they're not going to go, and you can't run your mission by remaining immobile. So all you can do is settle for the situation and check every shadow, every sudden movement, and try to make sure there'll be time to duck. And of course ignore the snivelling little organism that's so busy anticipating what it's going to feel like with the top of the spine shot away, *why don't you run for cover*, trying to make you wonder why the hell you do it, why you have to live like this, *you'll never see Moira again if you let them get you*, trying to make you give it up when you know bloody well it's all there is in life: to run it so close to the edge that you can see what it's all about.

A chill at the nape of the neck. Ignore.

Cerebrate: start worrying over something real, the way they'd switched tactics. As soon as I'd arrived on the island they'd got on to me and moved straight in for the kill, failing with me and succeeding with Flower and taking not the slightest interest in asking questions. Suddenly they'd decided to ask a whole lot of questions up there in Room 39, without even leaving anything terminal for me to walk into. I knew it wasn't from consideration for innocent persons: this was a Peking operation and if a Hong Kong chambermaid went in there first and caught the blast it'd serve her right for having deserted the Daughters of the People's Liberation Army to work for the wicked capitalists across the water. One aspect was fascinating: did they really think anyone from London would leave his cypher key stuffed in a lamp bracket for them to find? They must be thinking of the Russians.

The Taunus was all right: I'd left traps. There wasn't any need to look under the cowling but I looked just the same, from habit. The face was at the window as I straightened up.

"Are you visiting the hospital?"

A Chinese, nobody I knew.

"No."

He wagged his head. "Would you please not park here unless you are visiting hospital."

"All right."

"We have sometimes many people park here, and no room for——"

"I won't do it again."

"Thank you. Hospital is for emergency, and if people park here, we cannot get ambulance up to doors, so——"

"Oh use a bloody shoehorn."

Start up and back out and turn, not at all polite, but it was beginning to look as if I'd missed the boat and I wasn't very happy. There were two chances left: ring every restaurant and supper club on the island, and set up a temporary base at the Golden Sands Hotel.

It was in Telegraph Bay and there were some hill roads to it but I took the major route through Victoria and down past the University, peeling off along the meandering drive that led to the beach. The Golden Sands was long, low, exotic and recently built, with vines and creepers still trying to cover the pagodas and terrace walls. A small group of people were down on the private beach, playing with a dog; the only others I could see outside the place were a man and a woman stowing the sail of their boat at the jetty. Two or three motor launches were throbbing in the channel, one of them leaving a wake that had curved away from nearer the shore, possibly from the jetty here.

"D'you have a room facing the beach?"

At the Golden Sands the focus of social life would be on the beach, at the poolside and along the two lower terraces.

"I will see," he said, looking a little worried that he might have to disappoint me, but with only half a dozen cars down there and the terraces deserted I had an idea things might turn out all right. "We can offer you this one, sir, if it's just for one night."

Room 27, second floor, view taking in the jetty. The Hong Kong life style was maritime and there could be as much traffic to and from the hotel by sea as by the road. I stayed in the room for less than half a minute to check security points and then went across to the terrace bar at the front, because you could watch the road from here and anyone arriving by boat would take the lantern-lit magnolia walk past the end of the building, coming around to the entrance.

Small girls in glowing cheongsams, their feet making no sound.

"No," I said. *"Indian tonic."*

There was a phone and I started work: ten rings for Jade Imperial Mansion and then the rounds, beginning with the ones in her known pattern—the Bayside Club, the Danshaku, Gaddi's, the Eagle's Nest.

Even from the front of the building you could hear the noise of the powerboats, and I kept one ear open in case any of them came across to the jetty. Two cars arrived: two couples, their voices floating up through the dusk, *way to come, I know, but Felicity said it was a simply fabulous place for fish*, headlights moving along the main road through Pok Fu Lam.

"Yes, I think table reserved in name Tewson."

The Harbour Room. A hit and a miss, because I was here, not there.

"For tonight?"

"Yes, sir."

"What time?"

"I think—excuse me. Lady cancel table."

"She what?"

"Lady cancel table. Not come tonight."

Hugo's, the Man Wha, the Tai Pan Grill, trying Kowloon now as well as the Island, no go, every time a negative, trying the Miramar as the low grey Jensen came round the curve of the drive and parked under the row of lanterns.

She was alone.

19:07.

Small neat steps that would have left footprints in a deadstraight line, not turning her head as she came

towards the doors, not looking upwards. I had a cover line
if she saw me here but it might be dangerous, better she
didn't see me. Turquoise tonight, a discreet shower of se-
quins, her midriff bare, where the mole was, though I
couldn't see it from here. The Honda arrived within ninety
seconds and although the driver didn't get out I could see
it was the short Chinese, the one I'd taken to the Hotel
Mauritius. A whiff of exhaust gas came on the air.

I went to the top of the double staircase and looked
down. Not every word was distinct but there wasn't any
delay at the desk: the room had been reserved. The boy
was taking her to the lift, her short hair bright as she
passed below the lamps. It stopped at this floor and I was
in my room when they came past, a breath of something
by Fabergé, she'd told me she always seemed to go for the
expensive ones, she didn't know why.

She wandered, for the next half an hour, among the few
people who had moved onto the lower terrace, not speaking to any of them, not looking anywhere in particular but
sometimes at the sea, drinking three vodkas in a row—I
could hear her voice when she turned this way—twice going along the lantern path under the magnolias, so that I
had to use the binoculars to keep her in sight among the
shadows there. Then she got fed up and came back, her
steps quicker and her bag swinging, and sat at one of the
tables not far below my windows, clasping her bare arms
and swinging one foot all the time, now and then swatting
at insects.

Taking calculated intervals I got out the map from the
briefing material and spread it on the bed, looking at it for
half a minute in every five, Directorate of Overseas Sur-
veys Series L882, Sheet 20, Hong Kong 1:25,000, Cape
D'Aguilar (Hok Tsui) Area, Grid Zone Designation 50Q.
Very close to Grid Ref. 2:14–24:60, roughly in the centre
of Tai Tam Bay, Macklin or Egerton or someone had put
a red cross: *Tewson drowned from boat here.* Peripheral
features: Tai Tam Village, prison at Tung Tau Wan, Lo
Chau Island, Turtle Cove Beach. A second reference, blue
cross: *Slipway where Tewson hired boat. Also Witness 3
and 4.* This was 1,650 yards from the centre of the bay
where the red cross had been marked. Witnesses 3 and 4
were two of the Chinese fishermen who had seen Tewson
in trouble. A green cross marked the point on Turtle Cove

Beach where Tewson's papers had been washed up later. Submarine contours gave only five fathoms within a hundred yards of the shore near the slipway, ten fathoms for the general bay area.

She hadn't moved.

The report was attached to the map. *Approximately twelve noon Tewson hires boat from Mr. T'sai, game-weight tackle. Alone on board as before.*

There were some bits about Tewson's being noticed by several people: coast guards, narcotics officers, the crews of fishing junks.

Approximately 16:00 hours several others, including the four key witnesses, see Tewson in "some kind of difficulty." Mr. Fu Jen-chang sees boat rocking, flurries in water (normal surface conditions smooth throughout bay), "silvery flashes on surface." Mr. Yung Lung-kwei, fisherman on junk within 100 yards of Tewson's boat, sees him "struggling" with what appeared to be a fish, just prior to his overbalancing and falling in. Another witness—

A woman laughed suddenly below and I went to the window, thinking it might have been Nora, but she hadn't moved, and no one was talking to her. From here she looked small and somehow significantly alone, untouchable, sitting there with her secrets, trying to drink some of them away. I wondered where she'd been, that day: whether she'd been on the slipway watching the distant blob of the boat when her husband had struggled with his fish, and lost. I wondered whether she had known it was going to happen, this event that had brought so much change in her fortunes.

There were still boats out on the channel, their lights making patterns across the still water; and one of them was swinging in a curve towards the jetty, the throb of its motor fading to a murmur. It was the fifth I'd counted since Nora had gone out to the terrace, and three of them had left their mooring again. She'd watched each of them as they'd arrived, and she was watching this one, not leaving the table but keeping her small head angled attentively.

I picked up the 7×50's again and focussed them on the jetty. The glow of the lanterns left shadows, and I could have seen better by the more diffuse light of the moon that was just rising. A small group of men, one of them remaining with the launch as the others began moving towards the building. The woman's laugh came again from below but I didn't look away. There were four of them, three wearing white shirts or jackets. As I went on adjusting the focus I saw that two of them hung back a little. As they came under the terrace lights the details were immediately clearer: three Chinese and a European, two of the Chinese hanging back quite a few yards (big men, possibly bodyguards), the other Chinese walking side by side with the European, who wore some kind of bush jacket and a pair of sunglasses.

I got this man into sharp focus and studied his face for a moment and then put the binoculars down as he saw someone and gave an awkward little wave of his hand. Nora had left her table, smoothing down her dress and going to greet the two men, the Chinese holding back a pace, the two others remaining by the pagoda some dozen yards away. The European embraced Nora, kissing her on the cheek, a shade embarrassed, Nora a shade cool and breaking away rather soon, perhaps because they'd all kept her waiting for nearly an hour.

I shut the window quietly and went to the phone.

A girl answered and sweat broke out on me at once because we were going to have to work very fast: Mandarin had shifted gear again, kicking hard into phase three, and we had to go with it.

"He come," the girl said.

Briefing said the arrangement was that Chiang would remain on close call continuous throughout this operation but that didn't mean he could go and—

"Yes?"

Goose, gold, so forth.

"For London, urgent, immediate, coded numerals."

He didn't answer. Getting his pad.

"Ready?"

"Yes."

I gave it to him in Cantonese: there didn't have to be any mistakes. There were two signals but the first was the most urgent.

"*Saam—yat—baat—saam,*" extended phase digits, "*Leong—say—leong—sup—saam,*" reverse transfers for the sake of speed, "*Yat—look—baat,*" throw in a suffix group of three fives repeated to cancel any inadvertent alert in case he left an omission in the blanks. "Read back."

He was quicker in his own tongue, only just giving me time to phrase it mentally in English, but he'd got it all right, first go:

Need director fully urgent. Tewson alive.

7

Overkill

The sea was dead calm, a flat blue shimmer of light reaching to the hills of Lamma Island, half seen through the haze. The water near my feet lapped softly across the big smooth stones, swirling around the piles of the breakwater. It was nearly dawn.

The man under the looking-glass tree hadn't moved.

I put the binoculars up again. The jetty of the Golden Sands Hotel was half a mile away, and the launch was still there. A figure was moving about on it, opening the engine hatch and half disappearing, and I thought if he was going to start it up it would mean they'd be leaving soon and there was nothing I could do about it. Nothing.

Relax. You've asked for the impossible so don't start bellyaching because it's not going to happen.

Five minutes later the island across the channel became suffused with a rose light, and the man under the looking-glass tree lifted his arms, beginning the movements of *tai chi chuan*. He was about sixty or seventy yards from where I stood, and hadn't yet seen me.

Part of my frustration was due to the fact that nothing apparent had happened since I'd sent the two signals last night. Chiang had got them off before 20:15 hours and I'd sweated it out till midnight to give Egerton time. Then I rang Chiang again.

Will make attempt, London had said. Chiang told me the signal had come in at 21:13 hours. That was pretty fast considering the action they'd had to take. My first request wouldn't have been any problem: Macklin had told me during field briefing that they'd probably fly someone in from Peking to direct me in the field, and he was probably here already, holed up with all those bloody snakes and asking Chiang where the hell I'd gone. It was my second request that would have shaken them up a bit: I'd asked for a high-speed powerboat to make rendezvous with me at this precise point, the twelve-pile breakwater half a mile north of the Golden Sands Hotel in Telegraph Bay, soonest possible, essential before dawn.

London was six thousand miles away and I didn't know how they were going to do it. I just knew they had to.

If Egerton hadn't played it so close to the chest they could have put a director into Hong Kong with me and there wouldn't have been any trouble: he would have tickled up the Navy or a private small-boat fleet operator and I would have been on board by now, that's what a director in the field is for. Sometimes Egerton is too clever by half.

The man under the looking-glass tree was bending and swaying, bringing his spirit into harmony with the rhythm of the universe as the rose light turned gradually to gold on the hills of Lamma.

Binocs: nobody moving anywhere outside the building itself, two Chinese boys trying to get a sail up near the end of the jetty, could only be to air it, there wasn't any wind. The man on the launch was shutting the engine hatch and in a few seconds I heard the slight thump of the timber. A minute later the throb of the engine began.

Fatalism now necessary. Either London would do something in time and we'd still have a mission or London would be too late and we wouldn't. Nothing I could do.

Of course I wasn't certain it had been Tewson, the European in the bush jacket and sunglasses. But he'd looked like the photographs—the one in my briefing file and the one in the *Hong Kong Standard,* and his greeting of Nora and her response had been precisely in character with what I knew of their relationship. They'd been meeting, probably, for the first time since Flower had tagged her to the Golden Sands, and they'd met in the presence of strangers, or at least alien acquaintances. They'd kissed, but not like lovers: it had been a gesture of almost anything but love—habit, convention, the need to demonstrate a token affection, leaving nothing for the neighbours to say.

I wasn't sure it was Tewson but I'd bet on it because the whole thing fitted in with her attitudes towards me and her behaviour at Jade Imperial: as a young widow released from a sexless marriage her eagerness, archness and inexperience had been predictable, but it hadn't explained her sense of guilt and intrigue. She wasn't just having an affair: it was an *extramarital* affair.

Hindsight makes you look a fool: I should have known two nights ago that Tewson was alive.

The engine of the launch was still running and I lifted the 7×50's again, not wanting to, making myself, because if Tewson put to sea and I couldn't follow and find out where he went, the only lead would be Nora again and she'd have to be worked on and that would mean asking London for one of the psychos and he'd have to come all the way out—unless they could rake one up from the embassies or consulates in Peking or Taipei or Tokyo—and start from scratch and it could take weeks to break her down and get what he wanted without her knowing. And all I'd get out of it was a free ride home and a stomachful of adrenaline, what the hell was London *doing*, I didn't want the bloody Guards called out, I just wanted a boat, for Christ's sake, and I wanted it *now*.

It wouldn't have made much difference if I'd used speech code instead of cypher: it would have saved maybe a few minutes but no more than that because C. and C. were open twenty-four hours and there'd only been two signals to unzip and besides, it would have been highly dangerous. *They picked the flower* was perfectly safe because even if it was intercepted and its meaning understood, it didn't say anything they didn't already know. It was a whole lot different asking for a director to come out to the field: it not only meant the operator had got hold of something big enough to need direction, but that he was going to try for immediate penetration, a tacit declaration of war that would bring in their troops—and their supply line was a few miles long, from here to the South China coast, with ours having to stretch half across the globe.

The second signal, ordering a boat and specifying the rdv, couldn't have gone in any other way but cypher: it was fully urgent and strictly hush and if the opposition had intercepted and decyphered it they'd have just sent someone down here to the twelve-pile breakwater half a mile north of the Golden Sands Hotel in Telegraph Bay with orders to tread all over my face.

The man had finished his calisthenics under the look-

ing-glass tree and was walking slowly up the beach to his
fishing boat. I wasn't worried about him: he could have
tagged me here from the hotel and semaphored the entire
Book of Mao if he'd wanted to, but he hadn't. His movements had been genuine *tai chi chuan* and I'd made certain that no one was tagging me when I'd come down
here. The immediate field was totally secure.

There was movement now and I refocussed: two figures
detaching themselves from the edge of the building, one
white, one darker, indistinct because the line of magnolias
was in the way. More movement, this time on the far side
of the pagoda: two figures again, both white, the same
stature, their motion coordinated. A slight burst of noise
from the launch as the seaman cleared the cylinders.

The darker figure stopped, looking up at one of the
first-floor windows, and even at this distance and with no
depth of field I could see his awkwardness as he waved his
hand. Then they were filing down to the jetty, forming the
same kind of procession I'd seen last night.

I estimated that Mandarin had another two minutes to
run.

London was six thousand miles away but they'd got a
radio hadn't they, got a telephone for Christ sake, this
wasn't an alien state, it was a Crown Colony and they
could pull some rank couldn't they, and what the hell was
the Minister doing about this, the one they were so bloody
proud of because he could cut through the red tape in ten
seconds flat, hadn't anyone picked up the blower and got
him off the pot?

Sweating like a pig.

The seaman was in the stern, handing his party aboard,
and the launch heeled slightly to their weight. Two of the
figures were going into the cabin, one of them the man in
the bush jacket, George Henry Tewson, the man from
London, dead on paper, killed off by bought witnesses at
the dictates of clandestine necessity, the man at the centre
of Mandarin, alive and well and vanishing from sight as
the stern went down and the exhaust note bubbled to a
roar. Within thirty seconds the launch was a small indistinct blob half lost in the morning haze, and I lowered the
binoculars.

Mission aborted. Am returning to London.

Because there wasn't anything else I could do. Tewson

was being released periodically on some kind of parole
and he might come here again but it wouldn't be for another week, unless they changed the pattern. I'd already
got as close to Nora as I could without getting killed and
if I stayed in Hong Kong for another week I wouldn't
have time to do anything but keep out of their way and
hope to stay alive: but that wasn't what I was here for. All
London could do was send one of their tame mind benders
to work on Nora Tewson and by the time he'd produced
results I'd be somewhere else and stuck into a different
jumble sale—Helsinki, if I could twist their arm, there was
a ministry scandal blowing up and we all knew it was Ni-
kolai again and we'd have to stop him. Aware, at the edge
of my thoughts, that the sound of the launch remained
steady, even though it was on the horizon now. They were
going to go straight through the roof in London because
they hated a mission to abort, it meant someone had blun-
dered. I supposed it was something to do with the acoustic
properties of the East Lamma Channel, there was an echo
coming back from the hills over there, making it seem that
the launch was stationary at full speed. So what did we
do, we lost yet another of those poor little wretches they
always put in the field too early and we had all the paper
off the wall at the Hong Kong Cathay and we ran out of
toothpaste. London was going to fire Egerton from a cannon every Tuesday at the Horse Guards Parade for as
long as they could find anything to put back in the barrel.
But the *direction* of the sound had altered too, and I
turned my head.

The damn thing was nosing inshore, losing way; some
kind of police boat—I hadn't seen it because the binoculars had been stuck in my eyes—the engines dying to a
slow boil, three smart-looking officers in the stern and
watching me but not making any sign in case I was the
wrong man. I went along the breakwater like a monkey,
jumping from pile to pile and trying to keep my balance
along the horizontal timbers. The launch was standing off,
quite a big vessel, twin screws, couldn't come in any
closer, take time to lower the boat, it was up to me, really.

One of them grabbed me as I fell aboard.

"Can you move off?"

"Are you Mr. Wing? We received—"

"Can you move off *immediately*? Look, you see that boat on the horizon?"

His head swung like a perched hawk's when it sights prey. He was a neat young Chinese, thin as a string, all cap peak and cheekbones, his eyes locked on the distant sea.

"You wish me to follow?"

"If it's not too late."

He moved a hand in a signal to the bo'sun and nearly had me in the water as the stern dipped and the deck lurched, sending me against the rails. He was calling something to me above the roar of the engines.

"What?" I shouted.

"Are you Mr. Wing?"

"Yes."

"Captain Liu Tse-tung, Narcotics Division."

The wind was whipping at our faces now and he led me into the cabin. I caught the scent right away and he saw my expression, giving a quick laugh.

"Fifty kilos," he said. A couple of the bags had burst and the stuff had spilled across the top of the locker. "We were taking it in when we had the signal about you."

"When was that?"

"At 05:40. We were north of Green Island."

"You didn't waste any time."

Peripheral anxiety: Nora Tewson might conceivably note that two minutes after the launch had left the hotel mooring a police boat had put to sea at full speed half a mile north along the shore. We didn't carry any markings visible at that distance but we had radar and we didn't look like a cabin cruiser. Nothing to be done about it: ignore.

There were some charts framed under glass on the bulkhead and I looked at them. Hydrographic Department, Hong Kong Approaches. The relevant sheet was No. 341: Islands South of Lantao.

"What's your bearing, Captain Liu?"

He looked at the compass. "Two-four-oh."

We were heading roughly southwest, passing the north coast of Lamma Island by Pak Kok Point and moving into the West Lamma Channel. I'd assumed that a Peking-based operation would take the launch northwest towards the South China seaboard but I was wrong, unless it was

going to round Lantao from the south and head north after leaving Hong Kong territorial waters. We could see its
dark blob through the windscreen, larger now and growing
clearer. The sun was almost directly behind us and still
only two diameters high, right in their eyes if they looked
astern.

"Are we flat out?"

"I am sorry?"

"Are we going at full speed?"

"Yes."

"All I want is to see where they go. Do what you can to
stay up-sun of them."

"To stay—?"

"Stay between them and the sun."

"Ah yes, understand."

It occurred to me that London had taken so bloody long
because they'd had to screen the whole of the Hong Kong
police through local agents in place before they could give
me a boat crew I could trust: Macklin had told me to use
utmost care in approaching the police or the Special
Branch. Egerton must have worked his chilblains to the
bone getting me this toy; it was a shame.

In ten minutes we began passing junks on their way out
to the fishing banks and I looked at the chart again.
Lamma was to port and falling astern, with Cheung Chao
Island coming up on the other side. The deck had been
tilting a bit and I took a look at the compass. We'd begun
heading a few points more southerly at 235 degrees. Five
minutes later Captain Liu spoke again.

"You wish me still follow?"

"Yes. Why?"

"We are leaving territorial waters now."

"What difference does that make?"

"Only if you wish me to put a shot across bows, or
go aboard. We have no more authority now."

He was looking slightly disappointed, and I thought
what a dangerous world it was.

"They must *not* see us, Captain Liu. They must remain
totally *unaware* of our presence. Now is that understood?"

"Oh yes, understood."

He turned away slightly, probably embarrassed, peering
with great concentration through the windscreen. I suppose
if you're a young ambitious skipper of a police boat you

spend a lot of your time looking for an excuse to blow someone out of the water.

There wasn't a lot of shipping about, but enough to give us a bit of cover. Liu went to stand by the bo'sun and we altered course twice in the next ten minutes as he brought us almost parallel with the launch, keeping between it and the sun. Then he ordered half speed.

07:03.

"What's that thing?" I asked him.

"An oil rig."

"Who does it belong to?"

"Communist China."

I watched the distant shape of the launch slowing towards the oil rig, then looked at the chart again. The date on Sheet 341 was 1972, but someone had marked the rig in ink later, slightly west of longitude 114° by east, latitude 22° by north, some two miles south of the Sanmen Island group.

"Stop both," Liu ordered.

The bubbling of the exhaust died to silence, and we began drifting, suddenly isolated on the expanse of the sea. Water slapped sometimes under the stern, and a cable strained at its cleat somewhere forward of the radio mast. The sun was already hot, and threw an oily shadow on the starboard side. Captain Liu stood without moving, his cap peak set like a pointer at the horizon. The superstructure of the oil rig stood like a splinter against the sky, and within five minutes the shape of the launch had merged with it. I took another look through the 7×50's, but we were still too distant to see much detail.

"All right," I told Liu.

"You wish to return?"

"Yes." I got him over to the charts. "Head well to the north here, above Sha Wan, and come down the coast, keeping as close to it as you can."

He spoke to the bo'sun, and as we turned and got under way I stood looking at Sheet 341. Mandarin was still running, and we now had a target zone centre: 114° by 22°, South China Sea.

In the first two seconds I forced a *yoshida* on him but he knew this one and broke it and his foot razored the air edge-on, fast and powerful and deadly but missing me and bringing down some of the jars. They crashed to the floor and my scalp rose but there was nothing I could do. The man was my first concern, not the reptiles, because he was trying to kill me and they would only attack in fright. We rolled and glass crunched under me and he gained a lock and I think it would have finished me but I was lying half across one of the snakes and it began striking at my arm, again and again, and I had to do something because I couldn't stand them, they nauseated me, again and again, coiling and releasing, its scales livid and the tiny black eyes glistening and the jaws gaping at right angles in a regular rhythm as it coiled, released and struck, coiling again as the pain burned in my arm.

It made me feel sick and I had to do something because there were some others free too, slithering around among the broken glass. They'd send me mad if I couldn't get away so I used my other knee and brought it against him in a jackknife drive that would have been quite useless without my horror of these things to give it force, and the hold eased and came on again and then broke and I tried the only trick I had, the third movement of the *toka,* going straight in without the first and second preliminaries to open up on the target, but he took it and waited, knowing I didn't have the leverage to make the kill. For nearly a second we lay locked and immobile, one body, a two-headed eight-limbed freak with its fierce internal energies at variance and on the point of blowing it apart as the electro-chemical forces sought to regain stability.

I didn't know anything about him. There had only been Chiang here when I'd walked into the snake shop, and at first he'd acknowledged me with a slight nod; then his eyes had shifted quickly to look past me, over my shoulder, and I had moved. There wasn't time to do anything consciously: in extreme danger the organism cedes control to the primitive brain, and the cortex is required only to compute data and supply intelligence. Of the several hundred thousand facts, impressions and implications, these were salient: I was presently listed for elimination by an alien network heavily infiltrating the field; there was alarm in Chiang's eyes; in the Orient the bare hand is the traditional weapon; Chiang's eyes had shifted only once, so that there was probably only one man behind me; my hope of survival in these circumstances (unarmed combat,

close confines, one adversary) lay more in a blind lightning move than in a considered and organized attack. In
the fifth of a second it would take me to turn and consider
the ideal defence he could fell me with a hand blade to
the neck.

So I'd gone in low, spinning and reaching for his legs
and finding them, bringing him off balance and chopping
at the kneecap to paralyze, since it was the first target
presented. If there'd been a mistake, if there'd been no intention on his part to attack, I would have known it at
once and could have withdrawn, leaving him only bruised.
But there hadn't been any mistake: I'd known from the
stance of his feet that I'd caught him halfway through a
blow designed to kill.

During this second of suspended time there was near-
silence around us as we lay locked together in mortal inti-
macy on the fragments of glass. I had managed to shift
my weight and roll sideways a little so as to bring one elbow down across the small scaly head, crushing it by
degrees until its movement stopped. A heavy slithering
came from somewhere close and I wished they weren't so
quiet, I wished they'd scream in their fright or bang into
something, to take my mind away from their oily legless-
ness.

Something else moved now: Chiang. I didn't know anything about Chiang either. He ran a safe house for the Bureau with global transmission facilities and had no love for
the mainland Chinese but that was all I knew. I didn't
know what he was prepared to do for me at this moment;
and it would be fatal to believe he'd do anything at all.

I think he was going to shut the door of the shop, and
in part of my vision field I could see the faces of two boys
peering in from the street, perhaps wondering at the crash
of glass just now; but this street, at this hour, was filled
with its own din and probably no one else had heard.

The man on the floor with me moved. I couldn't do
anything immediately because this new advantage was his
and we both knew it and we'd felt it coming: one of the
hazards of close combat is sweat, and for the past few seconds it had been springing on our skin, most critically on
the fingers of my left hand that were gripping his wrist.
He had felt them begin to slip and so had I and we were
both ready but he was faster and the air brushed my face

as he chopped hard for the temple and missed and chopped again and tried for a third time, too greedy or too impatient, spending his strength and letting me work for a throw and letting me get it, a blinding light in my head as I called for more force than I had, pain under my palm as broken glass went in, the throw succeeding to the point of taking him off balance and leaving him vulnerable, not defenceless but open to anything I could do with my right hand. There wasn't a lot of opportunity because he was spinning away from me through the terminal phase of the throw, his shoulder smashing against the shelf of jars and sending them down, his face passing for the first time across my field of vision: a youth with thick black brows and flattened eyes, a Chinese from the north or northeast, Mongolian or Manchurian. Glass flew as the jars hit the floor and a black and yellow trickle ran, forming a coil and rearing, but I blocked my mind and tried to concentrate totally on the need to survive.

Forebrain processing was taking over the gross elements of the task while the primitive creature conditioned itself, the nerve signals triggering the medulla and pouring adrenaline into the bloodstream, the pulse rate and blood pressure rising as sugar flowed in to feed the muscles, the senses increasing in their refinement so that the input of data should receive almost instantaneous assessment by the cortex.

But time moved slowly and at present the overall data was derived from a scene that was near stationary: the youth was still reacting from the momentum of the throw, his head jerking as his shoulder bounced from the shelf. Somewhere at the edge of the scene was Chiang, slamming the door.

Forebrain. The youth was coming back in a rebound from the shelf and I could take him with a single bracket throw if I waited long enough: it would need a tenth of a second. His face had blenched and I thought it was only partly because his blood had receded to supply the internal organs: his shoulder had smashed fairly hard into the edge of the shelf and the muscle would be in trauma. I went on waiting, letting him come, working out what I wanted to do and planning the best way to do it. The bracket was still viable, right hand in a swinging chop at the nape of his neck to add force to his own momentum, left hand bunched and driven upwards into his abdomen. Supplementary moves: my left knee to his groin if the bracket spun him towards me, a chop at his shoulder to increase the degree of paralysis made by his impact with the edge of the shelf.

It was getting near time and he was already working for some kind of initiative but we were too close for foot blows and he wasn't moving his left hand or arm: they were hanging from the shoulder and I knew why his face was white. The heel of his right hand was coming up but he wouldn't be able to make the blow because his right foot was too close for support. Then it was time and I put the bracket on him, connecting but not strongly enough for a finish because my foot was slipping on something and robbing me of the support I needed. He buckled over the abdomen blow and my hand hit iron muscle and there wasn't anything I could do about it because the bracket was on and he was still alive and very active, hooking at my leg and swinging a close fast throw that turned me and sent me down. He could have done it then because my spine was exposed and he still had the strength in one hand but what he didn't realize was that he was throwing me back into that bloody snakepit *and I wasn't going to have it.*

The forebrain shut off almost completely and the organism took over and I was vaguely aware of the action being triggered by the emotional syndrome: horror, desperation, fury—each emotion contributing to the next and powering the physical body with speed and strength otherwise unavailable. No science, no cerebration, no technique. Blind rage. In this way murder is often done, and the well-known statement is heard later in court: *I don't know what happened. Something just came over me.*

I think he reacted twice, but nothing remained in my memory except an impression of heat, redness and a form of unearthly joy. It probably took two seconds, three at the most. I wasn't on the floor any more because that was the place where the organism had been determined not to go: it had been quite adamant about this because it had known that if it fell down there among those things again it would go mad.

I was standing in a crouch with my back against the wooden counter. He was on the floor, facing upwards with his eyes still open. Blood was dripping from my hand where the glass had gone in. It was dripping into one of his eyes and I moved my hand away, thinking vaguely that if it went on dripping there he wouldn't be able to see, though of course it didn't matter what went into his eyes now.

It was very quiet except for the sawing of my breath. I didn't hear anything but sensed a movement to my right, and looked up at the man sitting on the stairs holding the gun.

8

555

"Put that bloody thing away," I told him.

I meant it. I wasn't joking.

He'd had me worried for a second, till I'd recognized him. I'd thought it was more trouble and I wasn't ready for it.

He was Ferris.

"Tried to tread on you," he said, "did they?"

He gave a wintry little smile, putting the gun away.

Ferris had directed me in Hanover, last time. He was sitting on the steep flight of stairs, thin and sandy and owlish, an eccentric don, his hair all over the place, what was left of it.

"Why didn't you do it?" I asked him, still annoyed at the start he'd given me.

"You wouldn't keep still."

I suppose he didn't want to make a noise, either, not that sort of a noise. And he might have got Chiang in the leg or somewhere. He would only have done it if he'd seen I couldn't do it myself: that was Ferris, he always made you bloody well work for your living.

My breath went on sawing. I'd used an awful lot of muscle in the last few seconds and I needed the oxygen back and my lungs were going like bellows. When I could I said:

"Chiang. What kind of venom is it?"

He didn't answer. He was standing quietly looking down at the boy on the floor, his expression benign. It could have been Chiang who'd done something at the last minute, thinking I couldn't manage: he was a belt, the briefing said. Maybe I'd ask Ferris. Or maybe I didn't want to know.

"*Chiang.*" My nerves were still sensitive.

His head snapped up.

"What kind of venom have these things got?"

"Venom?"

"Poison—come on, I want to know if it's—"

"No poison." He shook his head. "Snake not venomous, no. Law not allow, in shops." He took a step towards me and dragged my sleeve back, his fingers very strong. There were fang marks all over the place and I tried not to think about it. "No trouble," he said. "It happen sometime with me too, is like little nails." He called suddenly in the direction of the stairs. "*Chih-chi!*" As he moved impatiently towards the stairs I caught the smell of the incense that clung to his gown. I straightened my back slowly, letting the nerves explore the bones and ligaments. There didn't seem to be anything wrong, just the hand burning, and the punctures in the arm.

Chiang moved past me again, taking the boy's wrists and dragging him through the broken glass, leaving him behind the counter. One of them slid across the floor in a series of smooth curves, black and yellow, and I said:

"Ferris. Where are we going to talk?"

"Up here."

I walked to the stairs, watching for another one and ready to kick out. A girl was coming down in a cheongsam, not looking at me, looking at Chiang. He spoke to her in Cantonese, with no particular urgency in his tone. They had to see to the *Sai-yan*, his hand was bleeding, then they had to clear up all this mess and find the reptiles, they would keep the door locked, so forth, and she kept saying yes, yes, quickly and repetitively like the chatter of a bird, expressing her fright at the mess, looking down at my hand, then fleetingly up at my face. She went back up the stairs.

"Chiang," Ferris said. "What about *him?*"

"Ah!" He threw his head back quickly. "I will make all in order." He came shuffling quickly to the stairs, scattering bits of glass and flicking the dead snake aside with his pointed shoe, folding his strong stubby hands and speaking softly and emphatically to Ferris. "Will cost money, to take him long way and bury with *fung shui*. There will be many others to pay, tea money and for not speaking of this. Will cost two thousand dollars," watching our faces to catch our reaction.

"You will be paid," Ferris said thinly, "what London decides you are to be paid." I remembered he hated mercenaries, even though we had to depend on them for so many things. It was nothing to do with morality: he knew they were dangerous. "And there will be no *fung shui,* because he was our enemy, not yours. And there will not be 'many' others to help. You will use *one* other, and you make damned sure he's deaf, blind and dumb. You should be ashamed of yourself: in London Mr. Chiang is not said to be a greedy person. I would not like to report otherwise."

Chiang gave a breathy little laugh to cover his loss of face, and said nothing more. Ferris didn't look at me, but turned and went up the stairs. The girl, Chih-chi, was at the top, beckoning me to follow her. She sat me on a wicker linen basket in a bathroom on the first floor, with my wrist across the edge of the cracked hand basin, and used running water and a pair of eyebrow tweezers while I looked at the two rust stains running down beneath the taps, and the toothbrush and Lifebuoy soap and the bottle of black hair dye, one of Mr. Chiang's little secrets. She didn't speak English, or was too shy, so we spoke in Cantonese: she was the third daughter and working in a doll factory before going to the University next spring, if she could pass the examinations; but she found English difficult, "like Chinese puzzle," with a sudden warbling laugh at her own joke, her eyes darting to mine again, wondering who I was and who had smashed the jars and released the snakes down there and what had happened to my hand. The things she told me were only the record I'd asked her to put on.

She used the tweezers delicately, her hand pecking at mine like a bird, flicking the pieces of glass into the basin while I sat there feeling the reaction and feeling it more strongly because I didn't want there to be any; I had to start thinking again. But all I could think was how bloody chancy this trade was getting, it could have been me down there lying in all that hideous mess, with Ferris getting on the radio, *Wing broken,* or whatever phrase he'd use for immediate and urgent speech-code transmission to Norfolk and by direct private phone to Egerton's bedside at one in the morning. *Deceased during mission* on the right-hand page in the book before it was closed, and nothing to show for it, nothing like Thornton had shown, just a vulgar brawl with a hit man, almost an accident.

Hadn't you better think?

Well I'm bloody well trying to.

She had to grip my wrist to keep my hand still: I was shaking all over, muscular reaction, nervous reaction, could do without it, had to get back on form because they'd dropped in a director for the field and he was waiting to local-brief me. She got some bandage and a dressing and I tried to blank off my mind, clear it of all references and associations and start all over again. It worked, up to a point, and the question came in pretty sharply: *Hadn't you better think about what he was doing here?*

Well he didn't tag me from the car because I checked, all the way. And he didn't tag me from the Golden Sands. So he—

Did that hurt?

No.

Must take great care, so forth. She tied the knot.

"How did he get here?" Ferris asked me when I went up to the radio room. He assumed I knew, and it made me touchy, because I should know, and didn't. He was fiddling with the set, his long body angled and propped on one of the sacks that Chiang kept here.

"How the hell should I know?"

He turned his narrow sandy head to look at me for two seconds with his yellowish eyes. They were rather bright, with shifting lights in them, but just about as expressive as a cat's-eye on the road. He wore plain glass in his spectacles: we all knew that. It was some kind of image he was trying to identify with, and it was very successful because you only had to imagine Ferris without his glasses to realize you'd never recognize him. He looked away, with the faintest smile, and went on fiddling with the set. He knew I didn't mean how the hell should I know, I meant shut up I'm trying to think.

There'd been no tag from the Golden Sands and no tag from the Taunus. Either he was one of the people they'd drafted into the field to keep watch for me, or Chiang had blown me.

"Ferris."

He looked up. I said:

"Has Chiang had recent screenings?"

"Oh please be serious," he said, and gave a token giggle, concentrating on the set again, trying to clear the signal identification bleep from the background noise.

I realized I must be in mild delayed shock because if that boy had been one of the people who'd been drafted into the field to watch for me he'd be doing it at the Hong Kong Cathay and the Mauritius and the Orient Club and places like that where I'd been sighted and identified, not here at the safe house. No one had ever seen me come here: no one. *Except him.*

There was something I was missing and it wasn't anything to do with Chiang. When London sets up a safe house it doesn't leave anything to chance because if one major operator gets blown at any given time and in any given place it can shake the whole of the network and do irreversible damage and we all know that and I'd forgotten and Ferris had reminded me.

I was forgetting too much.

"Ferris."

He looked up again.

"I've got something for them," I said.

"London?"

"Yes."

"I'm holding open for them now. Can it wait?"

"If you like. But I know where Tewson went to."

"Oh Jesus Christ," he said and switched over to send.

I told him where the thing was, 114° by 22°, and he began sending in cypher.

Forgetting too much, but some of it was coming back and I went down the stairs and found Chiang putting those bloody things into a canvas bag while Chih-chi swept the glass into a cardboard box marked *Nestlé's*.

"Chiang, are there any more of those things loose?"

"Is all now," he said, "all home." He was looking despondent and I didn't know whether it was because I'd finished off one of his most expensive delicacies or whether he was still annoyed with Ferris for not letting him screw the Bureau for a couple of thousand Hong Kong dollars.

I went behind the counter and bent over the boy and he stared at me with one eye as I found his wallet, checking it, yes, a picture of me, a copy of the one they'd found in their Western networks file, not so good as the one I had of Tewson but quite recognizable, some kind of minaret in the hazy background, it could have been a stray they'd shot while I was doing the Bangkok thing. I took the wallet upstairs for Ferris to go through, and put a match to the photograph and waited until he'd finished sending.

923–843–01 blank 267–783–14 . . . the same as the one they'd given me, because that was the cypher for Mandarin. He was telling them about the boy downstairs while he was at it: *no smoke necessary, contact will deal immediate, any dossier to follow.* There might be something in the wallet he could send, but the boy was only a hit and wouldn't know anything about the Peking cell, any more than Flower had known about the Bureau.

"An *oil rig*," said Ferris, and swung round on the sack of herbs. "Now there's a funny place." He sniffed the air and looked at the curl of black ash. "Your picture, was it?"

"Yes."

"They must have it on file." He looked up at me critically. "Would you like a tetanus shot or anything?"

"Not really."

"Are you ready to fill me in?"

"There's not much." I slid my back down the wall and sat on the floor and told him everything I could think of. He broke in only when he wanted me to know something or when he wanted me to see that he already had the background . . . yes, his parents are flying out to take his body back home . . . yes, they sent me a microfilm on the lady Nora . . . all right, I'll deal with that, when you've told me what sort of damage they did . . . It took only ten minutes but by that time I'd formed a conclusion about Egerton: he was a worse bastard than I'd thought. Because Ferris had too clear a picture for London to have jumped him in from Peking as a reflex action in the last twenty-four hours.

"When did they bring you in on Mandarin, Ferris?"

"Six weeks ago."

"Did they tell you who you were going to direct?"

"They said they hoped to get you."

"I bet it wasn't Egerton who said that."

"No, it was—" then he broke off and looked at me and the faint crinkles began at the corners of his eyes. "Did the Egg say he didn't have a director for you?"

"Macklin said so."

"Macklin?"

"He's in Field Briefing."

"Oh he is, is he? Well we're not taking any instructions from him, old boy, he gets all his maps back to front. Oh I *see*," he said suddenly, giving a soft whinny. "The Egg thought you wouldn't take it on if he couldn't drop you straight into the action, is that it? Took you in, did he? Serves you right, you're always trying to pick and choose." He was looking me all over with critical eyes. "You feeling uncomfy, are you?"

"It was those bloody reptiles, I can't stand the things."

"Oh really? I thought they looked rather jolly old fellows."

He got off the sack like a stork taking off and went to the top of the stairs, waving a finger in the direction of the set. "Keep an ear open, old boy." Then he was shouting for Chiang, telling him he'd got some shopping for Chih-chi to do, poking his head back in the doorway. "What are your measurements?"

"Which ones?"

I wished he'd shut up and settle down and let me think because I wanted to know how it had happened. I suppose he was being very decent about it, giving me time to work things out: a director like Sargent or Loman would have slung the whole book at me for turning up at a safe house for initial local briefing with a tag right on my back. It must have shaken him.

"Need a new suit," he said. "Get arrested if you went out of here in that one, blood all over it."

I gave him my measurements and told him to change the image and felt an immediate fool because it was the first thing he'd think of. He pretended he hadn't heard. I sat watching the carrier level and tried again but all I came up with was another negative finding: they hadn't raided Self Drive or if they had it didn't give them a lead because I'd put my address as the Hong Kong Cathay and I'd never been back there.

"Thing is," Ferris told me as he came back and sat on his sack, "there were only two characters who were ready to look at this job, but the Egg said he didn't want them because they probably wouldn't live. No names and all that, but they're a couple of clowns, knives in their teeth, that sort of thing." Feldman, I thought, and Ptack, neither of them long enough out of middle Europe to develop style. "They wouldn't have looked twice at the toothpaste, for instance, and you know what the Egg always says: 'There are old agents and bold agents, but there are no old bold agents.' "

There was a fly buzzing at the window and he got up and began stabbing at it with his long pale finger until I heard a light brittle crunch. He came back and sat down, wiping his finger on the sack, and I remembered him in Hanover and before that in Tangier, going out of his way to step on a beetle and coming back without any interruption in what he was saying. We don't know much about our directors but one thing I knew about Ferris was that he'd been sent into Brussels three years ago with express orders to hit a man who'd been turned, and he was back inside twenty-four hours and nobody asked anything or said anything but the next day the tin came round to all departments and we dubbed up for the widow. At the time we didn't know it was Ferris but we knew it was someone in the top echelon, active branch, and it didn't take some of us long to work it out.

Even his choice of phrase was significant: *Tried to tread on you, did they?*

"They probably saw you in the street," he said consolingly. There was some static and the S meter reacted and he looked at it and away again. "Despite what the chamber of commerce says, the two chief industries in Hong Kong are narcotics and espionage, I dare say you know that. They're all here, including M.I.5, the C.I.A. and of course half the population of Moscow. More to the point, almost the entire population of Peking is here, and you may have noticed how the walls of the Bank of China appear to be bulging."

The set came alive and he adjusted the band spread, listening with his head on one side and perfectly still, like a praying mantis. It was a brief request to stand by and he acknowledged.

"So you may have been seen in the street. Unpalatable but not unthinkable."

I didn't say anything because he was interested in the set now and anyway there wasn't a lot to say. By "unpalatable" he didn't mean it was unnerving to think one could be sighted by pure chance; he meant that even if it was a fact it left you with the feeling you were dodging the issue and saying oh well, it was probably a bit of bad luck.

That could be fatal.

Still a point I was missing so I shut it right out of my mind and let the subconscious work on it without any pressure from the forebrain: it was the quickest way. I could hear Chiang in the shop below, clearing up the last of the glass, and Ferris said:

"He's all right, you don't have to worry. One of those who got across just after the purge. They shot his wife before they were a hundred yards out but he kept on swimming: it's ten miles, you know, where he did it. They'd been married three days. Of course, he doesn't remember her now, or not much, but the barb went in and it won't ever come out, you know how it goes. Notice how content-ed he looked when that character down there stopped moving? Hates their guts." He gave a titter. "Doesn't stop him trying to ride the Bureau all the way to the bank."

He was simply telling me that if I thought I was tagged here because Chiang had blown me I was wrong and I'd better think again. I gave it a try and for the first time came up with a positive: the Honda had still been outside the Golden Sands when I'd left there and the Taunus was in view of the windows so I'd got a boy to bring it across to the steps, told him I'd strained my ankle: it had been the best I could do and it had given me full cover from the upper floors but it was just conceivable that the Honda tag had sighted me from somewhere below.

"Dear oh dear," said Ferris. "They really are terribly constipated today, aren't they?" He fidgeted with the band spread again but he could tell he was spot on. Then he stopped fidgeting and sat absolutely still, perhaps as an ex-ercise, to prove he could do it. It worried me a bit because he shouldn't have to. Certainly I'd brought a tag right into the safe house at the initial rendezvous and had to kill him in front of a witness but as far as we knew the situation was secure again, and Chiang seemed confident he could lose the body.

As far as we knew. It could be that. The tag could never go back to his cell or send them a signal or in any way blow the safe house, but *somewhere he'd picked me up* and if he could do it so could someone else, the minute I left here. Until I could find out how he'd got on to me I couldn't come back here once I'd left: so the safe house was blown anyway, in that it was no longer usable except for transmission.

I wanted to ask Ferris his thoughts on this but I didn't think I'd like the answer so I left it and went on sitting on the floor with my hand beginning to throb, watching his insect-like stillness.

"What happened to North?" he asked me. "You were there, weren't you?" He eyed me obliquely through his glasses.

"I thought you'd been stuck in Peking."

There wouldn't have been any signals on a thing like that. On the contrary, half the staff at the Bureau would have been put on special duties, brushing it under the rug.

"We get the *Telegraph*," he said innocently, "by diplomatic bag. Just for the crossword."

"He shot himself."

"I know. It said so."

In the press his name had been given as Dorkins, and he'd been a charter pilot for some unheard-of outfit.

"Well that's what happened," I said.

"That all?"

"He didn't blow anything, if that's what you mean."

"That's what I mean."

"He was still peddling his cover, even to Connie, just before he went and did it. I thought that was pretty good, considering the state he was in."

"Oh very," he said quickly and looked at the wall. "Poor old North."

I didn't say anything, just to make it difficult for him.

"He was doing something for Liaison Group, in Moscow, went and fell hook line and sinker for an actress. He always was a bit corny, remember? Actually she was working Venus traps for delegates from Finland—the roof's coming off Helsinki any time now, did you know? Anyway she fell for him too, snap crackle pop, not just drawers off and the door shut, the whole red rosy rigmarole, hearts entwined forever, going to get married and everything. Then dear old Auntie KG found out and shot her dead in front of him when they were getting on the plane for Antwerp; both had perfectly good papers, he'd fixed them for her. He was all right, travelling separately, clean as a whistle, but I suppose it broke him up. Only known her for three weeks; some people are funny, aren't they? Do *you* like girls?" He gave a soft little whinny and got down in front of the set, spinning the band spread and moving the main tuner to make sure it was working.

"I heard," I told him carefully, "that he'd got out of Lubyanka."

He didn't turn around.

"Oh really, the things people say."

I knew he wouldn't have brought up the subject of North without a damned good reason. Bureau policy demands immediate smoke out to cover "any event of a scandalous nature or an event considered to jeopardize security," and this policy has spread a mortuary silence throughout the corridors of that dreary hole in Whitehall. I'd talked for a minute to Dewhurst the night I'd left London because we were alone and both shocked by what had happened. Policy apart, we still don't chew the fat because a lot of it's too depressing and we'd end up neurotic. Most missions are dangerous and all of them impose a strain and every so often you'll see an operator come back too shot up physically or too shaken spiritually to be sent out again, ever: at this time Macklin was one of them and North, God knows, was another.

When something like that happens, we do not ask for whom the bell tolls. We don't want to know.

Watching Ferris at the set, I thought there was only one reason why he'd brought up the subject: that's why I'd made it difficult for him, to bring him down a peg. It's nearly always a part of the executive-director relationship, especially when a mission hots up: you're both having to think like hell just to survive and you keep your wits sharp with a bit of one-upmanship. The North thing had shivered the whole of the network and London was putting smoke out world-wide. As my director in the field, Ferris was giving me the official version of the affair and that was the one I would adopt if there were any questions asked by anyone, anywhere, even—or especially—under duress.

"Ferris?"

"What?"

"Did North have anything to do with Mandarin?"

"No." Then I suppose he thought the answer had come too pat, because he spun round on his heels to face me and said slowly: "Nothing whatsoever. And that is gospel."

"Fair enough."

He spun slowly back again. London doesn't tell you more than you have to know when you're briefed because you can work better with your head clear of extraneous data, but you're never misinformed, and Ferris was just reminding me.

"Thing is," he said over his shoulder, "if they don't—"
555–555–555–555.

The call sign for Mandarin, very clear. He acknowledged and stood by. "Four blocks," he said, "aren't they getting fussy? You'd think old Parkis was running this one."

I sat a bit straighter, waiting, as Ferris was, knowing the signals were going to come on stream. I smelled the herb-and-sacking smell of this room under the roof and listened to the rising din of the narrow street below where the letter writer would be setting up her stool and the boy lighting his charcoal under the first trussed duck, but I was thinking of London at two in the morning, the wide wet streets and Egerton's battered Rover slipping through them with a bow wave on the gutter side and his pale academic face peering through the windscreen wipers—because this was obviously what was happening over there: he'd taken the earlier signal at his bedside, the one about Tewson's being on the rig, and had got dressed and gone down to the garage for his car. Now he was inside the building and loping at his own pace along the corridors, heading for the radio room. They knew he'd come in, and had flashed us the call sign, four blocks to indicate direct communication from Control to the director in the field, not really necessary because Egerton would announce himself. They must have someone new at the console.

A full minute went by and Ferris began showing his nerves, leaving the set and sitting on his sack again, crossing his legs and huffing. "Did you hear the one about the sailor who got his finger stuck in the keyhole? They tried to—"
555–000–000.
Mandarin: Control at console.

Ferris squatted on the floor again with his head near the integral mike and acknowledged. Within five seconds the signals came on stream and I sat upright with my eyes shut reading London, extending the digits and reversing the transfers and trying to place the tone and failing: they had in fact got a new boy in there, rather prissy but first-rate on his pauses and repeats.

After a minute Ferris swivelled round and looked at me.

"You reading?"

"Yes."

He turned his back again and went full out for almost thirty minutes, getting the details from me as Control asked for them: estimated number of opposition observers in the field—identity of principals if any known—location of opposition base and disposition of other field quarters, safe houses—degree of insistence—so forth, most of it routine with key contractions, the kind of things they always wanted to know at the outset of a mission. Then the questions got specific: Egerton wanted to know Mrs. Tewson's attitude towards her "deceased" husband, whether she appeared venal, disloyal, opportunistic. Was she promiscuous?

I did what I could, catching the questions in the air before Ferris had to ask me, and in fifteen minutes I was sweating hard and wishing to Christ I didn't feel so ragged: the little bastard had forced a throat block for ten seconds or so before I could break it and I was still getting flashes in front of the eyes. Then Control went on to the mundanities and the only question I had to answer was about the damage to the Hong Kong Cathay: I said they'd want some new wallpaper and a plumber and an electrician but no windows smashed, telephone okay, so forth, while some poor bloody clerk put it all in the book—you could tell this was Egerton's mission. The Hong Kong Cathay Hotel would in due course receive a cheque "in compensation for any damage sustained during the sojourn of one of their guests." If the manager took it into his head to try tracing the cheque to its source he'd grow old before his time. Egerton was particular about what he called "the public domain." Dewhurst would have just said they must be insured against drunks, bookies and acts of God and left it at that, his point being that as a British taxpayer he wasn't going to fork out for things the insurance companies ought to pay for.

298–363–586 . . .

Flower. No further action required on our part.

What would actually happen was that his parents would be met at the airport by a senior secretary of Welfare Section, and all their expenses would be paid.

398–277–972 . . .

I began reading alertly again because I could tell they were getting round to instructions. Egerton had probably gone into another room to work things out either alone or in consultation while his second-stringer key-contracted the routine advisories: further movements and establishing of access, liaison and security left to discretion of director in field; transmission schedules to be as per current pattern, Far East theatre; emergency signals to follow established rulings as to times, form and code; allocation of stand-by periods to conform with current schedules, bi-hourly (diurnal), hourly (nocturnal); heavy traffic bypass key: 555–000. State of mission reports were specified, right down to the last micro-dot.

Then they went off the air for fifteen minutes.

Two stand-by signals and then four blocks of 555. Then they began on the instructions, the first of which we'd already been expecting: I was to go out to the oil rig and try to get aboard.

9
Shield

Then I stopped dead.

I suppose there wasn't anything to get excited about but it had worried me, having to kill him like that, and he'd left a lot of muscular strain in me and there'd been those bloody things slithering about. Oh fair enough, all in the day's work, but look, we hadn't even got any target access figured out yet and already there were two dead and I wasn't beginning to fancy my chances all that much.

I stood in the street, close to a doorway, very close, looking between the buildings towards the open square in the distance, wanting to shout at them: *Can't you leave me alone?*

I just didn't feel ready for more, that was all, at least for a while. Give me a day, or even a few hours if that's how it's got to be. *Bloody well leave me alone.*

I stood in the street with the morning sun dazzling in the shop windows, the temperature in the eighties and warming up to another lovely day in exotic Hong Kong, Pearl of the Orient: this morning we shall be taking you on yet another fascinating tour, this time beginning with a tram ride to famed Victoria Peak, then down again to explore the fabulous Tiger Balm Gardens, pride of the island; stood in the street feeling how cold it was, how perilous.

From this distance I could see the Taunus easily enough, and the traffic passing it. There'd been a slot and I'd backed it in and it was still there where I'd left it. The square was a lawful parking zone but I'd taken the last slot and there hadn't been any vacancies since then, or they'd only just arrived. The Humber was double-parked with the bonnet up, some kind of engine trouble so the police couldn't move it on in a hurry. The red van had

Typhoo Tea on it in gold letters but there wasn't a grocer's or a café or a tea shop anywhere near: they were all souvenir shops and cheap jewellers' on that side of the square but the van was parked with two wheels on the pavement and the roller door was down as if there was a delivery being made. The Chinese on the bike was just sitting there with his arms folded watching the traffic, not even bothering to fetch a paper or something to read.

The others I couldn't see or hope to recognize. There'd be others, I knew that. This was about the roughest static surveillance job I'd ever seen but that wasn't the point. The point was that the Taunus was a death trap.

The left eyelid was flickering: it always did when the nerves got close to the edge. And I was cold, standing by the doorway in the sunshine, because I knew Ferris was up there in the room below the roof, thinking I still didn't know how that tag had been on my back when I'd gone into the snake shop; well he was bloody well wrong because I knew, I knew now. And the unnerving thing was that I'd known for quite a while, and could have told him, put him out of his misery. It was just that I'd had other things on my mind and hadn't taken too much notice.

I wasn't prepared to dodge the issue by saying that boy had sighted me by chance, even though Ferris had offered me the option. I *might* have been sighted by chance, but it was damned unlikely. And the only *other* way that boy could have got onto my back was by a communications pitch and the only way they could have found any use for communications was by having a signals source and he could be only one man: the one in the Honda at the Golden Sands Hotel. He'd been somewhere on the ground floor and seen me and recognized me and got onto the phone and told headquarters, and headquarters had put out an all-points bulletin and from that moment the Taunus was a marked target. I'd checked and double-checked on the way up to the safe house but there were limits to what I could do in a narrow winding street already crowded with Chinese, and the boy had been the first one to sight the Taunus and he had my photograph—they all did—and he came to make the hit.

The people down there in the square didn't know that. He'd been an isolated case on his way from base to station or nosing along the Capri travel pattern of two evenings ago and he'd been lucky, if that was the word. Then some-one else had sighted the Taunus but I wasn't there so there was no one to follow, so he signalled headquarters and brought the pack in: there could be twenty or thirty down there in the doorways and behind windows, besides the people on station near the van and the Humber and on the bicycle. They would be deployed along the streets leading to the square, the surveillance spreading tentacles in every direction to make sure I couldn't get within a hundred yards of the Taunus without being seen. Or two hundred: the distance from there to where I was standing now, close, very close, to the doorway.

My hand was throbbing. Must take care of it, she'd said. The feeling of deathly cold wouldn't go, and I got fed up because I ought to get more bloody control over myself: the mission was still in its access phase and I ought to be feeling right on my toes and I wasn't and there was no excuse.

"Tui mm chiu."

I stood back, keeping clear of the actual doorway but remaining close enough to use it. Two other people went in, a woman and her small boy, and it wouldn't do if the wrong people saw me and recognized me and went in, say three or four men, and turned round and blocked the door-way while the rest of them came up. I wouldn't know any of them. I wouldn't have time to know anything at all, if they came.

I began working back up the shallow steps—it was a lad-der street like most of them in this area—having to push my way through tourists and vendors and groups of shopkeepers gathered in the bright morning sun, *want roast duck?* The scent of cheap perfumes and the drains, long time no rain, people said, working back towards the snake shop but turning off as soon as I could to avoid the cardinal sin of visiting a safe house with surveillance known to be active, *want haircut?* The sudden clatter of a mahjong game in a doorway, a stall with wardrobes for the dead, *is this the place where you can get to see those fruit sellers, do you know?* A child's laughter as a for-tune-telling bird picked a card from the basket; turning into the alley and walking faster, checking twice and going on, using every pane of glass there was, bumping into people because I had to watch the reflections, *tui mm chiu*, sometimes attracting attention and that could be dangerous, slowing down, taking the next street, a wider one, looking now for a taxi. Finding one.

"Lane Crawford's."

When we reached there I went through the front and out by the back way, climbing over a new delivery of merchandise, finding a bar and calling Ferris.

We listened for bugs.

"My car was covered in ticks."

"Oh I see," he said. He meant that was how the boy had got on to me.

"It could be rigged as well."

"Of course. Anything in it?"

"A suitcase."

"Everything all right apart from that?"

"It is now."

I rang off and sat down in the corner of the bar with my left shoulder against the wall, the mirror on the other side of the room and the door facing me. I was clear of the Taunus trap but they were getting very insistent and I could be picked up anywhere, anywhere at all, because of the photograph.

"Coffee."

To help chase some of the adrenaline out of the system: there was no chance of physical exercise. The eyelid had stopped flickering, I should bloody well hope so, I must be getting old or something. Relax, switch off, leave things to Ferris. He'd be on to the police by now, telling them where to find the Taunus and what to do with it: check it for an explosive device, check the suitcase, take the car back to Self Drive and put the case into the harbour or wherever they liked, because I wouldn't get it back: they'd hold it for me but they wouldn't part with it or with me either without asking me an awful lot of questions. Hong Kong is just like other places: the police don't like being rung up and told to look for bombs in abandoned cars without wanting to know why. Ferris could pull enough rank to tell them to shut up but it'd mean revealing the fact that we were on the island and we didn't want to advertise it.

I'd asked him to do a couple of other things for me while he was about it: pay my bill with Fleetway and Self Drive, and get a dozen gardenias sent to El Caliph before eight o'clock tonight with a message: *Please forgive, been called to Rome due to the devaluation crisis, tried four times to ring you but not home. Will never forget you. Clive.*

I put on the mask.

The nerves were back to normal and it hadn't taken so long as I thought: for three hours I'd been moving around Central as free as a tourist and nobody had tried to raid me or even get on my tail, besides which Ferris hadn't been mean: it was a white summer-weight linen suit and quite a good fit and I felt a bit less like a lavatory brush with the mange. I'd kitted up again at Lane Crawford's: new suitcase, shaver, toilet things, shoes, so forth, and the case was genuine leather because I can't stand plastic, so that scaly old hell hag in Accounts was going to cough up her brimstone when she got the bill.

I breathed in through the nose and the face plate tightened satisfactorily and I took it off. We spent a lot of time getting a good fit for the fins: he was a helpful little man, five feet high with a crew cut and a jolly smile and the right hand off at the wrist, said it was a shark and I believed him.

"You from England?"

"Yes."

"What part?"

"London."

"So! I have sister in London! Beshnill Green!"

"Well I never."

I asked him for a double hose regulator and three standard single cylinders of compressed air with reserve mechanisms and nickel-plated interiors, capacity 71 cubic feet each.

"Can you recharge these for me if I need more air?"

"No." He shook his head, beaming. "Used to have charging room, but had also assistant who broke valve one day. Tank went through wall here and flew three streets away, finish through side of bus!" Peals of laughter. "Nobody hurt, but take permission from me. You get them filled at another place, I give you address."

"Thank you."

Tank harness with instant release buckle, lead belt, depth gauge, compass, underwater watch.

"Dry suit?"

"No, wet. Foam neoprene, have you got one?"

"Oh yes."

Diving knife, saw-tooth edge one side, straight edge the other.

"You want shark repellent?"

"Yes."

"Spear gun?"

"No."

"Abalone iron?"

"No."

I had to try three wet suits on before I found the right one. It had a yellow insignia on the back as a safety marker and I'd have to cover it with black adhesive tape later.

"Do you stock chains?"

"What sort chains?"

"To secure the tanks to the boat."

"No. Tell you where to buy." He gave me another address.

"I need a lamp."

He kicked the stool over to the shelves again and jumped up and hooked down the box, catching it in the crook of his elbow. We tested the batteries and I signed a traveller's cheque, sweating a lot after trying on all those suits but feeling much better, almost back on form, even the muscles feeling smoother. Tonight I'd be getting some sleep because Ferris wouldn't be able to rustle up everything we needed before the morning. God only knew how he was planning to send me in to the objective but if it was going to be an air drop we'd obviously have to make it by night: that would be tomorrow at the earliest.

I'd hired a dark-grey station wagon from Avis so that I could lay the air tanks flat. I stowed the gear and found the place where they sold chains and noted the place where they could give me a recharge if I needed one and bought some black adhesive tape and reached the Harbour Hotel on the north shore of the island by noon. That was where Ferris had booked me in.

There was already a message for Mr. Wing: please call TWA about my reservation. I used the phone in my room and we listened for bugs and then he went straight into speech code, switching to cypher where he had to and rattling off the numerals. The code was standard operational for this date, Far East theatre, listed arbitrary with no mnemonics: October for briefing, Monday for rendezvous, Gin rummy northeast, Yellow left hand, so forth. I went into the same pitch and thought Christ, he's got something moving.

"I want you for briefing," he said.

"When?"

"20:00 hours."

"Where?"

He gave the directions: there was a junk tied up in the Causeway Bay typhoon anchorage, the *August Moon*, the seventh along from the base of the northeast breakwater, left-hand side of the utilities stanchion.

"What's the flap?" I asked him.

"There's no flap. I'm sending you out to the rig, that's all."

"When?"

"Midnight tonight."

I slept six hours in Room 31 at the Harbour Hotel with traps at the door and the window and then got up and showered and took the stuff out of the canvas case and tried on the wet suit again and tested the mask, putting talc on the fins and taping the safety marker to black it out: they might just as well have painted a bull's-eye on the back of the suit, bang on the tenth vertebra.

19:00.

It was only a ten-minute run to the typhoon anchorage, allow another five to park the station wagon with decent security and find the *August Moon*. That gave me forty-five minutes to spare and I didn't like it: Ferris must have got a panic signal from London with orders to arrange immediate access and put his executive into the target zone, Bureau signals phrasing right out of the book. It meant they wanted the ferret thrown into the sea. That was all right: the thing I didn't like was having to hang around for three-quarters of an hour before I could even get to the briefing and find out what kind of access Ferris had fixed up and what kind of communications we were going to use and what kind of chance there was of my coming out of that particular target zone alive.

The oil rig stood in international waters but it was

Chinese territory and at a rough guess I'd put its defence armament at about the same strength as a pocket battleship.

I knew from earlier missions that Ferris was terribly fast and it was possible they'd picked him to field-direct this operation because they knew we might have to hurry at any given phase or at *some precise* phase they'd been able to anticipate in the initial planning. They might have shot him out to Peking as a cultural attaché or some kind of Embassy stooge the minute they'd seen Mandarin coming up on the agenda. I began wishing I knew a bit more about this job and that was a perfectly normal reaction at forty-four minutes to final briefing: the blood starts moving a few degrees quicker and the nerves start exchanging energy a few microseconds closer to optimum speed and you start wondering why the hell those zipper-lipped bastards in London couldn't have told you a bit more or preferably a bloody sight more about the operation they'd decided to pitch you into—in this case by Egerton's thrice-accursed subterfuge.

Relax.

I picked up the phone and gave it ten rings and put it down again and that was a perfectly normal reaction too at forty-three minutes to final briefing: the closer you move to potential death the more you think about women. Poor little bitch, we'd got her hormones moving again after all that time and all she was going to get at the El Caliph at eight o'clock tonight was a bunch of gardenias and all I was going to get was the shakes.

Phone.

19:11.

Ferris.

"London wants to send a shield."

"Oh for Christ sake, Ferris, be your age." We were using cypher and all I could give him was the circumscribed phrase: *Instructions refused.* But I got what I meant into the tone. Trust those bloody people in London to get you to the brink and then pull you back while they sent someone out to hold your hand.

"They're postponing the operation twenty-four hours," Ferris told me, "while they fly someone in from Taiwan. He's due to—"

"Ferris."

He waited.

"You let those pox-ridden bastards try sicking a shield on to me and as far as I'm concerned they can screw this mission and find another ferret. You know me and you know I mean that. I'm going in solo repeat solo or not at all."

Difficult finding the right cypher phrases, *request no support,. am withdrawing from mission*, like trying to blow someone's head off in a foreign language without knowing all the pronouns, but some of it I put across in straight English, *pox-ridden*, so forth, because it wouldn't give anything away.

"I think they're right," Ferris said reasonably.

I gave it five seconds because you don't get as far as the final briefing phase and chuck the whole thing in your director's face without another thought. This wasn't Egerton, or not totally: his chief talent was in knowing precisely what a given operator could do and how he was best able to do it. We all have our little ways and Heppinstall won't work properly *without* a shield because he's really a slide rule and requires peace of mind to do what he has to do, and while he's trying to feel his way in to the complex centre of some sophisticated shadow-summit configuration or whatever he's doing he likes to be free to concentrate while his shield keeps the competition away till he runs out of ammunition. Styles won't operate without a shield because he's shit-scared and London keeps a whole regiment standing by to support him through a mission because they know he's sensitive and brilliant and highly successful so long as he can keep his sphincter muscles under control.

I have to work solo because for me there has to be a risk. This isn't because I like a cheap thrill but because I need the stimulation of constant hazard to whip up the nerves and galvanize the organism to the pitch where I can do things I couldn't do otherwise. If I had to rely on other people to keep me alive I'd get sloppy and make mistakes and that can be just as fatal as if you haven't got a shield at all, look at that poor bastard Crowther——*I thought he was there*, his face puckered like a child's and his eyes watching me as we swayed along in the ambulance, *I thought he was there*, the last thing he ever said and I've never told anyone because he meant he thought

Jones was there, shielding his back while he went in and found he couldn't get out again till they dropped him over the railway bridge for someone to find, blown and cleaned out and dying while Jones was waiting for him in Lyons Corner House and stuffing himself on buns, a question of a missed rendezvous, that was all, a little misunderstanding at a critical time, the tears running down Crowther's face as he closed his eyes and gave it up—frustration, not self-pity or anything, he didn't leave anyone who loved him—frustration because he'd completed the access and was ready to strike and get out again, another beautiful job, beautifully timed, *how does he do* it, we all used to say.

Don't you give me Jones. Or anyone.

"Ferris," I said, "if you're not prepared to direct me without a shield you'd better say so now."

After a bit he said plaintively: "It's London, old boy."

"London knows bloody well I always work solo."

"It's because it's underwater," he said.

"Tell them they can pull me out, then. Send someone else in."

There was a short silence, then he said, "Don't go away."

I put the phone back and left an imprint of sweat on it and walked up and down, feeling soured and deceived and afraid because they could have settled this question earlier: Ferris had his access worked out, or he wouldn't have called me in for final briefing, and he couldn't have worked out his access before he'd signalled his plans. *That* was when they should have said all right but if it's under-water we're going to insist on a shield. But they'd had second thoughts and I didn't like that: it meant they were worried.

19:13.

Ferris couldn't have left the safe house yet because he was still in signals with Control. There hadn't been time for him to rig up a set of his own on the junk or some-where because he'd need to make directional tests and check out the interference patterns and he wasn't a radio man. And he wasn't signalling through Chiang: the present traffic was too sensitive. So even if he could get London to agree, it was going to take a lot of time and we were going to miss the 20:00 hours rdv and arrive late for the midnight jump and it was giving me the sweats be-

cause if ever there's a time during a mission when you
want everything to run like clockwork it's when you're
down for final briefing and taking up the slack on your
nerves so you'll be ready to do what you have to do, wherever it is and wherever it's going to take you.

Ferrets have feelings.

The phone didn't ring for twenty-five minutes and I
spent the interval in a limbo, not wanting to do anything
intelligent like checking over the briefing material because
the whole thing could have gone dead and cold by now,
very much wanting to phone Ferris and tell him to send a
final signal. *Executive withdraws from mission.* But there
wouldn't be any point because they'd know I'd started to
go gently round the bend. I'd never withdrawn from a
mission even when Loman was running me, even when the
bastards booted me into Tunis to pick up an operation already half wrecked and with two top-echelon ferrets out
of the running, one dead and one blown before we'd even
found access. That's why they shanghaied me into these
stinking rotten jobs, because they knew no one else would
take them and they knew I wouldn't back out once I'd—

Phone.

19:38.

No bugs.

"London," he said, "is going to compromise. You don't
get a shield but they're sending in a reserve."

I thought about this for so long that he had to ask if I
was still on the line. I said:

"All right. But keep him out of my way."

"I told them that's what you'd want."

"You didn't tell them anything they didn't know."

He said there was time to keep our rendezvous and I
said that was a bit of luck and rang off before I could say
anything else: because you don't feel relieved when the
pressure comes off, you feel like murder. It's something to
do with the organism using the quickest way to get rid of
the shock and I was quite happy about that, spending the
next three minutes murdering half the directors in the Bureau very slowly and with an awful lot of screaming as the
volts came on. While this was happening I put the gear
back into the canvas bag and shoved it into the wardrobe
with the track suit and the other stuff and rigged entry

traps and went down to the station wagon sixty seconds ahead of schedule.

I didn't object to a reserve. They were taking a risk, I knew that. Since my signal reporting that Tewson was alive they'd been logically assuming he was either in Hong Kong or on the Chinese mainland, where I could have got to him through the normal penetration channels. Ferris had then shaken them by reporting that he was in fact under guard in what amounted to a maximum-security block entirely surrounded by water and he'd shaken them a second time when he'd told them he planned to send me in solo.

He knew it was the only thing he could do. In the specific circumstances of this mission at this phase he knew it was the only possible access to the target zone: not by a fleet of ships or an airborne regiment, but by one man, And he knew we couldn't use a shield because this one man would himself become a target, and we didn't want to double its size. Ferris had told me he thought London was right because he wanted to see if I had any doubts. He'd seen I hadn't, and he'd got into signals again and persuaded Control to lay off.

A reserve was all right. A shield would have followed me about and tried to keep me alive and got in my bloody way, but a reserve would be told to stand off and do nothing: unless I was blown or killed. Then he'd move in. That was all right.

I drove steadily. The lights had come on in the dusk an hour ago and now they were bright, the whole of the Kowloon shoreline glittering across the night-black harbour where the shipping floated like patches of fire that had broken away from the land. The traffic was easing off towards Causeway Bay, but I was taking the narrower streets, doubling sometimes to check, finding it clear.

Waiting at a set of lights, it occurred to me that London must be terribly nervous, wanting to send in a reserve. People like Egerton realize the whole thing isn't a chess game: they know the shadow executive comes under strain the minute the mission starts running, and he's not expected to feel reassured if they send a man out to sit like a vulture on a tree while he's doing his best to stay alive and bring home a winner if he can. Normally London never tells you: they might tell the director in the field but he doesn't necessarily pass it on. Well they could screw themselves.

There were people milling around the car, trying to swarm across the road before the lights changed, and a Boeing went sloping weightlessly down the night sky towards Kai Tak on the other side of the harbour. Maybe they'd told me about the reserve because London was narked about my refusing a shield, and Ferris wanted me to know what Control's thinking was: he was very good about that, and tried not to keep you in the dark even if it meant telling you something you didn't want to know. There was no time to think about it anyway, because they were holding the gun hard against my left temple and I couldn't even turn my head to see who it was.

10

Mime

The Boeing drifted lower, its port light flicking on and off as it vanished behind the buildings and reappeared again, its attitude slightly nose up as it settled along its flight path. Most of the people milling across the road were Chinese, coming up from one of the ferry piers, but there were also a couple of American sailors and a group of Japanese tourists and an airline steward, Royal Dutch. The lights were still red.

Not many things in this scene were registering on a conscious level because they weren't significant, except for the lights. When the lights changed to green I'd have to drive off. The forebrain was very active, triggered by the sensation of pressure against the temple. Before we do anything physically we go through the performance mentally, as an automatic projection of intention to find out if it's really a good idea. If we think it is, the motor nerves are fired and the muscles ordered. There's still time to cancel the whole thing halfway or at any other stage: the freedom of choice is infinitely variable. But it's normally better to go right through with the intention once we're committed, because we've seen it happen mentally and we're fairly confident it's going to work: otherwise we wouldn't have put it into action.

There didn't seem a lot I could do. A mass of data was streaming in from the sensory systems and it had to be computed before anything useful could be done. Movement was restricted: with the people thronging in front of the station wagon I couldn't drive off. This was one of the countless combinations presenting themselves for review: a strike upwards with the right arm and a stab downwards with the right foot, leaving it for the sudden vacuum in the induction manifold to kick the automatic shift into low and send thrust into the final drive. Most of the combinations involved both movable components: man and machine. This one got an instant negative because I couldn't drive through the people and because the computing element of the cortex didn't estimate sufficient time for the right-arm action to hit the gun away before it was fired.

I assumed it was a gun but that was all it was: an assumption. Electrical impulse was pouring data into the brain and there was so much to handle that normal thought was ceding the field to imagination and instinct, and it wasn't logical to imagine they were pressing a fountain pen to my head, or a lipstick case. The image of a face flickered for one micro-second among all the others, the memory plundering its archives as a contribution to the welfare of the organism. It was a smooth round face, always rather sulky until you knew the man, Heppinstall's face, in my mind for this instant because we'd laid bets one day, the three of us (Stoner was the other), on whether it was possible to tell the calibre of a gun pressed to the back of the neck. We used several guns, alarming the fellow in Firearms because we weren't on duty at the time, and Stoner lost his money because he said one of them was a .38 and it was really the end of a scent bottle.

The lights went green.

A rickshaw got on the move, the other side of the station wagon, the man between the shafts butting his way through the stragglers. Two girls ran giggling to the crowded pavement, hobbled by their cheongsams, and on the far side of the intersection a bus driver began tapping his horn as he moved slowly forward. No one was taking any notice of what was happening around them: at this hour they were hurrying into the town from the ferries or along to the restaurants and brothels and bars of the Wan Chai district or eastwards to the hotels and supper clubs and theatres of Causeway Bay. A few were strolling, going where their fancy took them: this was their first sight of Hong Kong by night and they circled like moths.

He was a professional.

Quite a lot of the data concerned this man. Memory suggested he was Chinese because the competition on this operation was Chinese, and sensory perception tended to confirm this: he smelt of incense and the faint distorted image in the chrome strip of the window was Oriental.

The pressure against my head was steady and constant and I knew he was a professional because he was speaking to me and laughing a little, presenting the image of someone talking to a friend through the window of his car, even though he realized it was hardly necessary when the passers-by were preoccupied.

The station wagon swayed an inch as the rear door was pulled open on the other side. As far as I could tell there was only one man getting in. Then the front passenger door came open and someone else got in and slammed the door and pushed the muzzle hard against my left side, below the rib cage. The taxi in the mirror began honking because the lights had changed a few seconds ago, but we wouldn't be long now because the man who had been talking and laughing to me took his gun away and got into the back, leaning forward on the edge of the seat to talk again, bringing the gun to the nape of my neck and covering it with his left hand: I could feel the warmth of his little finger just above the muzzle.

The man beside me spoke now, prodding me, and I drove off across the intersection, going east. It was obvious what he'd told me to do, though I didn't understand: he spoke in Mandarin, the common language of the new China, as the first man had done.

"What do you want?" I asked them in English. Just a slight tremor of alarm in the voice, a couple of snatched glances at the man next to me. My cover was that of a man who dealt in rare coins and bullion and I must have had a few brushes with violence or attempted violence in my profession: a safe break or a mugging or a bag snatch, things like that: so I shouldn't be too frightened by this turn of events, but merely alarmed.

There was a flat half-muted singing of Mandarin again and I shook my head hopelessly. I was waiting for a bit of Cantonese but I wasn't going to understand that either because there's a distinct advantage in the language barrier: it invites the competition to speak freely among themselves in their own tongue and it slows the action down quite a bit when they bark out an order, because if you don't understand what they're barking out they can't expect immediate obedience.

I was now being searched, as far as was possible in the confines of the station wagon, and they were surprised not to find a gun. The ones they carried were now pressed a little harder against me, possibly because they were suspicious. Intelligent agents normally use guns.

Some more Mandarin, then some rather inept attempts at Cantonese when I kept shaking my head. These were hit men, recently arrived in Hong Kong, uneducated and no more than action-trained. Probably they'd been flown in from Peking when the people down here had found my photo in the files. There were a lot of them here, anything up to a hundred, and it didn't even have to stop at that because the population of China is embarrassingly large. They were here in force, presumably, because one operator can often mean a whole cell has moved into the field, and a cell would depend on a network.

"Down along!" he kept saying in Cantonese, while I looked suitably puzzled. He jerked a hand across the windscreen, showing me where I had to go: down towards the harbour.

I looked at my watch, being careful not to take my hand off the wheel, just angling the wrist, because they seemed rather excited and I didn't want any accidents. Both guns were suddenly pressed harder against me and I had a verbal warning. The time was 19:52 and I noted it because it's often important to remember what time an event happened: or this could be just rationalizing the subconscious need for orientation. To know the time was to control the situation, if only in terms of being informed, of being able to measure one of its elements; and I suppose this was a sop to the whimpering little organism as it tried to get my attention—*they're going to kill you . . . it's three to one and you've had it and there's nothing you can do but I don't want to die, don't let them—*

Bloody well shut up.

Sweat on my hands.

"Down!" he said at the next intersection and his thin hand pointed across the windscreen. By the reflection of its striking edge in the glass he was still having trouble with the bricks: it was swollen and inflamed. In a couple of minutes we came to a quay on the west side of the typhoon shelter and the man made me put the station wagon through a narrow gap between ropes and warning flags where the parapet was being repaired. Nobody was here, because at night there was nothing to come here for.

"Stop!"

There was a lot of sign language: I had to get out and stand with my hands raised against the wall of the rope store while they patted me all over for the gun, beginning to chatter when they couldn't find one. I could hear two of them back inside the car, pulling up the seats and snapping open the glove compartment.

"Where gun?" they asked me, frustrated.

"What the hell would I want a gun for?" Getting irritable now, a good mind to call a policeman, so forth.

It was possible they were brighter than they looked, so I launched a daring tirade of indignation in colonial English, mentioning the severe punishment they would receive at the hands of the judge, and the long years in prison they were risking by their infamous conduct. They let me go on for ten seconds or so, not because they were listening but because they were completely thrown by not being able to find my gun. Then they told me to shut up, and began on my wallet. They had a photograph of me—I could see it was another copy of the one I'd found on the boy in the snake shop—and they began comparing it with my face and the photograph in my passport, making me stand facing the tall lamp at the edge of the quay. They weren't too satisfied, but then I didn't see how they could be, because passport photos are only ever good for a giggle and the one their network was circulating in Hong Kong was grainy.

I stood as they'd placed me, hands by my sides so as not to attract attention if anyone came by. A gun was pressed against my spine while the other two went through my papers: driving licence, membership card of the British Numismatic Association, representative's card for Mendoza S.A. of Buenos Aires, the letters of introduction.

"You've made a mistake," I said.

They looked at me and then at the papers again. I don't think they'd understood, but I sensed they were pretty impressed by the cover material and for the first time it occurred to me that I had a chance of getting out of this alive. The feeling was quite heady, and an indication of how depressed I'd been getting before I'd seen the straws in the wind. The thing was that all they'd had to go on was the photograph: the copy of the one on file at the Bank of China. The station wagon was clear and so was the Harbour Hotel, and they'd picked me up on sight alone: part luck and part efficiency. There weren't many English in Hong Kong but the faces of Caucasians looked much alike to the Asians and they'd been very good and that was probably why they were so excited when they'd got into the car. Now they were beginning to wonder if they'd got the right man.

"You're looking for someone else," I told them, shaking my head. The two of them looked up again.

"What this?"

He held out one of the letters of introduction, trying to sound accusing. He could have questioned any of the other papers just as well: he wanted me to react, that was all.

"Coins," I said. The Mendoza letter heading carried three gold pieces, sumptuously embossed and gilded. With great care I moved my hand, pointing to my pocket.

"What coin?"

I took a risk and tapped my pocket with a stiff finger, making my small change clink, then bringing my hand very slowly to point at the letter. "I am a coin dealer."

"How this?"

He meant my left hand.

"Accident." I didn't want to go into that one so I produced a short embarrassed laugh. "Look, I thought you were going to rob me, but now I can see you're looking for someone in particular." I spread my hands till the gun prodded my spine. "I am not the man you are looking for."

It was the only possible hope. They were young and inexperienced and would fear their superiors; and they weren't keen on knocking off an innocent party before they'd made sure who he was. On the other hand they felt frustrated about this: they were three of the toughest young thugs I'd ever seen and they were longing to make a killing for the hell of it because that's what their Peking instructors had been training them to do for so long.

"You come Londan?"

He had the inhuman stare of the disciple newly ordained: with all the power of Mao behind him, he was addressing one of the imperialist vermin he had learned about at the desk and on the blackboard. They'd stuffed his head with *ta tzu-pao* and his stomach with government rice and sent him out crusading, a true Son of the Socialist Revolution, a brave Soldier of the People's Liberation Army, neither lance in his hand nor falcon at his wrist but just an itch in the pit of his guts to do in reality what he had done so many times in make-believe, spilling the saw-dust out of the sacks in the sweaty gymnasium, sending them swinging on their ropes at a chop of his hand or a kick of his foot without even hating them, and dreaming of the day when his masters would give him something alive, something to hate, something to kill.

Something like me.

"No," I said, "I don't come from London."

I didn't think he could read Roman characters. He couldn't: he didn't react. The passport and the other papers didn't mean anything to him and that was why he found them impressive: their very unintelligibility was mystic and had power over him. He went on staring for a moment and then turned suddenly away to talk to the other man: not the one with the gun at my spine, the one with the blepharitis. They spoke in Mandarin still, the *Kuo-yü*, and I couldn't follow; but it seemed as if they thought they'd made a mistake and didn't know what to do next, so I began rehearsing a speech in simple English. They wouldn't understand but the words would implement my gestures and provide the vehicle for tone: and the tone was very important—rueful, conciliatory, half admitting myself as party to their unfortunate mistake.

"Listen," I said, and they looked at me. "If you will let me go, I will tell no one. It is a silly mistake. I will go away quietly, and forget." I rang the changes on this theme, bowing myself out of their ken, taking a step towards the station wagon, shaking my head sorrowfully about our foolish misunderstanding, the bloody thing poking sharply into my back as I took that one step nearer the car. I stopped and waited for them to react.

There were chimes sounding somewhere, probably from one of the English churches. Eight o'clock, the hour when a young married widow with a taste for Ming and emer-alds and *soixanteneuf* would be going through the doors of El Caliph to receive in surprise a dozen gardenias in lieu of dalliance; when a thin owlish man with a thing against insects and a scar on his soul would be waiting in the shadows on a Hong Kong junk and listening to these same chimes, checking his watch; and when Clive Wing, coin dealer, was standing on a deserted quayside wondering how many minutes longer he was going to live.

They'd listened to what I'd said and their rather bright stares had followed my gestures attentively: the language of mime is universally understood, even by children. They seemed to be waiting for me to go on, but I decided to leave it at that, as if I felt confident and didn't need to protest. It was quiet here, and we all stood perfectly still as we considered, in our divers ways, what should be done.

I thought I could neutralize one of them: the one with the gun at my back. It would take him a long time, relatively, to pull the trigger, because I would induce nervous trauma in him first. That's why I always disappoint those people in Firearms when they try to sell me their goods: I just don't trust the bloody things. They're heavy and awkward and unreliable and of course an absolute giveaway, and I don't like the bang they make. When these ticks had hijacked me just now in the car I couldn't have used a gun even if I'd carried one, and they wouldn't have accepted my cover: they'd have known right away they'd pulled in the spook they were after. No go.

It takes time to pull a trigger because the chain of events is long and intricate. This boy would have fast reactions but that would only narrow the time gap: it wouldn't close it. Whatever move I made would surprise him because he was holding a gun and I wasn't and this gave him enormous confidence and left him wide open to surprise and all its hazards: he'd lose something in the region of a tenth of a second right at the outset because the flood of incoming data would be blocked off by the condition of shock. He wouldn't be able to think what I was doing because his ability to reason would be suspended until the shock phase was over. Added to this critical delay would be the normal physiological requirements in terms of time: the time needed to assess the data, decide on the appropriate action, envisage it, analyze the image, reach the decision to act and order the action. The transmission of nervous signals would take very little time, the electrical impulse travelling at a hundred miles per second and in this case probably a little faster since the organism was trained in unarmed combat. But once his trigger finger had become active under its muscle contraction he was going to run into a phase of gross delay in the overall operation: the flesh of his finger alone would absorb several minor fractions of a second, and the spring mechanism of the gun would then begin using up the greatest proportion of the total time demanded from initiation to completion.

They stared at me, at my rueful smile.

Somewhere inland the clock in the church ended its chimes.

None of us moved. None of us.

So maybe I could neutralize one of them: the one with the gun. But there was too much against it. I'd have to move sideways instead of forward and down, and even then his gun hand would follow until I could mount the blow. And if I brought it off there'd be one dead man and that was all: there wouldn't be time to cripple him or put him out of action—it'd have to be a *shikana*, the force of both arms swinging the elbow in a murderous curve for the diaphragm, a rising blow that wouldn't call for sight, since I knew precisely where his diaphragm was at this instant.

But if I did it there'd be another death a second later because the nearer of the other two, the one with the blepharitis, would recognize the blow I was using and come for me with any one of the forward-killing kicks while my neck was exposed to him at the end of my own movement. He'd be too frightened to do anything else: because this is the way with the graduated belts—their powers are so deadly that they recognize the dangers of an equal.

So there wasn't a chance but you have to think of everything or you'll miss a trick and they'll go in there and switch the lights on and lock the door and pull your dossier out of the safe and drop it into the document destruction thing, just because you didn't think of *everything*.

"You're making a mistake," I told them again.

They didn't understand and it worried them in case I was saying something they could use for their profit. They told me to shut up: I didn't know the word but I knew the tone. Then the thin one folded my papers and put them into the passport and I waited for him to hand them back to me and give a shrug and let me go, because the imperilled psyche becomes undisciplined and clutters the mind with false hopes, however you try to reason.

He said a word and the gun was pushed harder against

my spine and we moved at last, the four of us, towards
the station wagon. I was forced back into the driving seat
and they took my wrists and put my hands on the wheel
rim. Then they all climbed in and slammed the doors and
one of them tugged out the street map from the glove
compartment and got it open and stared at it for a moment and finally stabbed his finger near one of the folds.

"Here." He looked at me with his blank animal eyes to
see that I understood. "Go here."

The dash wasn't lit but there was a chemical glow from
the quayside lamps and his finger was stabbing again at
the point on the map: the corner of Statue Square, where
the Bank of China stood with its great brass doors and its
garrison of armed guards and interrogators, the place
where they were going to take me and after a while make
me wish to Christ I'd drawn a capsule.

11

Target

"Have you seen this chart?"

"Yes." I told him.

"On the launch."

"What launch?"

"The narcotics boat."

"Oh yes."

He had it spread across the table: *Sheet 341—China—Southeast Coast—Hong Kong Approaches—Islands South of Lantao.*

"Have you studied it?" he asked me.

"Not in detail."

His head turned slightly and he became very still for a second or two. Then he went across to the bulkhead and put his foot down and there was a light crunch and he came back.

"I wish to Christ you wouldn't do that," I said.

He gave a titter but watched me with unamused eyes. "Cockroach, old boy, the mariner's bane. How are you feeling?"

"Bloody awful."

Physically I was all right but it had put an edge on my nerves, those three little ticks trying to get at me like that within minutes of final briefing.

"You've got three and a half hours yet," said Ferris. "Take it easy." He leaned over the chart again, moving the lantern so that its light featured the bottom right-hand corner. This was the target zone, centred on longitude 114° by east, latitude 22° by north. The oil rig was two miles south of the San-men Islands and I saw he'd marked it in: I suppose he'd asked the Navy or someone where the thing was.

"Have you seen any other charts?"

"One or two."

"On the narcotics launch?"

"Yes."

I hadn't studied them. He got another one and unrolled it and spread it out and began topographical briefing while I sat in my track suit and tried to get my left eyelid to keep still: they could have wrecked the whole mission for me, those little bastards.

"Hong Kong is pretty well surrounded," said Ferris, "with these little islands, a couple of hundred of them belonging to the Colony and the rest of them garrisoned by the Communist Chinese."

I didn't ask any questions yet but I was already wondering how the hell he was going to drop me into the target zone with any kind of security, even by night.

"You'll be going in by sub," he said without looking up from the chart.

It wasn't telepathy: he was just a very bright director and keeping one step ahead of me. I let him go on talking, trying to get the other thing out of my mind.

They were probably dead.

"This group is perfectly barren, with the nearest garrison on this island here, five nautical miles to the northeast."

I was beginning to steam now so I unzipped the track suit to the waist and let it hang open. Ferris had gone to fetch it for me from the Harbour Hotel, mustn't catch a cold he'd said with a whinnying laugh, and left me here on the junk with a towel round me. I hadn't dried off enough before I put the track suit on and that was why I'd begun steaming.

It hadn't taken a minute, but it had seemed longer. There wasn't time to plan anything elegant because once they got me inside that bloody place I wouldn't come out again alive and they'd have a go at getting the whole lot before I was too far gone to say anything. There wasn't anything useful I could tell them about Mandarin: we wanted to reach Tewson and we weren't even in the access phase and they knew a hell of a lot more about him than we did. But they'd try for general background: what was my cell, what network, what bases, so forth, and if they worked on me for long enough—I mean for months, not hours—they might get a picture of the Bureau and even some of the organizational features. Names wouldn't mean anything: they were all code.

The thing about having the 9 suffix after your name in the dossier is that although it means you've proved yourself reliable under torture it doesn't mean they won't start doing things to you one day that'll finally break you down.

I don't like pain any more than anyone else does.

My hands were on the wheel where they'd put them and the thin one turned the ignition key to start the engine and then told me to drive off.

"Go now," he said, and I thought how Chinese it sounded, even though he spoke in English.

So the first thing to do was blow my cover.

"I can be quite useful to you," I said.

The thing that surprised them was that I said it in Cantonese.

They'd been half sure I was the man they wanted: it was only when they couldn't find a gun that they began having serious doubts, and even then they'd thought it was worthwhile taking me along to the interrogators. Now they had all they needed: I could speak Cantonese and I'd been concealing the fact, on top of which I'd told them I could be useful to them.

They all three started to talk at once and the thin one told the other two to shut up. He leaned forward with his arm across the top of the dash, turned sideways to watch me.

"You are from Londan?"

"Yes."

"Your name is Clive Wing?"

"Yes."

His Cantonese wasn't much better than mine but we got along.

The man behind me was pressing the gun into my neck so hard that I couldn't sit up straight. They were excited again now, ready for the execution, but the thin one had a certain basic intelligence and thought I could conceivably be more use alive than dead.

The thing I needed was speed.

"Drive to the Bank of China," he said.

"If that's what you want. But I've told you, I can be useful to you."

The engine was ticking over.

"You will tell them at our headquarters," he nodded, his tone cocky and his whole attitude like that of a master spy running an entire operation. "I shall arrange full interrogation."

I kept quiet for a couple of seconds and then got the right degree of reluctance into the tone. "All right, but I can put one of my agents into your hands, if you'll be lenient with me later."

I looked at my watch.

"What agent?"

"We're working together. But we'll have to hurry because we had a rendezvous at 20:00 hours and he'll leave if I don't show up."

It was terribly basic stuff and I felt a bit embarrassed. The hit men of any network are never much more than muscle, but these were from a state where most of the population had been trained to regard the life of the ant as Utopia. If I tried any kind of subtlety with them we'd get bogged down in misunderstandings and all I needed was speed: speed in terms of actual miles per hour. Also I needed a valid reason for hurrying.

I looked at my watch again and the gun poked harder into the neck muscle, sending my head forward, and one of the men behind me laughed but the thin one told him to shut up.

"Where is your rendezvous?"

"On a junk, just this side of the Naval Dockyard."

He wanted me to show him on the map so I pointed to a spot near the Dockyard. There were a thousand junks along the north shore of the island, and anywhere would suit me, so long as it was west of this quay, because I needed three left turns and a straight to bring me out where I wanted.

"How many men are there?"

"One man."

He thought about this and someone behind us said they could take on an army and he told him to shut up again. Then he reached his decision, slapping the top of the dash a little dramatically.

"Very well. We will go."

"You've left it a bit late," I said. "We'll have to hurry."

He nodded quickly and I used my right foot and the acceleration caught them by surprise and that bastard in the back lost his balance and the gun came away from my neck and it was quite a relief.

That was about all there was to it. I didn't go too fast round the three left-handers because I didn't want to worry them and there wasn't any need, but I gunned up along the straight bit past the warehouse and they all sat waiting for me to slow and turn at the T section but I didn't because this was where the repair work was being done to the edge of the quay and by the time they began calling out we were going through the ropes and the warning flags fast enough to pull the uprights down and clear the edge without hitting the underside of the chassis.

They didn't shoot or anything because there obviously wouldn't be any point and in any case they were sitting there now with a cold wind blowing through their guts as the water of the harbour came swinging up at us in a great black wall. I had the window down because if we hit the surface at any angle within ninety degrees each side of the vertical the door was going to slam shut again and I wanted the water to flood in before they could do anything about it, not because it was necessary to kill them but because I didn't want them getting out and swimming around and trying to get at me again: if I could reach the junk in the typhoon shelter we could keep Mandarin running and go into the access phase. I wanted that, a lot.

One of the road-repair boards flipped up and smashed the windscreen as we cleared the edge and a rope tautened and broke and whiplashed past the open window and then there was the long curving drop and I tried to work out the angles and the timing but the surface wasn't far below the edge of the quay and I had to hit the door open and kick clear of the bodywork and strike the water feet first with the impact wave from the station wagon knocking me sideways, most of the breath gone and not much idea of the way things had worked out except that I was still in a fair condition for swimming.

The door slammed shut as it hit the water but it was a muted sound, metal on bone, one of them probably trying to get out while there was time, not making it. Then there was one colossal bubble as the whole thing went under, then a few smaller ones, then nothing, just the waves across the surface as I began a slow crawl.

"This island here," said Ferris, "is your only possible

refuge if you get into any kind of trouble. Heng-kang Chou, with a steep south shore inclining to an average of sixteen fathoms within twenty yards or so of the water-line."

"No garrison."

"No garrison."

He wandered off to the stern deck and took a quiet look around and came back, whistling softly, and I waited for him to tread on something again, then I was going to rip right into him because it had only been yesterday when the bus had left the long red smear on the roadway.

He couldn't see anything to tread on.

"You think any of them got back to the surface?"

"Possibly."

I didn't want to think about that either because there are some ways of going that you don't wish on your worst enemy. The thing was that they'd spent a lot of time in the gymnasium but they'd had no security training or they'd have known the last thing you do when you have a captive is let him drive the car.

"Got any questions?"

"Only general. What's the sea temperature?"

"The average for the past week was eighty-two degrees."

"This oil rig." I got up and peeled off the top half of the track suit and turned it inside out and spread it across one of the bunks. "How close can anyone go, in international waters?"

"You feeling the heat?"

He was watching me with that quiet glitter in his eyes.

"Oh for Christ sake, it's a hot night isn't it?"

It brought more sweat out and I was duly warned: with only three and a half hours to go I'd better start shutting down the spleen. This access was about the most sensitive thing I'd ever had to handle: that was why London was sending in a reserve.

"Just wanted to know, old boy, that you're feeling on top form." He looked at the teakwood dragon that held the bulkhead lamp in its jaws. "In international waters maritime law prohibits uninvited vessels approaching nearer than five hundred metres. That's about what? Fifteen or sixteen hundred feet. Last year a Soviet ship sailed to within a hundred feet of an offshore rig in the North

Sea and began taking photographs, and the Navy sent a
destroyer out there to warn it off."

"How close is the sub going?"

"Within a mile. That's well clear of the illegal limit."
He gave a giggle. "Mustn't upset anybody."

I asked him about stand-off, liaison, rendezvous patterns, so forth. Some of it hadn't been worked out yet
because there hadn't been time. "You know what their
lordships are—you ask them to lend you a piddling little
submarine and they think you're trying to scuttle the fleet.
But we got it in the end—she's in the harbour now, been
rusting there for weeks. H.M.S. *Swordfish*—you must have
seen her when you came in from—"

"Yes."

"No more questions?"

"Not really."

He'd briefed me on night signals, rations, panic-button
limits, the whole of the access routine.

"What've you got?" he asked me, lifting his wrist.

"21:54."

"That thing waterproof?"

"Yes."

"Okay." He pulled the winder and reset and pushed it
back. "I'll be filling you in on the rendezvous patterns and
that sort of thing after we've left harbour. The skipper's
had to call up the Admiralty to get various permissions—
aren't you glad you're not a bell-bottomed *matelot*?"

I said I was going to take ninety minutes' sleep and he
seemed rather relieved and said he'd go for a little walk,
by which he meant he'd take up station out there and vet
anything that moved. He'd already fetched the scuba gear
when he'd gone to the hotel for the track suit, and there
wasn't anything else to do but wait.

"Ferris."

"Old boy?"

"Is London going to put any fresh tags on Nora
Tewson?"

It was nothing to do with briefing, and I was a bit surprised at my own question. A touch of jealousy, I suppose: I didn't want anyone else to know what I knew of
her, that strange double image of the innocent and the
tigress, at least for a while. I didn't count Tewson, of
course: he'd never known her like that.

"I very much doubt," Ferris said, "if they'd put any more tags on that girlie, considering the state of things out here. The Egg doesn't care at all for sending people on suicide stunts."

We went aboard *Swordfish* at midnight.

Her lights resembled a fishing boat's and I didn't recognize her until the tender began slowing, then the configuration came up in silhouette against the lights of the Kowloon shoreline: radar mast, conning tower, diving planes. The sea was glass calm.

The lifeline was still rigged on deck but a couple of hands started bringing it in as we went on board. There were two or three figures standing on the bridge and Ferris peered at them in the inadequate light.

"Wing," he said, "this is Bill Ackroyd, captain."

We said hello and a seaman reached down and took my stuff from the man in the tender. One of the air bottles banged against a stanchion and someone said, "Easy now . . ." I looked down.

"Careful with that bag there—it's fragile."

"Aye aye sir."

It was the short-wave Hammerlund transceiver Ferris had dug up for me and we'd put it in a waterproof bag along with the lamp and the rations.

People were speaking in low voices and I noticed the main bridge lights were shrouded: except for her riding lights *Swordfish* was in wartime rig. The tender backed off and swung in a wide curve away from us, leaving a scimitar of iridescent light across the sea. I could feel the vibration of the diesels under my feet.

"What's that over there?" I asked Ferris. It looked like some kind of launch, standing off at a hundred yards.

"Escort," the skipper said.

"For the whole trip?"

"Just out of harbour. Would you like a drink?"

He took us below. There was gin set up in the wardroom and I asked for a straight tonic and Ferris wanted to know if they had any milk and Ackroyd began looking at us as if we were a couple of freak sea anemones they'd dragged up with the anchor chain.

"Frank Topper," he said close to the chest. "Diving officer."

We all said hello again and I wished to Christ we could cut out the garden party and get moving. Ferris had a nervous smile switched on against any doubts in his mind and I began feeling bloody annoyed because my left hand should have had some kind of treatment and I was still in mild aftershock from the station wagon thing and London was pitching us right into a crash-access operation and that meant something had come up on the board and they'd started to panic.

"Cheers," one of the officers said.

There seemed to be a lot of noise from the fans and blowers but nobody took any notice. Then there was the slam of a steel hatch and two seamen came down and disappeared through a doorway and Ackroyd took us back into the control room. The helmsman was in his seat and there were needles crawling all over the dials and Ferris stood there watching everything with his bright glass eyes and a ruff of hair sticking out where he'd brushed his head on the companionway coming down. Everything had suddenly gone quiet.

"All right," Ackroyd said. "Slow ahead both."

There wasn't any appreciable movement but the bug started glowing across the chart on the DRT and in ten minutes we were out of the harbour. Five minutes later there was another sudden period of inactivity and Ackroyd said:

"Pull out the plug and ease her down to periscope depth."

The deck began sloping by degrees and I looked at the instruments.

Time 00:31. Course 220°.

Ferris was watching me and I felt like kicking his teeth in because his stare was critical and I knew that if I showed any signs of nerves or fatigue or anxiety he'd have this ship turned about and taken back into harbour. I didn't like being assessed at this phase of a mission: if I felt incapable of going in or doing a decent job I'd say so, he knew that. Better than Loman, perhaps, or Porterfield: they'd send you into the target zone with your nerves in rags and your eyes out of focus from fatigue if they thought you could finish the course without dropping dead.

"We'll slope off," Ferris said with a bright smile, "and

do some more chatting." He led me into the wardroom and we sat down and went over the whole thing again. I got it right at the third go and then he filled me in about the liaison and rendezvous patterns. "The routine rdv's will be prearranged by radio. Ackroyd says we can't risk coming in closer than a mile from the rig, so if you can swim that distance you'll navigate by the north star and listen for the call of the sea swallow—I'll play you the tape in a minute. *Swordfish* will pick you up on the sonar and move slowly to rendezvous."

This was typical Ferris: in less than twenty-four hours he'd had the call of the sea swallow put on tape and dug up a radio from the American stores and pushed London to give us a ship through the Navy.

"If you're not in a condition to swim as far as that—or any distance at all—we can do you a straight emergency pick-up through the distress channels and send in a Coast Guard chopper with a net. If—"

"You can't do—"

"Oh yes we can. It'd expose our hand but if I can get you back alive without blowing the mission that's what I'm going to do."

I knew he meant it but as I looked at him in the flat white light of the wardroom I wondered whether he'd always been so considerate towards his executives in the field, or whether he was trying to atone for what they'd sent him to do that time in Brussels.

"Can I come in?"

The captain was standing in the doorway.

"Of course," Ferris told him. "We were just chewing the fat."

For a submarine skipper Ackroyd looked too young but that might have been partly due to the apple-red glow on his cheeks, which I put down to the gin. His eyes were small and quick and he gave explosive little laughs, trying to cover them by tugging at the creases of his tropical slacks or scratching an ear. He looked about the last man to want to creep about under the sea in the confines of a tin coffin.

"Would you like to know anything about this tub? She's S Class, commissioned only last year and built for patrol—got two diesels and all mod cons. She's fast, silent and difficult to detect. Just the job for you, what?" He tugged energetically at his creases.

Through the doorway I could hear the pinging of the sonar transducer above the rush of the blowers. There was almost no vibration from the screws.

"Lucky to find ourselves on board," said Ferris.

"Don't know about *luck*," his small quick eyes glancing from Ferris to me and back, "I understand you put such a squib under their lordships they haven't come down yet!" He scratched his ear, his cheeks glowing. "What are you chaps," leaning forward suddenly and lowering his voice, "intelligence wallahs or something? M.I.5?"

"That's right," said Ferris. I suppose he thought if Ackroyd had the impression that M.I.5 worked overseas he might as well leave it at that: a classic piece of disinformation. "By the way, do you think they'll use depth charges?"

Ackroyd's face snapped shut and he looked down at his hands.

"You know, that's why you chaps had so much trouble getting us to help you. If I were to take *Swordfish* into Chinese waters, only a few miles north of here, we'd have depth charges dropped on us. No question at all." His bright eyes came up and scanned us in a series of flicking glances. "I mean, unless we surfaced and explained our presence or signalled we were in some kind of trouble. Now, they can't do that in *international* waters. But they might try." His glance took in the doorway and he began speaking close to his chest again. "It hasn't escaped their lordships that if we are to drop off a frogman within a mile of an offshore oil rig whose structure is Chinese Republican territory, we might encounter objections—and of the most tangible kind. It wouldn't be *legal*. But it would be *understandable*." His laugh exploded and he tugged busily at the lobe of his ear.

Ferris gave a companionable whinny.

"So it's like that," he said.

"It is like that, gentlemen."

"Cross our fingers," said Ferris, and Ackroyd glanced at him. We could both feel the chill coming out of him, though he'd been trying to deal with it. Ferris was claustrophobic, and the idea of being inside this thing when they dropped depth charges on it wasn't making him feel any better.

"Let me explain," said the captain. "If they were worried enough about our presence so close to the rig they might try to blow us out of the water and later claim they did it when we were inside their territorial waters and that we drifted south before we bottomed. They'd have to knock us out at the first shy, or we'd start sending radio messages to the effect that we were being attacked in international waters." He shrugged with his small pink hands. "Provided they could drown us to a man before we could use the radio, how could anyone dispute their claim?"

We didn't say anything.

"That is the position, then. Of course I'm going to make every effort to avoid an incident. I have seventy crew on board." His face went shut again and he looked down at the table. "For the duration of this voyage, gentlemen, *Swordfish* has been placed on a war footing."

"This was our only way in," said Ferris. "I'm awfully sorry."

"Give us something to do. You called on the right people—the Silent Service!" A short burst of laughter while he plucked at his ear.

"What time," I asked him, "do we expect to arrive off the rig?"

"Come into the control room."

The glow of the bug was moving across the chart between Lamma and Cheung Chao islands. "We're heading north of this one, Hei Chou, and turning approximately southeast, instead of rounding this group here. The long way round, but safer. As you see, all these islands are Chinese territory and most of them maintain garrisons and of course Coast Guard units." He glanced up at the chronometer. "I estimate we'll reach our position in half an hour. Let us say 01:15."

We went back into the wardroom to keep out of their way.

"Everything going nicely," Ferris said, but he didn't look at me. He was behaving rather well: every time one of the bulkhead doors was slammed somewhere in the ship he gave a quick blink but that was all.

"Piece of cake," I said, and began sorting out my gear. I didn't know what the conditions were out there: in an

air drop you can study the target zone on your way down
and pick out any features that could be dangerous or difficult, but all I knew on this trip was that the sea was calm,
the temperature was in the region of 82° and moonrise
had taken place twelve minutes ago. It wasn't much to
know.

In ten minutes the ship began heeling slightly as we
turned southeast and headed straight for the rig, fourteen
or fifteen miles distant.

At 01:00 I went back to the control room, leaving Ferris looking at a copy of *Penthouse*, not really his cup of
tea. His face had lost all its colour now and had a sheen
of sweat on it. I noticed he'd pushed back the tuft of hair
that had been sticking out.

They'd changed the chart on the dead-reckoning tracer
and we were now on 341 with the glow of the bug moving
midway between Yai Chou Island and the San-men group.
Our heading was 142° and the oil rig was four sea miles
distant, dead on our course.

It was quieter now in the control room and I looked up
at the blower grilles.

"We've shut some of them down," said Ackroyd.

The engine room telegraph was at half ahead both: we
must have been slowing. Nobody was slamming doors any
more. I looked at Ackroyd.

"Same ETA?"

"That's right." His small bright eyes were very steady
now as he watched the console.

01:04.

I went back to the wardroom. Ferris had pushed the
copy of *Penthouse* to the end of the table and was sitting
motionless, looking slightly upwards. I suppose that was
where he was expecting to hear the crump, but the bloody
things could go off anywhere, dead on our beam or below
us, anywhere. He turned his head.

"Are we still on our ETA?"

"Yes."

"Time to suit up, isn't it?"

"Yes."

Talc floated up under the lights as I got into the wet
suit and zipped it to the throat and started on the final
checks: tank pressure, valves, harness, backpack, buckles,

a quick exhalation through the mouthpiece to clear the check valves. All normal.

"Have you seen the rig yet?" Ferris asked me.

"Not yet. But it's there."

I hit the valves a fraction to blow out any dust, making him flinch.

"Sorry."

"Don't mind me."

I aligned the regulators, turning the butterfly bolts fingertight.

"Are we slowing?" he asked.

I stopped work and listened.

"Yes."

There wasn't anything more I could do before it was time to put on the scuba so I went into the control room. Ackroyd turned his head fractionally.

"We're rigged for silent running," he said.

"Understood."

We spoke very quietly. All sound background had gone: the engines were running at slow and they'd shut down all fans, blowers, pumps and auxiliary motors. Next to me I could hear the diving officer breathing.

"Want to take a look?"

I went to the periscope.

The oil rig was dead in the sights, a black skeleton structure rearing from the moonlit surface of the sea. Longitude 114°, latitude 22°. The target for Mandarin.

12

Solo

It was a quick piping note: the call of the sea swallow.

Ferris left the tape running while he helped me with the scuba.

"This side okay?"

"Another notch on the buckle."

The weight of the tanks shifted.

A seaman came to the doorway.

"The captain wants you to know they've got radar."

"On the rig?"

"Yes sir."

The bloody harness still wasn't right.

"Back another notch on both, will you?"

"Will do. There's no hurry."

But I could hear his breathing. We'd passed through Chinese territorial waters between the islands and the last report from the control room was that we were now standing off the rig at one mile.

"Feel better?"

I shrugged the scuba a couple of times.

"Yes." I tipped my head back as far as I could, without feeling the regulators.

The nearest naval base was probably at Kitchioh or somewhere to the west along the South China coast, and even if they could send anything seaborne from Namtow they wouldn't get here before *Swordfish* was under way again: it was airborne attention Ackroyd was worried about. The chart gave the depth in this area of the continental shelf as eighteen fathoms and if the garrison sent a chopper out from the rig or one of the islands we'd have to crash-dive but with periscope depth at sixty feet there'd be critically limited room to manoeuvre: with the sea calm and the moon clear we'd be a sitting duck for any kind of aerial reconniassance.

"For Christ sake switch it off, will you Ferris?"

That bloody bird was getting on my nerves.

He went over to the tape recorder and pressed the stop button.

"Anyway, you'll know what to listen for." I thought he said it rather deliberately.

"If I don't know now I never will."

"What we call good briefing, if I may say so."

There was an edge on his voice, the first time I'd heard it.

"Are they going to put it through the loudhailer?"

"With discretion." A wintry smile. "It's not meant to be a peacock."

Ackroyd was standing in the doorway.

"How are things getting along, gentlemen?" He said it in a half-whisper.

"Fine. Where's the head?"

"Through there." As I turned away he said quickly— "Don't flush it. We'll do it for you later."

"Fair enough."

They were still standing there when I came back. The silence was almost total now and I could hear the rustle of a sleeve as someone in the control room moved his arm. Nobody looked at me, but I was the only man among the whole of the complement they were thinking about. As soon as they could spit this bloody frog out of the escape hatch they could start engines and get the hell out of here before some yellow bastard spotted them.

"Skipper," I said, "I'd like to take a final look."

"By all means."

He led me into the control room.

I knew they wanted me out of *Swordfish* as fast as possible but I couldn't help that. I had to establish the image of the rig and I had to do it now and from this precise position because later it wouldn't be stable and I could lose my bearings. We were to the northeast of the thing and midway between it and the San-men Islands and I wanted to memorize the rig's configuration from this exact angle because if a sea haze covered the pole star and the rig's structure sent my compass wild I'd have nothing left but this image as my guide.

"Up 'scope."

Ackroyd stood aside and I took the grips, turning the

sights until the crosshairs swung to centre on the rig. At this distance it reached twenty or so degrees from the horizontal and I could see its riding lights. There was some kind of flood illumination hitting the cranes and derrick from lamps on the top deck, and a flare pilot was burning with a steady flame from the tip of a stackpipe.

At one side I could make out the black aerodynamic shape of a helicopter, the object we most feared.

"Thank you."

"Our pleasure."

The 'scope was brought down and I went through to the wardroom. A young seaman was coming the other way and stood aside for me, his leg catching one of my reserve air tanks: it hit the metal bulkhead and someone said *shit* under his breath and the seaman's face went white. We all stood perfectly still for a minute, trying to replay the sound in our memory to judge how bad it was.

It wasn't very good so I did a final synchronization check with Ferris and tugged the flippers on and carried the reserve tanks and the other stuff along to the escape hatch. Ackroyd led the way personally, which I thought was civil of him.

Ferris helped me stow the gear against the bulkhead and I checked the face plate for misting.

"Better you than me," Ackroyd murmured. He had a very held-in smile.

"I wouldn't want your job either," I said and put the mask on. They swung the door shut without making a noise and the last thing I saw was the pale and watchful face of Ferris, not much of his mind on me, most of it going through a lightning series of checks to see if we'd forgotten anything, overlooked anything, anything that could catch up on us a minute from now or an hour from now or at noon today when I was alone in the target zone and out of reach.

Flooding began.

The sickly rubber smell of the mask.

I shifted the lead belt around an inch, unnecessarily.

The water was waist high.

The thing I had to do was simple. Difficult but simple. During final briefing I'd asked Ferris why the hell didn't we take up station at the Golden Sands Hotel and do a snatch on Tewson the next time he was brought ashore to see his wife? There were three reasons, he'd said. One: Tewson might never go there again. Two: London wanted the evidence. Three: London wanted to know what the evidence *was*.

The water touched my chin. The mask had started to mist up so I pulled it off and spat into the face plate and wiped it clear and put it back.

If Tewson never went to the hotel again we could lose him forever: he could disappear into mainland China and that would be that. Presumably the evidence London wanted was to be used against Tewson or through diplomatic channels against Peking or maybe both. And the evidence London wanted was the evidence of what Tewson was doing on board the rig.

Water above my head. Vision distorted, sound magnified as the water gushed in from the pipes. Left hand stinging: salt in the wound.

Ferris would tell London straightaway: he'd have to, because Egerton always insisted on phase situation reports going in on time and it was no good telling him later that you were up a steeple or down a drain. The moment this watertight hatch opened Ferris would have to say so, either through Admiralty Signals and Crowborough or ship-to-shore cable to Chiang in cypher, the standing contraction: *Access phase open, executive in target zone.*

The hollow ringing sound of the water died away and there was just the steady inspiration and expiration of my lungs, with the soft cathedral echoes. Then hinges turned and a circle of pale light appeared above me and I pushed gently upwards, floating away.

The sea was dead calm and the light milky, with the waning moon trailing a pale gold disc above me on the surface. Minutes later I thought I heard the pulsing of the sub's engines but I wasn't sure: the senses were having to adjust to the laws of this other world where the ears must listen under pressure and the eyes see things as larger than they were, and closer.

Halfway to the rig I turned and floated on my back, sighting along the surface through the face plate. The island was there on the near horizon: Heng-kang Chou. I'd been moving off course, and when I turned again I saw the rig's configuration had altered noticeably. This worried me because there'd been no figures we could hope to work out for the target-zone duration: I could hold out for three days in terms of rations and drinking water but that didn't have any reference to the amount of time I'd spend submerged. Standard practice was to economize with the air supply and leave a ten percent margin of error in making calculations, and you don't economize with the air supply by going off course.

Watch what you're bloody well doing.

I'd been using the compass because they had radar and there'd be lookouts on the rig. The phosphorescent dial was clear enough to read accurately but the steel substructure was beginning to send the needle wild and from now on I'd have to risk it and take direct visual checks at intervals with the face plate clear of the surface till I could pick up the base of the rig below water. I was moving almost due south and the moon was climbing in the east and I'd have to avoid tilting my head to the left when I surfaced the face plate, to minimize reflection from the glass.

They didn't have sonar. We'd known that, long before we'd reached our position. If they'd had sonar they would have sent the chopper aloft to investigate our sound and we'd have seen it and Ackroyd would have turned about or surfaced, signalling difficulties. The main danger would have come from divers below the rig: if the substructure was under repair or there were modifications being made they'd have divers down and they would have picked up the sound of our screws.

I submerged again, moving a few feet below the surface, low enough to prevent the kick of the fins from making a disturbance, high enough to preserve buoyancy. I began looking for the outlines of the substructure ahead of me now but the water was cloudy in patches: it could be just plankton or weed debris, or the machinery on board the rig was perpetually disturbing the sea bed. I began worrying about exhalation bubbles but there wasn't anything I could do: they'd still break the surface from whatever depth I went down to. Ignore.

The world was silent around me, my own sound alone disturbing it: the hollow and echoing rhythm of my breathing as the living bellows of my lungs fed on the inert reservoirs of air and blew it out, each breath exhausting it by degrees, and irrecoverably. Sometimes the reserve tanks and the other gear caught an eddy from my fins and pulled me sideways a little, dragging on the nylon cord, and every time this happened I rose and broke the surface with the face plate to correct my course: but I didn't like having to do it because this whole operation was so *bloody* sensitive.

This was a Ministry of Defence thing and they'd got something so big on the board that they'd panicked and thrown us a crash access and the Bureau hadn't been able to stop them. Control had been kicked into motion with almost nothing to go on: we had to reach Tewson as fast as we could and we didn't have to ask any questions. There was obviously a chance that he'd show up again at the Golden Sands but they couldn't give us time to mount an orderly snatch and that was all right but they couldn't have it both ways: they'd hair-triggered Mandarin to the point where the target was so sensitive that I'd almost certainly blow it before I could get there.

Tewson was the target: Tewson and the rig. And the instant they realized we were getting too close they'd whip him into China. Tell you what London had sent me here to do: I had to stalk a bird bare-handed and catch it before it flew up.

Bloody London for you.

The cord tautened again and I was pulled sideways, getting fed up with it. When I broke surface with the face plate I saw the configuration had altered, but not too much: I was learning how to do it better, every time. The flare at the tip of the stack made a diffused glow and I took off the mask and demisted it, pulling the mouthpiece away for a moment to drag in the dry taste of ozone.

The rig looked about half a mile away and as far as I could see there was no movement on board: the lights were stable and their pattern didn't change. I'd have liked to audio-survey for a few seconds but it wouldn't be easy: it wouldn't be any good just pushing one ear above the surface because it'd be full of water: I'd have to drain it and that'd mean putting the whole of my head out and if they had any short-range scanners they'd pick up the blob.

I went down again and listened below water, holding my breath for five seconds. Nothing.

From the information Ferris had picked up from local sources the oil rig had been operational for three months:

the crude was said to be already on stream and they'd set up a tanker shuttle between the rig and the refineries along the South China coast. If they were burning residual lean gas at the flare pilot they must be running at production capacity and they ought to be working round the clock because on an operational oil rig there's no difference between night and day.

There was on this one. No sound of machinery. No sound of life.

I checked the time at 01:46. Airstream normal, buoyancy easy to manage, the spare tanks no real problem. During the next long haul I made two brief visual checks from the surface and then stayed below: the faint yellow stain of the flare pilot was now on the surface and I used it as my lode star until the dark trellis pattern of the substructure began showing against the sea bed a hundred feet below.

The glow of the derrick bases flared softly for two or three minutes on the surface and then dimmed out as I arched my back slightly and brought my head down, diving to twenty feet on the gauge. I was assuming there were lookouts and the air tanks on my back could pick up scattered light. It was almost totally dark at this depth and I stopped kicking and drifted, using my free hand to bring me more or less upright. My eyes had been used to the moonglow for some time now, and the flare pilot and then the white reflected light from the derricks had closed the irises to something like half their original diameter, and I needed time to accommodate. The trellis pattern of the rig was very faint now, although I was closer, and the sea was a dark wall around me.

Silence.

Then the long-drawn sound of my inhalation, hollow and strange, as if I could hear only the echo, and not the sound itself. Silence again and then the bubbling as my breath rose from behind me and floated above my head. At each interval between inhalation and exhalation the silence was total.

Slight stress beginning because of this, and because of the dim light. The onset of disorientation: normal but uncomfortable. The organism was starting to ask where it was, what it was doing here where it couldn't see things very well, couldn't hear things. To be ignored, or better still contained. Keep still and keep quiet, listen to what you can: the sound of your own life-giving breath. Look at what you can: the faint pattern of the girders, and above them the square configuration of the superstructure, delineated by the night glow of the sky, and the diaphanous cloud of debris drifting past as the current flowed from the south.

Breathe. See. Hear. All is normal. Relax.

The nylon cord tugged slightly as the current moved the reserve tanks, turning me gently round. With one hand I spun myself slowly back, to keep the girders in sight. They were becoming clearer, darker against the sands beyond, except where the cloud floated, moving nearer against my face plate, and lower. Its edge was blotting out part of the girders, as if it were opaque, and becoming larger. One of the background girders ran straight upwards from it, thin and perpendicular, and I looked down to follow it, then up again to watch the cloud itself. Its configuration had altered suddenly, and protrusions appeared, perfectly equidistant; and as it bumped against me I put my free hand out to push it away, but it wasn't easy because it was a cable above it, not a girder in the background, and these protrusions bumping against me in the current were detonation horns.

The shock was explosive because the nerves were being hit by imagination as well as fact and in an effort to keep me alive the imagination was picturing for me what would happen if I touched that thing again and for an instant I saw the blinding light and felt the tearing apart of life in the roaring waters and then the inrush of eternal dark.

Christ sake stick to the facts and think, try to *think*, get back to where you were a second ago, the bloody thing hasn't gone off and you're still alive so do something to stay that way. *It could have blown us right*—shuddup, you snivelling little tick—*you'll never see Moira again if it*—get out of my head, it didn't go off and we're just the same as we were before but we have to *think*.

There wouldn't just be this one.

It drifted away a little on the current and then came back, tethered by the thin steel cable. I moved away slowly, fanning the water with both hands, retreating from it but not too far.

They wouldn't have put just this one here. There wouldn't be any point. I was in a minefield.

Fanning with my hands, keeping upright, maintaining the organism in the vertical attitude it was used to, so that it could operate without too much stress. But more data was being rammed into the brain, a whole mass of it to do with my hands, information about my hands, information and questions, why were they both free, my hands, where had the—

I don't know.

Turn. Spin slowly *and mind the air tanks because if they hit that*—take care, take normal care, if it was a beach ball the tanks would never hit it, it's only because it's full of TNT that you *think* they might, relax. Turn slowly and look, look everywhere. It can't have drifted far.

Instinct is devoted almost totally to keeping us alive and it functions at nerve speed and it doesn't even refer to higher authority: it doesn't waste time asking the brain what to do. It acts. It short-circuits the normal system that processes the data and presents it for decision making and signals the motor nerves and contracts the muscles. It doesn't demand cerebration because that would slow the action. And it can't think for itself: it thinks as much as a gun thinks after the trigger's been pulled. If it sees a spark coming it shuts your eyes and if it sees a snake it stops you dead in your tracks and if it sees a high-explosive mine it frees your hands and drives them flat against the water to push you away and that was why I'd lost my hold on the nylon cord and that was why the reserve tanks and the radio and the rations were drifting somewhere in the gloom where I couldn't see them.

Where I had to see them.

But it was getting darker.

Water pressure felt the same but I could be mistaken because in these conditions of dim light and silence and weightlessness the threshold of disorientation was low and if I couldn't maintain psychic stability the senses would have to start struggling to bring in the data and if I missed any data it could be fatal. I wanted to check the depth gauge but the idea of moving my arm, of moving anything at all, was unnerving: but it was the only way to find out if I was sinking imperceptibly to the sea bed and increasing darkness.

I kept my arm to my side, bringing it up by the shortest path until my wrist was in front of the face plate and I was peering at the gauge like a man going blind. No information. The luminous dial had lost its brightness and the light around me wasn't enough to pick out the shape of the needle. I tilted my head by degrees, moving slowly, the sensory nerves of my skin beneath the rubber suit alerted for tactile signals. Above me it was less dark: a greyness was diffusing the faint light from around the platform of the rig. So I wasn't sinking and they hadn't doused their lights and there was nothing in the water to cloud my vision. I'd been sweating, that was all.

The shock had raised the blood heat and brought the sweat out and the face plate had misted over and in normal conditions I'd have known what was happening but in these conditions it had taken a lot of finding out and the idea wasn't pleasant because if a diver doesn't know when his face plate's misted over he's pretty far gone.

Christ sake relax. Take the bloody thing off and wipe it and put it back and do something about that stuff drifting around.

Or do nothing.

Mental blocks were getting in the way of rational thought because the organism was still frightened: not about what would have happened if I'd hit that thing with one of the heavy metal air tanks instead of my chest, but about what might happen if I went after the reserve tanks and came on them just as they reached a mine.

I took off the face plate and put it back and blew out through the nose. It wouldn't stay clear for long but I didn't want to surface yet and use saliva. A decision had to be made and the whole of the mission would depend on it: I was going to look for that equipment and try to find it before it struck a mine or I was going to get out.

All decisions are subject to chance and chance is incalculable. You can only predict likelihood and I thought it was likely that the reserve tanks would hit a mine if they went on drifting with the current. If they hit a mine there would be debris on the surface and the crew of the rig would see it and examine it and fit the clues together: a buckled radio component caught in the remains of a waterproof bag, an air pocket bringing it to the surface; a carton of protein concentrate, some biscuits still in their waxed paper. They'd know how close we were getting and they'd double the guard on Tewson or fly him out. Either way, Mandarin was blown.

But I'd be alive. The island of Heng-kang Chou was two miles away and I could get there underwater with the air I had left in the tanks. The break-off rendezvous for this access phase was twenty-four hours from the commencement of solo operations by the executive in the target zone: 01:29 hours today when I'd left *Swordfish*. Location was Heng-kang Chou Island, rotating quarter zones as per standard practice for this topographical situation: the northshore if I could find caves or some other refuge, east shore if there was nothing available in the north, south shore if both were blank, so forth. Life support was no problem in terms of food and water: thirst would develop but that would be containable for the short period involved. I'd be in good condition when Ferris picked me up.

Mission aborted: executive withdrawn.

Because it'd be no good sending in the reserve: there'd be nothing for him to do. George Henry Tewson would be somewhere in the three and a half million square miles of the Chinese mainland. *Reserve recalled.* And close the file on Mandarin.

Egerton wouldn't like it.

He works for the good of the cause. They all have their different motivations, the London Controls. Loman's working for a knighthood and he doesn't give a damn for his ferrets: look at what the bastard wanted me to do in Tunisia—blow myself up. Parkis is working for some grand and distant checkmate when the board is cleared of the pawns and in the meantime he moves us around and he doesn't care whether we live or die so long as we block the knights and the rooks while he plans his strategies. But Egerton works for Queen and Country and his morality is First World War, with tattered banners and muted bugles and the Greatest Game of them all to win, except for one thing: he won't send you over the top without a chance. As Ferris had put it to me on board the *August Moon*: "the Egg doesn't care at all for sending people on suicide stunts."

The alternative to getting out was going in.

Egerton wouldn't like that either.

But he'd never know, because there's always a phase in the mission when you're suddenly and critically in need of Control direction on a major issue and can't get it or don't want to. There's nothing London can do about it. They can plan the whole operation from initial briefing and access down to the final support liaison that's designed to get the executive into the target zone and out again with a clear exit path and a whole skin and the merchandise they're buying with what they pay him to do it. But you can't always stick to the blueprint and unless you're lucky you're going to find yourself cut off in a red sector one fine day with the access blocked or the radio jammed or someone treading all over your face because you opened the wrong door and then you're going to want field direction or something from Control and you're not going to get it.

They can bust a gut designing a set-up that'll get you past all the pins without flashing a light but there's nearly always a time when you've got to go it alone. We know that. It's why we're in this thing, most of us: the ferrets have got their motivations too. We don't go looking for trouble but if we get it we think we can deal with it and that's when we try very hard because if we fail we're going to have to live with ourselves forever afterwards and that's tough because we're vain.

So when we get close to the edge we don't go back: we look over. It's just another way of getting rid of infantile aggression and if you don't like it you can do the other thing.

There wasn't any real problem. If I let that stuff go on drifting it'd either blow a mine or move free and wallow around in daylight tomorrow and attract attention and if either of those things happened it'd finish the mission and that wasn't the object of what I was doing here. I was here to complete Mandarin according to plan. It didn't look as if I had a chance in hell of coming out alive but that wasn't a reason for not going in at all: it was gut-think.

Immediately around me was an area of dim light and beyond it was a soft gathering wall of dark and somewhere on the other side that stuff was drifting in the current: two steel cylinders, each of them charged at a pressure of two thousand pounds a square inch and capable of smashing through the wall of a building and flying three streets away and going through the side of a bus and that was just if the valve broke. They could do better than that if they went the wrong way through a minefield.

The one factor that had any value for me was that of time: the longer that stuff went on drifting the less chance I'd have of finding it before it hit one of those bloody things and blew the sea apart. So I thought I'd better start now.

13

Directive

The water was grey-green, growing lighter and darker as I rose and fell, gliding through the grey-green world, going my way in silence.

Three minutes.

They drifted past me in the shifting light and shadow, their steel spheres glowing as they caught a gleam of light from above, their copper horns thrust outwards from them, naked and quiet.

Two minutes.

I threaded my way between the cables, sinuous and slow and taking care. Nothing lived here and nothing moved except this black rubber creature as it passed through the cloudy avenues of spheres, but a presence was here, of a kind so different from my own that I felt its hostility: the blind trapped presence of a thing unborn, a thing that once free would hurl the sea apart. I made my slow way through it.

One minute.

Sometimes a bubble rose from the sea bed, turning dull silver and then shimmering past my face, vanishing above me. One of them passed close to a mine not far from where I moved: it touched and broke against the tip of a copper horn and for an instant sent me mad as the firestorm roared raging through my head. Then it was over: the sound died away and the seas subsided and the hollowed echoes of my breathing slowed again. The potential packed inside these deadly fingers had grown too much on my mind and I wanted nothing to touch them: not even a bubble.

Zero.

02:30.

Break-off point. I'd been searching for half an hour and hadn't seen anything and this was the time when I must break off and let the stuff go on drifting. Beyond this limit I'd start using the air that was reserved for taking me as far as Heng-kang Chou if I had to get out of the target zone and go to ground. I'd covered most of the minefield and drawn blank: in daylight I would have seen the loose gear long before this but I'd been working in near-darkness and without a hope of using the lamp because the mines were cabled on outriggers below the surface, well clear of the rig's substructure, and if there were look-outs posted on deck they'd pick up the glow of the light.

Twice I'd doubled back on my tracks without knowing it until I'd seen the faint image of a pontoon leg on the wrong side, a hundred feet below, and realized I must have turned too far where the mines made a right angle. Once I'd wasted time going down to fifty feet, seeing a patch of shadow that had turned out to be a mass of drift-ing weed.

I turned obliquely and dived in a long curve, coming up inside the minefield and heading for the great trellis of girders, hearing the sound when I was almost halfway across the open space. It was the sound of a ship's bell, cracked and muted, its rhythm irregular. In five minutes I had the direction worked out, turning full circle to orien-tate aurally and then moving across the slow southerly current and through the network of girders to the far side, reaching the minefield again.

I didn't have to search far, once I'd got there. The stuff was looming in front of my face plate, stationary except for the slight tug of the current. The nylon cord had fouled one of the cables and was wrapped around it, and the sound of the ship's bell was being set up by the valve of one of the reserve tanks as it kept hitting against the mine.

I stood off, watching it, my hands fanning gently to keep me upright. The waterproof bag containing the radio and the rations was creating resistance against the current: part of it had caught around the cable, leaving one of the tanks to swing against the mine. It wasn't any good trying to make an estimate and work on its findings because there were too many unknown factors but it didn't look as though I had long because the shoulder of the cylinder was nudging one of the detonation horns and it was a strictly shut-ended situation so I kicked with the fins and moved in, freeing the cord first and then working higher up, keeping my head back and the face plate clear of the horns as I pulled the reserve tank clear. It wasn't easy because the mine was fixed to its cable with a turnbuckle and cotter pin and the pin kept catching against the valve guard.

Normal thought process had ceded to a form of specialized attention: the conscious field had narrowed to contain only the essentials I needed to work with—the shape and size of the valve guard and the cotter pin and the horn of the mine, the angles and direction in which the manipulation had to proceed, the forces against it and the means of combatting them. But somewhere in my head there was panic trying to get loose, like an area of pain the anaesthetic hasn't quite reached.

Ignore.

This thing wasn't long out of the armament factory: the steel had a satin sheen and the copper of the horn was catching the glow of the flare pilot burning above the rig. The cotter pin was bright and a blob of grease still clung to the thread of the turnbuckle. There were Roman characters indented around the rim of the mine itself: they weren't clear in this light but it looked like *Hitachi, Japan*.

The valve guard came free and I backed off, bringing the gear with me. The time was 02:51 and I was alive and the mission was still running.

Just after 03:15 I went aboard the rig.

The storm-wave height of the lower deck was fifty feet, leaving a gap between the deck and the surface of the sea; but in this area it was almost dark and the girders gave a network of cover. I left all four tanks and the rest of the scuba gear lashed to a girder below surface and climbed one of the iron ladders. I didn't expect to find lookouts on this first deck: they'd be surveying the open sea beyond the limits of the minefield. There was a radial series of catwalks and I took one of them as far as the central ladder that served the drilling complex, going up again and reaching the top deck.

A single main lamp burned alongside the derrick, flooding most of the deck. A blizzard of bright moths blew around it and a lone bat circled, gorging itself, sometimes rising to the height of the flare pilot flame and circling again. Most of the deck was taken up with the drilling rig, skid-mounted and abutting on the control cabin. The turbines took up the rest of the space and the helicopter pad was raised on a separate platform clear of the derrick and the two auxiliary pedestal cranes.

There were more radio facilities than I'd expected: two masts cantilevered off the top deck and carrying microwave dishes, and a third mast with a booster-type unit that looked very like a tropospheric scatter system, conceivably for data transmission, rig-to-shore.

The one on my left hadn't moved for three or four minutes: he was using binoculars on the sea through a ninety-degree vector. The other man was pacing, his back to me because I was in the central area and he wasn't looking for anyone there. They were both in some kind of paramilitary uniform but carried only sidearms. The deck was three or four hundred feet across and I assumed there were other lookouts on the far side of the derrick and to the south of the engine-room installations.

It took me nearly an hour to locate the control console, not because it was far from the central area but because I had to move by inches, getting back into cover and staying there for minutes at a time while a lookout patrolled the area I was working. I couldn't have moved around at all if the cover hadn't been exceptional: the whole of this deck was broken up by cranes and winch gear and powerhouses, and most of the enclaves were in deep shadow. The dangerous areas were the catwalks and corridors and I kept out of them except when I had to evade one of the patrols. The cover story Ferris had worked out for me was better than nothing but it wouldn't stand up to professional interrogation: it was an extreme resource to keep the opposition stalled while I tried for an emergency getout from the target zone.

If one of those patrols sighted me it could blow Mandarin as effectively as a mine.

The control console was housed in a building like a concrete bunker and the only window was made of smoked plate glass with an intergral mesh of extruded steel. Lamps burned inside and the control panels were visible through the glass but the place didn't seem to be manned at this hour. The signs above the main door were in Chinese characters followed by a number.

It was now an hour before dawn and I began getting out, hanging back in deep cover and moving only when the risk was calculated. The most interesting thing on the middle deck was the work site where they were building some kind of platform into the main structure of the drilling derrick: the area was cluttered with welding gear and pneumatic rivet hammers and there weren't any signs that the job had been abandoned. I had to signal Ferris and I couldn't do it from anywhere near the rig unless I had adequate noise background to cover my voice and if those riveters started up I could get some sort of message out through the interference if the set was any good.

By 08:00 hours I was beginning to feel the shakes.

I had a lot of information for London and I wanted to give it to them as soon as I could because the future wasn't too certain. But I couldn't do anything about it until I had some kind of noise background and all I could hear was the low-pitched sound of the diesel generators and that wasn't enough: the human voice range would cut right across it.

There were two things wrong: geometry, chronometry.

They wouldn't leave a minefield to look after itself: there'd be a strict surveillance routine to make sure none of those things got loose or trapped flotsam and that meant they'd be sending someone down in daylight and he'd use one of the four iron ladders that ran from the lower deck to the sea bed down the substructure legs. They provided access to the pontoons and anchorage for repair and maintenance and the trouble was that I couldn't hope to find any effective concealment here between the lower deck and the surface of the sea. The geometry was wrong.

I was wedged in the angle formed by three girders and it was the best cover I could find anywhere in the storm-wave gap between the rig and the water: there were twenty other places like this but they were *exactly* like this and therefore no better.

If the work crew on the middle deck had started riveting at first light I could have sent my signal to field direction and got out. I'd been thinking of Heng-kang Chou Island in terms of a refuge in emergency but now I'd surveyed the rig I knew I'd have to go out there and hole up till tonight if London wanted me to extend operations: but I couldn't leave here before I sent my signal because the waterproof bag was showing some wear and tear and I didn't think I could get the Hammerlund as far as the island in working conditon. One drop of sea water in the wrong part of the circuit could block off the information I had for London and there might not be another chance. So I had to stay here and hope the riveters would start work before anyone came down here to look at the minefield but they hadn't started work yet and that was why I was getting the shakes: the chronometry was wrong.

At 09:00 I was sweating hard in the rubber suit with the sun eight or nine diameters above the horizon and sending out heat. There had to be a change of plan because I was a sitting duck and the best thing to do was leave the radio here and go down and put on the scuba and wait with my head above water, ready to submerge as soon as anyone came down from the deck. They wouldn't see me and wouldn't see the radio unless they were looking for it and I could stand off below water and get back here when I could. One of the things I didn't like about it was that I'd use up a lot of air but none of the arguments against this plan made any sense because if I didn't put it into action I risked being seen and taken on board for interrogation and the longer I waited the higher the risk would become.

I tilted the Hammerlund along the inside line of rivet heads against the girder and swung down and went sideways along a horizontal section till I reached a pontoon leg three feet above the surface and then climbed all the way back because the noise had started.

09:14.

Frequency 8MHz.

222.

Executive in the field to base: Wing to *Swordfish.*

A hell of a bloody din from the deck above me, louder than I'd expected, the rivet hammer trapping the sound and sending vibrations throughout the whole of the rig: I could feel it against my thighs and shoulder as I slid one leg along a girder and lay almost prone with my head against the set.

222–222–222.

He'd told me he was going to stay on board *Swordfish*

until I could send him a situation report: Ackroyd had a much bigger radio than anything Ferris could carry around and I might flash the sub to come and pull me out in a hurry and he'd want to be there.

I kept on talking, giving them blocks of three with my head against the set and my nerves getting tight because it was going to be a fifteen-minute exchange of signals and I hadn't even raised an acknowledgement yet and as soon as anyone came down one of those ladders the whole mission was blown.

Treble two thrice.

All right, I was in the middle of seven thousand tons of steel girders waving a six-foot aerial around and trying to hit the ether with it while half a dozen diesel generators were pushing out enough electrostatic squelch to jam any transceiver within ten miles of here.

222–222–

The riveter stopped and I hit the volume control in case *Swordfish* came through too strongly. The squirt of the welders kept up a low background so I thought I'd try it and spoke right against the mike, treble two, three blocks. Why the *hell* didn't those bastards—

345–345–345.

Swordfish.

Very faint. I acknowledged and turned up the volume a few degrees and waited. They were going to get Ferris. He wouldn't be far away. He'd give me fives: that was Mandarin. Sweat stinging my eyes. Nobody on the ladders. Oh for Christ sake come on, we're—

555–555–555.

Mandarin.

I went straight into the spiel.

We'd been Control-briefed to exchange signals totally in cypher when we were using the *Swordfish* radio, without any speech code thrown in to expedite the transmission. The Admiralty was a bit edgy about having spooks on board one of Her Majesty's ships and they'd obviously told London that if we wanted to use the sparks we'd have to do it in strict hush. That was fair enough: they weren't used to having a couple of torn-arsed mud larks playing about with their sub and the kind of stuff we'd be sending was pretty strong compared with the day-to-day signals normally going out—*Have polished anchor*—*Please send buns for captain's birthday*—so forth.

489—356—181—

Ferris was asking how I was and I told him to shut up and listen because I wanted to give him the whole picture before anyone came down here and stopped me.

369—376—210 ... Extending and reversing, leaving some of the transfers the right way round whenever they could stand in as a contraction ... *This isn't an oil rig it's a missile base* ... thinking up non-standard contractions when I thought Ferris would get it first go without risking delay while he queried it ... *No wellhead and false flare stack and crude reservoirs* ... *image from air would be perfect* ... *basic armament for defence: six eight-inch naval guns camouflaged as lean-gas coolers* ... *main structure under modification* ... *electronic and telemetric installations not yet completed* ... *assume Tewson involved as technician or supervisor* ...

"Him and his slide rule," Nora had said.

Ferris shot me a couple of queries about crew strength and the type of missile and I told him I thought there was only a skeleton unit on board while the boffins sorted out the stuff for the console. I couldn't tell him anything about the actual missile except that I hadn't seen any exhaust ducts or heat shields. There might be—

Then the riveter started banging again and I nearly fell off the bloody girder and Ferris began complaining about the interference: the generators had been bad enough but this din was affecting the air acoustics as well as the signal and I was getting fed up.

209—376—177—286—164—1.

It threw me and then I got it: I'd read *U.S. print Polaris* for *U.S. Sprint Polaris*. Both missiles had a compressed-gas launcher giving them a super-fast initial ascent with virtually no heat involved and getting them out of sight almost immediately and this could be the same type, which would explain why I couldn't see any exhaust ducts or shields.

He was asking me more about the camouflage but when I started off he cut in at the first interval and said he couldn't hear me through the jam so I told him to stand by and we sweated it out for twelve minutes till the riveter stopped and by that time I was right on the edge of my nerves because the logical time for a daily inspection of the minefield below me was first thing in the morning.

I turned down the volume for receive while Ferris put specific questions and then raised it for transmission and spoke close to the mike with the welders for background cover ... *configuration on both planes perfectly consistent with oil rig ... telemetry requirements identical in many respects ... giving similar installation images ...*

While I was filling in the picture it occurred to me that it made a certain amount of sense to build a missile base right on the doorstep of a U.K. possession and call it an oil rig. The Chinese Republic had silos all over the mainland for reaction-takeoff missiles but they were being photographed regularly by the American SR71 from eighty thousand feet and by the Soviet Turo-9 from somewhere just under that altitude: it wasn't possible to hide things any more. Aerial surveillance by high-altitude plane and satellite units had been jacked up to the point where you couldn't plant a row of beans without getting a call the next morning from the C.I.A. or the K.G.B. to say that according to their photographs you'd put them in upside down.

There were immense problems involved in building a conventional-takeoff missile base on the continental shelf in terms of getting the exhaust gas away but if you first thought of an oil rig as a disguise and then considered the similiarities between an oil rig and a submarine and used compressed gas to pop the missile up the tube as they did with the Sprint and the Polaris then you'd build one of these things.

Question: how far was George Henry Tewson from the design concept of Polaris?

"He was with the Ministry of Defence," she'd said grandly, high on bubbly, then she'd remembered they'd told her not to say things like that, "actually his work wasn't important, to tell you the truth," poor little bitch, out of her depth.

287–387–498–190–54 ...

He was on mission factors now: how long did I think I could stay on board the rig with any security? What was my life-support status in terms of rations, air, essential rig-to-island gear? How long would the radio stand up in these conditions?

Necessary to leave rig immediately exchange concluded. Fair chance of returning at nightfall but—

Bloody riveter began banging away and I called a 20–20 into the mike for stand-by and cut it dead to save the batteries and started to sweat it out again, watching the iron ladders and trying to think what I could do if Ferris asked me to keep station while he got into signals with London. That'd take up to an hour in cypher and I couldn't wait that long: I couldn't wait another two seconds with any security and he knew that because I'd told him.

Banging away, the whole of the superstructure vibrating, the rivets going into my head.

09:37.

If they just found me clinging to the girder looking dead beat the cover story might hold up long enough for me to try some kind of a get-out but if they found me with a radio it wouldn't hold up at all. There wasn't anything I could do about that: the instant I saw them on the ladder I could knock the Hammerlund into the sea behind the pontoon leg but they'd hear the splash and investigate and find the rest of the stuff. No go.

09:40.

There had to be a limit and in five minutes I'd open up the set and keep sending fifteens: *Situation contained but leaving station.* London was in a panic or they wouldn't have pushed me into this kind of position but if I could get out to Heng-kang Chou and delay the action for eight or nine hours till nightfall and take it up again from there they'd still have a live executive in the field and total security in the target zone. If I gave it more than another five minutes on board this rig they'd have a dead duck.

09:44.

The riveter stopped and I hit the set with twos.

He came in straightaway with another question but I didn't answer it. I told him the situation was too insecure and I had to leave station.

He asked for a repeat and that brought the sweat out again. We were throwing each other contractions for this exchange: the phrasing was right out of the book because the executive was in a red sector and had to get out and the director was having to decide whether to let him go or punch in a priority signal while he had him on the air.

Contractions take very little time indeed but I didn't have any to spare because my instinct was yelling at me to get the hell out of this death trap: send him fifteens and shut down the set and drop into the sea and pull out.

10.

Priority message.

Blast his eyes.

I waited.

He wasn't going to ask me for time while he talked to London. He didn't have to. He'd already done that.

Basic contractions: *2–8–0.*

Executive will withdraw objective from target zone.

The objective was normally a file or a document or a chunk of strictly hush electronics but this time it was a man and what they were asking me to do was bring Tewson off the rig.

14

Flotsam

Something moved away from me in the sand as my fins touched the sea bed, and a flash of silver showed against the pontoon as a group of pomfret took refuge.

The depth on the gauge was 106 feet and I was aware of the pressure here at four atmospheres. Movement felt heavy and the silence brooded. The light was diffused, scattering down from the surface and leaving no shadows where the splayed legs stood braced on the sand. Visibility was twenty or thirty feet: the girders were sharply defined in the immediate vicinity but grew hazy on the other side of the pontoon, finally vanishing into the insubstantial wall where sight was halted.

I'd changed air tanks on the surface, buckling the full ones into the backpack as a routine safety measure and bringing the old ones down with me to leave here with the radio and some of the rations. There might not be fresh water on Heng-kuang Chou and I was taking one quart along with me. The Hammerlund would have to be left here and I'd been worrying about that but there wasn't any choice: if I took it to the island I'd be able to stay in signals with Ferris during the next nine hours and with minimum background interference, but the waterproof bag was showing signs of giving out and the two-mile trip wouldn't improve it. The radio was a component in the life-support chain on this operation and I'd have to leave it lashed to the rig with the other gear for picking up tonight.

I wasn't thinking about the London directive Ferris had thrown me because there wasn't any point.

I would have said no straightaway and shut the set down on that but Egerton always likes you to give it a bit of thought before you tell him he's run the mission into the ground. It wasn't that he didn't realize what he was asking me to do: when the executive's in the target zone the director in the field is normally in rapid and constant signals with Control. The moment I'd left *Swordfish* they'd lit up the red bulb over the mission board for Mandarin in London and it wouldn't go out till I'd left the target zone or blown the operation or got snatched or neutralized by the opposition.

Ferris had had all the time he needed to tell Egerton *precisely* what the situation was and Egerton therefore knew *bloody* well that I didn't stand a hope in hell of bringing Tewson off this rig. I'd set up a get-out action when I'd gone aboard but London didn't know that and in any case it was in the extreme-resource category and I put my chances at ten to one against getting away with it. This was nothing but routine procedure: when you go into the target zone you leave every possible door wide open behind you and if there's anything you can use for a last-minute hit-and-run get-out you give it a go because in a lot of cases the alternative's a ten-year stretch in a brain-wash facility or a six-foot hole where no one can see them digging.

I'd made no provision for pulling a man out with me and there wouldn't have been anything I could have done about it even if London had briefed me on it before we'd gone into the access phase: the rig was manned and guarded and Tewson was under the protection of the opposition and it was no go all along the line.

Ferris knew that. He'd been instructed to field-brief me with the signal and he'd done that. I'd received the directive and acknowledged it and all I could do now was hole up on Heng-kang till tonight and come back and go over the rig again to see if I could fill in a few of the gaps: try finding out what type of missile they were going to plug into this thing, take a closer peek at the unit that looked like a tropospheric scatter system, do a soft-shoe snatch on one of the guards and get him into cover and see if he could understand Cantonese.

But that would be all I could do before I had to pull out and when I pulled out I couldn't bring Tewson with me. They bloody well ought to know that.

Even at this depth I could feel the vibration of the riveter in the pontoon leg and when I lashed the used air tanks to the girder they began ringing to the percussion: at four atmospheres the residue of air was being compressed by seventy-five percent and the vibration was hitting them like a drum, so I took them off and looped some of the cord round the girder to damp out the metal-to-metal contact before I lashed everything tight and damn nearly knocked into him when I turned round because he was right behind me and reaching for his knife.

High cheekbones and light yellow eyes behind the mask, nothing on him except the diver's knife, no spear gun or anything. His move for the knife surprised me because you can't use any kind of a blade underwater with enough speed to do any damage: you've got to wait till you can get in close and then start ramming with it. He was shorter than I was and that meant he couldn't get in close unless I let him and I wasn't going to do that and he ought to know.

Conceivably it was just a defensive reaction when I'd turned round: he was offering the knife correctly, hilt down and blade up at forty-five degrees—he knew how to use the thing and unless I backed off it wouldn't be any good reaching for my own knife because he'd be ripping into me before I could get anywhere near it.

We looked at each other through our face plates for two or three seconds before we made a move. Everything was in the eyes: not communication but reaction. His eyes were alert and hostile, the lids narrowed and the pupils enlarged. He watched me with total attention. In my own eyes he'd seen shock and now saw decision. Man is one of the territorial animals and contact between two members of their species gives rise to an immediate issue when one or the other is on his own ground. For both of them—but particularly for the intruder—there is the primitive decision to be made: to fight or run.

But he hadn't been waiting to see what I would do. The situation was more sophisticated than it would have been for two of the lower animals: this diver had seen me lashing something to the base of the rig and it could be explosive and whatever it was he wanted to find out as soon as he could and take it aloft for close examination. He also wanted to know what I was doing here and who I was and where I'd come from and he was going to subdue me if he could and similarly take me to the surface and hand me over for interrogation.

There'd been a chance that I might have capitulated in

the instant of encounter but the time was past now and he saw that. The very fact of my standing here face to face with him was an expression of hostility and he was going to make the first move: by infinite degrees he was bringing his body lower and turning the trunk with the right shoulder coming towards me and the elbow at right angles, the blade of the knife cocked and steady, dull silver in the strange underwater light.

Combat at eighteen fathoms has its own rules and some of them run counter to the norm: you don't draw back to bring momentum into a blow because the pressure of the element is going to kill off momentum anyway. You have to streamline the strike and he did that and the blade hit the glass of my face plate and the point stayed there scraping on the surface as I held his wrist and we looked at each other, locked and motionless. He'd struck directly forward and into the aim and I'd known he'd have to do that because it was the only way and I'd worked fast and my forearm had driven straight upwards to connect my hand to his wrist but the water had built up resistance against the biceps area because it was travelling at right angles and it had slowed the blow but not critically: he'd struck for the throat or my breathing tube and hit the face plate and his wrist was locked in my fingers and I began squeezing.

The bone was thin and I began levering, working for a fracture, watching the pain start in his eyes. A foot blow was out of the question because of the drag of the fins so I knew he'd have to use his left hand and I was ready but he was wickedly fast, clawing for my breathing tube again and again as I jerked my head back and kicked upwards from the sea bed and dragged him with me, keeping the pressure on his wrist: but we were clear of the sand now and fighting in the manner of fish, and he used the element for his own defence, letting my grip on his wrist move his whole body, the kinetic energy travelling through the arm to the shoulder and beyond.

Breathing became difficult as the muscles demanded oxygen: the lungs began creating a vacuum, setting up pressure lag at the regulator.

He had stopped his left-hand action because I was holding the air tube out of his reach, my back arched and my head angled, but this was defensive because my right hand was immobilized and time was already running out: in scuba diving exertion of any kind is at a heavy premium and we were making demands on oxygen that weren't going to be met. I estimated we had two more minutes before exhaustion set in.

The current was taking us slowly away from the substructure of the rig and we were drifting higher, with the sand bars below us losing definition. The only purchase either of us had was against the other's body and we were using our legs now, not for striking but for leverage, my right foot working for pressure against his neck as one of his legs was hooked suddenly around mine when he went for a knee lock and got it and began putting stress into the movement with our ankles braced together bone on bone.

Our black-rubber bodies drifted, entangled intimately in a deathly embrace, a slow and freakish sea creature afloat on the current, the pressures and tensions of its own destruction working within it, the quadruple lung system starving for air, the twin heads close together in mortal enmity, each willing death on the other.

This wasn't how it was meant to be, this slow surrender to the sea itself, the drifting away to death of a four-armed creature, the light turning as the grey-green world revolved, the mind spinning in silence, in eternal peace.

Think.

A whirlpool of colours streaming, swirling, a singing of yellow in my eyes as the deep came, darkening.

Think.

Nitrogen narcosis.

Do something.

The consciousness ebbing as the rapture of the deep drew over me, the pain sharp in my knee and the brain waking, *Christ sake do something, finish him off and get up there*, his hand hooking again and the rush of salt water against my face as the mask was wrenched away, fighting him half-blinded now and with pressure against the nose and the shape of his other hand indistinct as his wrist came free and he hooked again and dragged my air tube away, taking my last hope of life.

Not good enough and had to try but salt water now in my eyes and in my mouth and no more air and he kicked with his fins to get clear while I drowned but *don't let him*, he'll leave you here to die and my hand moved, fren-

zied, part of the mind driving it, part of the mind striving
to clear a space for conscious thought like a bubble in
black water, a bubble of light, my fingers closing and
snatching at his head and dragging the mask off and going
for his air tube and finding it and tearing it away as he
squirmed clear of the knee lock and began fighting for his
life against the sea.

Then at some time our faces passed close to each other
and his looked as dead as mine must look, the eyes dulled
by the water and the mouth flattened as he held on to the
last breath of his life, as I was doing. Then we drifted
apart in the reddening light as the blood from the wound
in my hand began clouding against my eyes. I felt behind
me for the air tube but it was out of my reach: he'd
pulled the mouthpiece over my head and the tube was
hanging somewhere behind my shoulder blades. The longing began in my chest: the longing to drag air into the
lungs and breath again.

The sea darkened as he loomed suddenly against my
face, his shoulder hitting and turning me as his arm
hooked again and again behind him, his hand trying to
find the air tube as it drifted past my eyes. I cut it away
with my knife and kicked clear of him.

The effort had taken the last of my strength and my
chest was hammering with the need for air and I knew
that soon my throat must open and suck the water in, and
in the deep red singing I saw Moira, as I knew one day I
would, her long eyes and the flow of her copper hair, turning her head in the way she did, to watch me with her
smile as my mind became lulled in the soft-coming waves
of nothing, nihil, annihilation, while somewhere as if in a
different place the organism continued with its desperate
travail, my hand reaching overhead and the fingers searching, the breath held in the hollows of the sea and the mind
lingering, alive, the nerves subservient to the primitive nub
of matter at the top of the spine—the hand suddenly fren-
zied as the fingers touched the concertina rubber of the
tube and grasped it, pulling it over my head and trying to
force the mouthpiece against my teeth, *think*, as they
closed on it, on the life it could give, *but think*, as the
forebrain was roused from its narcosis—*face the surface*
and my legs kicked and I turned on my back, remember-
ing, my hand lifting, taking the mouthpiece higher than

the regulator with the opening downwards, *bring it down*, my face reaching upwards and my mouth hungry for the bubbling air and biting on it, *exhale*, the water turning me, *swallow*, my body drifting, *now breathe*, the sigh of the cylinders echoing in the deep vaults of the sea, *breathe*, the lungs greedy and pulling at the valve and sweetly filling, *breathe*.

I saw him once more.

He was slowly windmilling in the blood-red cloud, his arms open and his legs apart and his movement graceful as the current turned him, his eyes quiet as he danced alone.

His mask was still hanging at his neck, its strap holding it, and I pulled it over his head and put it on, squeezing the water out by degrees as I breathed into it. Then I kicked with my fins and my hands reached upwards, following the bubbles and slowly climbing their chain.

Don't hurry.

Let the bubbles go, there's no hurry.

Remember what you know: never climb faster than they do. Let them go.

The light grew stronger above me, its molten silver spreading in a pool as I neared the surface, following the bubbles, following. Globules of darkness began appearing and I watched them, amused, *think*, their effect mesmeric, their dark spheres floating psychedelically against my eyes, *remember*, their thin strings stretching above them, *remember the mines*.

The faint trellis of girders was on my left and I turned and moved in that direction, my heart thudding because the organism had been perturbed. Basic forebrain cerebration was starting up again as the effect of the nitrogen narcosis began wearing off: at the crude decision-making level I was able to plan what I was going to do for the next few minutes. Consideration of later problems was beyond me for the moment: it was enough to be alive.

When I reached the surface below the deck of the rig I removed the mouthpiece and turned off the air and hooked both arms across a horizontal girder and hung there, filling my lungs, slowly and deeply, again and again, sending oxygen through the system and driving the residue of carbon dioxide out of the body tissues, hanging as limp as I could and thinking of nothing, closing my eyes.

The water lapped at the girders, a slow swell moving the surface without disturbing it; I heard a sea bird call as it flew between the islands; another answered, far away.

Then the riveter started up again and the shock went through me and I opened my eyes, thinking I'd slept: maybe I had. It was time to go.

I didn't find it easy to put the mask on and the mouth-piece between my teeth because there'd been death down there and I didn't want to go there again, but I couldn't stay here by daylight: there was no certain cover for me above the waterline.

Orientate.

The island was to the north, and I could see it clearly: a series of humped green hills and a fall of granite rock where I knew there were caves. The sea between here and Heng-kang Chou was glass smooth under the climbing sun, except where the flotsam made a patch of black, its edges shining. They could see it too, because I heard cries and in a moment the riveter stopped and their voices were clearer. They were calling in Mandarin but I understood well enough: it was one cry repeated, *man overboard*, and interspersed with short sharp words of enquiry and response, *where? there*.

The hiss of the welding plant died away now and the only background was the murmur of the diesel generators. The men's voices were raised sharply against it and I heard the first order being shouted. Feet began ringing on the iron decks.

I dived.

Sound burst suddenly against my eardrums: the power launch was tied up on the far side of the rig, below bad-weather derricks, and its engines started up as I began a long curving path that took me through the girders on the north side of the substructure with the minefield ten or fif-teen feet above my head. I turned slowly on my back and saw their dark blobs against the flare of the surface. The body of the diver floated above them and the oblong shape of the launch went curving across, its draft too shallow for the keel to foul the outrigger framework that held the mines suspended. Its engines were loud now, filling the sea with their sound.

With fifty feet on the depth gauge I was invisible from the surface and this was as deep as I wanted to go because the pressure was already tangible and it was urgent that I stayed free of narcosis. There was also a lingering sense of fear as I moved again in the deeps, watching the enemy above me through a dead man's mask.

Ignore.

I kicked with the fins, setting a ready rhythm, still swimming with my face to the surface in the hope of navigating. The compass was useless at this distance from the rig and I couldn't go up and check my bearings: all I could do was to keep the pool of sunlight in my wake and on my left. But it was amorphous and diffuse, its glare dazzling me. I shut my eyes against it. The boat's engines were idling now as they took the body aboard and examined it.

Desultory thought process: Mandarin was blown. The cover story Ferris had given me had been thin at best but now it wouldn't stand a chance because they knew by now that the diver hadn't just got into difficulties down there: his mask was missing and his air tube had been severed with a knife. The three secret-service men who'd escorted Tewson to and from the Golden Sands Hotel were almost certainly on board the rig and there'd be a naval defence cadre with frogmen responsible for underwater maintenance and security and if they were good at their job they'd inspect the substructure down to the sea bed and find my gear and the radio.

I didn't see any point in going back to the rig when night came, just to get picked off by rapid fire or caught alive and grilled and taken to Peking and grilled again and thrown on the heap.

I could hear the launch again, taking him back to the rig.

The thing that narked me was that I couldn't tell Ferris we'd blown the operation and he couldn't tell London to switch that red light off and shut down the station on Mandarin. Ferris would go on brooding over the chart and haunting the radio room in *Swordfish* and Egerton would go on ordering trays of tea for his mission staff in Operations and punching out requests for a situation report and all they'd get was silence.

Well they shouldn't *bloody* well ask me to do the impossible.

All right I'd done it before but there were limits and this time they'd blown the fuse. Some stupid jerk in the Ministry of Defence had seen the news about Tewson's shark thing and got the wind up and hit the button and told the Bureau to go and verify and set up an operation to get him out of Hong Kong if he was still alive. That was all right till we told them he was under an armed guard on Chinese territory in the middle of the sea: that was when Control should have told them to go home and shut up about it and maybe that was what Egerton had in fact done but they wouldn't listen.

Well they'd listen now all right. Your bright little boffin's gone and run away from home and he's not coming back so you'd better change the combinations on the files and take that launcher off the secret list and stop his pension because there's nothing more we can do for you.

The sun was in my eyes.

It was all I had to steer by but it wasn't very precise: it was just a big dazzling area that changed shape sometimes when the swell ran heavy and created surface undulation, and if I went off course I'd waste time and air and energy and I didn't want to waste any of those things because they were the means of life. But the only hope of taking a straight line to the island was by surfacing and correcting my bearings and I was still only half a mile from the rig and the lookouts were alerted.

Sun in my eyes.

I closed them.

No go.

I had to watch the surface all the time to keep the flare of light in my tracks and on my left and I had to check the gauge every thirty seconds to keep at a constant depth.

Dazzle.

The sound of the engines was faint now but I could hear they were idling: they hadn't been shut off. The body was being put aboard the rig. Another sound was coming in, fainter still but regular, and I couldn't place it. I didn't think it was the riveter: That would make a sharper vibration through the water and they wouldn't have started work again so soon.

The sun was going down, its brightness flowing away to

my left and leaving me in twilight. A kind of peace was coming into me, a stillness, and my eyes were closing of their own accord, drawing darkness across the last of the day, while—

Watch it.

The twilight deepening to night, where nothing—

Christ sake watch it will you!

Been rolling over, I'd been rolling slowly over, hypnosis induced by the dazzle.

Orientate.

But it was difficult because there wasn't anything for the eye to fix on except that shifting pool of light and if I didn't stay locked on to it I could swim in a circle: in these weightless conditions with my only navigational reference tending to induce hypnosis there was no way of making the island unless I surfaced and took bearings and I couldn't do that because I knew what the sound was, the new one.

They were putting the chopper aloft.

I stopped kicking and hung there with the surface fifty feet above me and the sea bed fifty-six feet below. The rotor was producing a light fluttering sound, most of it screened by the surface, and the other noise was louder, transmitted directly to my ears from the screws of the launch. It was rising in pitch and increasing in volume: the thing was heading in this direction. The body had been found some distance to the north of the rig and I suppose it was the logical direction for anyone to take if they wanted to start a hunt for his assailant. They knew there hadn't been any kind of a boat near the rig and they knew his air tube had been cut clean through by a blade and it had happened underwater so they didn't have to make any guesses: they were looking for a frogman.

I'd shut my eyes while I was motionless and now it was dark again and I kicked with the fins to correct my attitude: I'd been drifting head down without knowing it. I had approximately sixty seconds before the helicopter picked out the faint blob against the sand bars and signalled the launch where to find me and I didn't like either of the two things I could do but I was going to have to do one of them. I could start swimming nearer the surface and wait till the chopper sighted me and then I could put out a cloud with the shark repellent and dive and leave it

for them as a decoy while I tried to get clear, or I could
go straight down to a hundred feet where they couldn't see
me and swim face up with the sun as a bearing and try to
hit the island before narcosis reduced me to a drifting
piece of flotsam and the air in the tanks ran out.

The launch was throttling down.

As near as I could judge it was at a horizontal distance
of a hundred yards: I could see its faint smudge moving
slowly across the surface against the dazzling light, cutting
a vee from the fluid gold and spreading it towards me.

Assume starting square search.

A shadow passed suddenly over me as the helicopter
swung in from the southeast, lowering across the sea. Both
the launch and the chopper would be armed and if I tried
the decoy thing they might decided to open fire instead of
bringing in divers to pick me up and hand me over for
grilling, so I jackknifed and put my arms to my sides and
felt the pressure mounting as I plunged to the dark sands
below.

15

Trap

I couldn't breathe.

His hands were at my throat and he pressed with his thumbs and I couldn't stop him. His eyes were slits and below the mask his teeth were bared with the effort as he went on pressing with his thumbs. Behind his yellow face the mountain reared.

I tried to move but his weight was on me and the water lapped at my head, its waves coming and going without any sound. The mountain was silent, gigantic, directly above me, and I began running but I couldn't breathe. He was blocking my throat.

Haze began covering the mountain and I pulled off the mask and the mountain was instantly clear. Something was in my mouth and I pulled it away and my lungs bellowed, heaving inside my ribs. There was something under my feet and I pushed upwards and got my head higher out of the water, and the mountain sloped away until it was a low hill, covered in green. I pushed again with my feet and climbed higher, getting a grip on the rocks with my hands, the left one painful and oozing blood.

Then I stopped moving and stood waist-deep in the water, wanting to do nothing but breathe the sweet air in: I'd always believed that thirst was the worst, but it isn't. The tanks had run out of air but I didn't need it because my head was out of the water: I'd been dying for the want of air when there was the whole sky full of it.

He'd gone. I'd been hallucinating.

This was Heng-kang Chou Island.

I couldn't have recovered full consciousness or I would have reacted faster. Situation data was coming in heavily and was so significant that I dealt with it first and the imaginative process was partially inhibited: I'd lost consciousness somewhere near the sea bed and drifted on the southerly current and exhausted the air supply in tidal breathing but I was still alive and had a refuge where I could hole up in safety and this situation was so satisfactory that I didn't look for problems.

Time check: 13:01.

I'd been drifting in the unconscious state for something like two hours and the current had kept me close to the sea bed or the helicopter would have sighted me. The rubber suit was ripped in a lot of places and my knees and shoulders felt bruised: Ferris had told me the south shore of the island was steep granite dropping away to sixteen fathoms within twenty yards of the waterline, so the onshore current had dragged me up the slope of rock to the surface.

Rotor.

There had to be more data before I saw the danger I was in, and it came aurally from across the sea and I went down slowly and was careful not to make a splash because if this was the south shore of the island it was in sight of the rig and at a distance of two miles a pair of medium-power field glasses could pick up an object the size of a man.

Bloody well wake up and try to survive!

I took off the face plate to avoid reflection and sank into the water with only my head clear, tugging at the quick-release buckles of the backpack and letting the air tanks go, pushing them down the rock face with my hands and then my feet to start them sliding to the bottom. Then I made a five-second survey across the sea's surface: three helicopters airborne, one of them this side of the rig and the other two well beyond it. Five boats visible, three of them cabin class, two of them smaller craft. I couldn't see from this distance whether they were Navy, police or Coast Guard, but they were flying the yellow-starred flag of the Chinese Republic in the stern. They would almost certainly have divers down.

The nearest cave mouth was this side of the southernmost point and I submerged with the mask on, surfacing every so often to breathe and keeping my head turned inshore, reaching the cave and crawling onto the fissured floor and flopping down on my stomach, drawing deep breaths, the mask still on until I remembered it and pulled it away. State of semi-exhaustion and it worried me because it hadn't been a long swim and the fins had cut down the work. Possible blood loss: I remembered the wound had come open while I'd been engaged with the diver. Possible residual effects of nitrogen narcosis: I'd been unconscious for two hours and there would still be a lingering retention of CO_2 in the tissues. Probably combination of both factors and therefore normal *but I didn't like it* because I had to think and all I could see was a flutter of light in front of my eyes and all I could hear was the *chop-chop-chop* of that bloody rotor amplified in the cave.

An irregular draught above my head and something pattering on my back, the sense of creatures somewhere near me. Take some interest then because *everything* is interesting if you want to live: all right, bats, flapping all over the place above my head; I'd frightened them.

I let my eyes shut again.

Be too dangerous to go inland and try to reach the far side of the island because the chopper was too close and there wouldn't be much cover in these soft green hills: there weren't any trees, only bushes and short scrub clinging to the rock where it could. I'd reached land but the only cover was in the sea and I'd no air left in the tanks and they were gone now anyway, so much junk, all I'd had to keep me alive not long ago.

Think of nothing. Relax.

Got to think. Want to live.

The break-off rdv for this phase was twelve hours from now and I was in place in the third rotating sector, Heng-kang Chou. The rations I'd been preparing to bring with me were still on the sand below the rig where I'd let them fall when the diver had found me there. I could last without food but I had a thirst beginning because I'd lost fluids in sweat and I wouldn't be able to graze on the scrub till nightfall. Ignore thirst.

The lights kept flashing and I shut my eyes again and lay prone, letting the whole thing go for a minute, leaving the organism to look after itself by automatic data analysis: squeaking sounds and air movement in close proximity recognizable and acceptable; volume of distant sounds constant; psychedelic display behind closed eyes attributable to nerve trauma, this data to be ignored.

The water lapped.

Relax.

Now.

I crawled higher and sat with my back propped on the rock and watched the bats dipping and swerving across the cave mouth, their wings turning pink as the sunlight shone through their thin membranes, turning black as they wheeled inside the opening again. Think. One of them coming very close, unaware of me until its radar picked me up, small ears and flat piglike face, vanishing as it weaved aside. Think of what must be done. Others hanging from the roof of the cave, for some reason undisturbed, asleep and enfolded in their leathery wings.

Face what you know. They're making a lot of effort out there, three choppers and five boats and probably more on their way; they want to find the man who killed their diver and they want to find him badly because he got near their missile base and they want to know who he is: they've got a lot of questions for him.

Check logic. Satisfactory. It would be nice to use this half-doped forebrain for cerebration above the Neanderthal level but for the moment it was the best I could do. There wasn't anything difficult to work out: there was a manhunt mounted for me and I must elude it.

But the thing I had to face was that they wouldn't deploy their forces on that scale without extending the search area and when they couldn't find my body dead or alive in the sea they'd start searching the San-men Island group and the nearest one was this one so they weren't going to have to look far. They'd start with the caves along the south shore and that was where I was now so I'd better get out but if I got out they'd see me.

Nerve light receding now. Left hand becoming numb because I was holding it above me against the rock face to stop the bleeding. So it didn't look as if I could do anything and what worried me was that red lamp over the board for Mandarin where they were sitting on their hands looking at the clock and the situation crossplot and not, very carefully, looking at each other when they got up and walked around and swallowed some more cold tea with the scum on and said no sir, every time Egerton came in, no sir, there's nothing new.

At that end of the mission there was a building full of people with talent enough to man an international chess

tournament and signals facilities in excess of the requirements of an operational Air Force base and a codes staff
capable of hitting our agents-in-place in Moscow or Peking with a telephone directory got up as Hymns Ancient
and Modern and a permanent hot line direct to the Minister of Defence and at this end of the mission there was a
half-doped ferret sitting in a cave and getting slowly covered in bat shit.

At a rough guess I'd say Mandarin was blown. All I
was interested in now was getting out alive and I didn't
think I could do it.

Swordfish would arrive in these waters at 01:29 tomorrow and the call of the sea swallow would be heard and
go unanswered and the sub would pull out and all Ferris
could do then was consider sending in the reserve, but I
didn't think there'd be one available because the Bureau
didn't have anyone stupid enough to take on a shut-ended
penetration job with a seaborne access problem except
possibly for O'Malley and for one thing he was in Athens
and for another thing he'd get pissed the night before and
go in with a sawn-off motor torpedo boat and they'd see
him coming before he'd started the engine and Control
knew that: he'd told Ferris to hang a reserve in front of
my nose just to make me go into this thing out of sheer
stinking pride.

Well this time it hadn't worked. If they wanted George
Henry Tewson off that rig they'd have to use a skyhook.

Aural data becoming significant and demanding analysis.

Increase in the volume of sound: and the only sound of
any consequence was that of the helicopter.

I dropped into the water and floated towards the cave
mouth and saw the thing was perceptibly closer. Two of
the boats were also moving in, one of them heading
directly this way with its bow wave appropriate to half
speed: they weren't hurrying because they hadn't seen anything and if there was anyone on this group of islands they
could head him off and pin him down without any trouble.
It would finally depend on manpower and they had unlim-
ited resources.

I thought the best thing to do was to start getting some
information on the cave system of Heng-kang Chou and
with that bloody boat heading this way I thought I had

less than a couple of minutes to get clear of here. This cave didn't offer anything: it was a cul-de-sac.

Preliminary hyperventilation is dangerous if it's pushed too far and I spent only thirty seconds on it, emphasizing the exhalation and taking nine or ten pints into the lungs before I slid below the surface and followed the undersea cliff.

I couldn't see them.

This cave was no better than the other one. It had a shut end.

I couldn't see them but I could hear them.

They were checking the other cave: two men in a dinghy.

When they'd checked that one, they'd come and check this one.

I waited. There wasn't anything else I could do.

The launch was standing off a short distance. The men on board couldn't see into the cave: they were base and support for the men in the dinghy. There were now two helicopters over the island: I could see one of them banking sharply across the southernmost headland and sloping down from the sky, *chop-chop-chop-chop*, coming closer.

I sank under the surface and lay prone in the shallows of the cave because even when you know you've finally lost a wheel you go on trying till the very last second: it's in the nature of the beast.

It's always someone else.

Always.

Never you.

Someone like K.L.J., Berlin, a long-range rifle shot.

Or Thornton. Hit a mountain head on with a Petrov X-7.

Or North with his brains all over the bathroom.

You never think it's going, one fine day, to be you.

The bloody thing slammed past the cave mouth, *chop-chop-chop*, the echo slamming back.

I waited five seconds and pushed my face into the air and started breathing again. The bats were going frantic, swarming into the sunshine and back, perfectly understandable, imagine what they must have thought, picking up that bloody great superbat on their little radars.

It would have been a piece of cake to hyperventilate and go down to fifty feet and come up on the far side of the dinghy and go into the cave after they'd searched it, but they had divers down in the area and I could see their marker buoys on each side of the launch. They were being very thorough.

I suppose Ferris was hanging around one of the islands in Hong Kong waters, Lamma or the Soko group, and from that distance *Swordfish* would probably notice the aerial activity. Conceivably he'd put a signal out: *a lot of choppers up, looks like a search, could be we're blown.*

You never think it's going to be you: they're looking particularly shut-faced when you go through Clearance and you know it must be Mario because it's the only one running, or you find you can't reach Parkis and you know his operation must have come unstuck because he told you to be here and he doesn't miss an appointment unless the sky's caved in and this time it's poor old Talbot, or you see two of the escape-crew couriers going into Debriefing as white as a sheet and that's either Fitzroy or Crocker and you don't ask anyone which.

This time they'll know it was you.

The sun was striking into the cave mouth, sending light dappling the rocks. Now that the helicopter had reached the end of its loop a mile away it was quiet in this stretch of water and I could hear voices from the power launch. When I sighted along the surface I saw three of the crew standing in the stern and watching the cave where the dinghy was. The men in the dinghy were armed and carried something heavy and chromed: I'd just seen the shape of it and the flash of the sun when they'd gone in there and it had looked like a portable searchlight taken from the launch.

There weren't any ledges in this cave, in this one where I was trapped. There wasn't a hollow where I could have crouched or a loose rock I could have used as cover. There was nothing.

And nothing I could do when they came. The divers weren't just making a random search of the rock face below water: they were keeping precise station, on watch for anyone swimming out of a cave when the search party went in.

All I could do was wait.

What's wrong with Egerton today?
Who?
Egerton.
Oh, his mission got blown.
Christ. Who was he running?
Dunno. Quiller, I think.

You never think it could be you and then one day you find out you're bloody well wrong and when I heard the splash of their oars I pushed with my feet and floated out of the cave face down so that they could see it wasn't anything worth shooting at.

16

Fuse

"I've got it," I said, "Redhill Golf Club!"

"It could have been."

"You were a member there!"

"For a year or two."

"You used to play a lot with"—I snapped my fingers, trying to remember the name—"Harry Foster! Not Foster, no"—I snapped my fingers again—"*Chester!* That's it—*Chester!*"

"That's right," he said.

"Well I'm damned—it really *is* a small world, isn't it?" I looked around, lowering my voice. "You know I left there under a bit of a cloud, I suppose?"

"Did you?"

"Well, chucked out, practically. Pro's little wife, remember her? Wow!" I gave a rueful grin. "Can't help it, y'know—I've just got an eye for the girls."

He laughed quietly, his teeth very white in contrast to his brick-red face. He was one of those Englishmen who never tan: they just get redder and redder. He looked suddenly serious, the laugh dying abruptly as he peered at me through his thick-lensed glasses.

"You know why I left the club?" he asked.

"No?" I thought quickly and began laughing—"Oh God, not for the same—"

"No. I got behind with the fees."

"Is *that* all? Of course I always paid up right on the dot—the only trouble was the cheques always bounced!"

We laughed again.

"How are you feeling now?"

"Oh," I said, "not bad."

"You've had a rough time of it."

The girl put the needle in and we watched it.

"It was a shock, that's all. Upset me, I can tell you."

"I expect it did," he said. "What happened, exactly?"

She went on pressing the plunger. I hardly felt it.

"Well," I told him, trying to think back, "I must have drifted here, pretty well unconscious. Then I saw this chap coming for me with his knife, and—well I had to do something. Woke me right up, I can tell you. He was a real *bastard*, came at me—" I broke off and looked around at the young nurse and the man standing by the door and the other one sitting on a stool near the sterilizing unit. "Do these people understand English, old boy?"

"It doesn't matter," he said.

"Well I mean I wouldn't like to upset anybody, but quite frankly, after what that—that chap did to me down there I'm pretty annoyed. Wouldn't you be?"

"I certainly would."

Someone else came in, looking at my hand without touching it, saying something to the nurse in Chinese and then slipping a white gown on and taking some surgical gloves from a sterile packet.

"He's the doctor," Tewson told me.

"Good afternoon," I said cheerfully, but the man didn't seem to hear me. I hoped he was good at his job, that was all: my hand was looking like a not terribly well-done steak.

"Go on," said Tewson.

"What? Oh. Well I mean there it was. That Chink came at me with his knife out and it woke me right up, as you can imagine. I'm pretty strong, and I know a thing or two about looking after myself, and—well, I suppose I must have been in a flaming temper, or of course I wouldn't have been so rough with him." I looked down for a moment, a bit ashamed of myself. "Poor little sod. But I mean he shouldn't have—" I broke off and shrugged with my right shoulder. "Well it's done now, I suppose."

The nurse inclined the articulated couch an inch or two lower, so that I was in a half-reclining position. The man in the white gown was working on my hand but I couldn't see it because they'd put a little screen round it.

"I can't feel a thing, you know. They're pretty good, aren't they?"

"Yes."

I looked at him very straight. "Listen, old boy, are they very annoyed about that poor little bastard? I mean sod?"

"He was only doing what he thought was right."

"So was I." I gave an ironic laugh. "At least, it was right for me!"

He was watching what they were doing to my hand.

"How did you come to be drifting so near the rig?"

"God knows! It was just the current."

He nodded slowly, still watching the operation. "Did you fall off a boat, or something?"

"Not exactly. I was in a rubber dinghy, with an outboard, and I'd put the anchor down while I was diving, you see. Then when I tried to pull it up, it wouldn't budge. So I went down again to free it. Thing was stuck in a whole lot of weed, I was about waist-deep in the stuff. Well I cut the anchor clear, and then had to cut myself clear after that because the stuff was all round my legs, Then I must have lost consciousness, or as good as. I just remember feeling sort of drunk—you know how it feels, do you? D'you do any diving?"

"Not a lot."

"Kind of narcosis. I'd been down too long—always overdo things, that's me." I shut my eyes and didn't say any more.

"It doesn't hurt?"

I opened my eyes.

"M'm? No. Can't feel a thing, old boy. No, the fatigue's just catching up on me, I suppose. Bit whacked."

I shut my eyes again.

"I expect you are."

"Sorry."

"That's all right."

He didn't talk again for a while.

Situation totally zero in terms of a get-out and I didn't like the way they'd brought Tewson in to put the questions because the other two men in here were obviously bugs and understood English perfectly and it meant the intelligence cell knew how to think and I don't like people thinking. They hadn't had more than a few minutes to brief Tewson and I didn't like the way they'd done that either: he clearly wasn't intelligence but he probably wasn't a fool either and they'd just told him to talk about himself as much as he wanted to, if it would help him put me at my ease, and that meant they were perfectly confident that whatever he told me I wouldn't ever be able to pass on.

The thing that interested me most was his present state of mind. It was so like his wife's: he was lonely, and he was scared. But I didn't think they were scared of the Chinese: they'd got into something deeper than it had looked and they hadn't given themselves a chance to pull out while there was time. In spite of his briefing there'd been no *need* for him to admit he'd lived in Redhill or that he'd been asked to resign from the golf club because he hadn't paid his fees: I'd been aware of his strong compulsion to reminisce with a fellow countryman just for a couple of minutes, until he'd remembered the others were listening and that he was meant to interrogate me.

That was why they'd taken him on a lead to the Golden Sands at regular intervals for sexual recreation and wifely reassurance: they didn't want their missiles to get stuck in the tube because their design consultant was spiritually disorientated.

"All over," he said.

"What is?"

I opened my eyes.

"Your little operation."

Reaction hit the nerves but stopped short at involuntary muscular stimulation. He wasn't looking at me as he said it: he was unaware of any double meaning.

"It feels fine."

"They're very skilled."

The surgeon was peeling off the thin disposable gloves and dropping them into a sani-bin and leaving the nurse to do the final dressing. She looked at me once, not smiling, looking away again, just wanting to know that the capitalist-imperialist dupe was exhibiting the correct clinical reaction following anaesthetized surgical trauma.

They wanted to keep me in good health and this tied in with the Chinese attitude towards captive political or intelligence officers of foreign extraction: they relied more heavily on indoctrination, mind bending and intensive exploration of the psyche rather than induced physical pain. It also tied in with the way they'd pulled me out of the sea an hour ago: there'd been a sudden alarm raised and for a few minutes I'd been a floating target for half a dozen guns, but after they'd made sure I couldn't do anything they'd got me into the launch and given me the appropriate rescue attention while I rolled my eyes and moaned and so forth.

. The only sign of enmity had come from one of the divers when he'd surfaced and seen me lying in the stern: his stream of invective had gone on until one of the officers had cut him short. Possibly he was a close friend of the man I'd killed, perhaps even his brother.

The nurse activated the very expensive-looking surgical couch and tipped me upright.

"Thank you," I said to her. "Thank—you," nodding and smiling.

Drew a complete blank so I turned to Tewson.

"This come under the National Health?"

He laughed pleasantly, rocking back an inch on his heels. I thought he probably hadn't seen an Englishman to talk to for a long time: "National Health" was a very English institution and the phrase had struck another chord with him. I could believe that if I just said "Piccadilly" or "God save the Queen" he would have broken down and sobbed on my shoulder. Served him bloody well right: he should've thought of what he was doing before he sold out to the Reds in such a hurry. At least people like Philby had the decency to go on hating our guts after they'd made the break.

But of course he hadn't sold out to the Reds at all.

He'd sold out to Nora.

"When were you in England last?"

I was certain he hadn't meant to ask.

"Me? Oh, couple of months ago. Why?"

"I just wondered how things were over there."

I gave a short laugh. "Price of bangers is up again, and you can still get into the *News of the World* if you leave your flies undone on the Tube."

We laughed together, real old pals.

He'd sold out to Nora: the girl with a taste for *soixante-neuf* and Ming. He couldn't give her the one so he gave her the other. A man short on libido doesn't have to be insensitive about it and she wouldn't have spared him: it had gone on for years and he hadn't been able to do anything about it because he wasn't earning enough. Then the chance came and he'd sold two things in the same deal: the design of the missile launcher he was working on, and his conscience. And he'd bought back his pride.

"So I suppose you never saw your dinghy again?"

"My what? Oh—no. Drifted off into the wide blue yonder. Cost me a packet. On my income, anyway."

"Where were you diving?" he asked casually, and I felt sorry for him: he was a genuine boffin and all he'd got on his mind was a slide rule and they'd told him to interrogate me and make it sound natural and he just wasn't capable. He was a simple-minded genius and this wasn't his field at all.

"South China Sea," I told him with a shut face.

"Just doing a bit of scuba fishing, were you?"

"That's right." Then I put my right hand on his arm and lowered my voice. "Fact is, old boy, I can't tell you what I was doing because I've been sworn to secrecy. Be breaking my word to a friend, get it? Awfully sorry."

"That's all right."

He was obviously relieved: he'd put the question they'd told him to put and if I didn't want to answer it he couldn't make me.

The nurse was putting my left arm in a sling and I looked into her blank young face as roguishly as my cover demanded, trying to make her look up at me. No go. She pinned the sling to the white tunic I had on: when they'd brought me on board the rig they'd cut away the remains of the rubber suit and put me into this Mao outfit and together with the sling it made a first-class change of image if I'd had any use for one.

The Chinese near the door pulled it open and beckoned us outside. He looked like the one who'd escorted Tewson to the Golden Sands Hotel. He went out first and we followed and nobody said anything till we were going along the deck towards the living quarters and suddenly I knew I had to make a move and I didn't know precisely what kind of move and I had to think and I thought fast, strolling beside Tewson near the rails.

It didn't have to be a physical move. The last-ditch getout thing I'd set up wasn't for now: it was for the dark and for the time when I was driven to do something suicidal. The move I had to make now was psychological and I was beginning to see its shape.

Situation: I was free to walk on deck in the warm afternoon sunshine and chat with my fellow countryman but appearances were deceptive because this was an opposition stronghold and they'd got me and they were going to keep me unless I could stop them and I didn't think I could stop them. In metaphysical terms I was at the wide end of a narrowing tunnel that would take me through the imminent interrogation phase with their professional from the Hong Kong cell and through increasingly restrictive incarceration and withholding of privileges to the final elaborate mind-bending sessions with the intelligence psychiatrists in Peking that would leave me psychically emaciated and with irreversible personality changes that would kill off any hope of making an eventual break because I would no longer be the kind of human being who could plan such a thing *or even want it*.

Probably it was my last chance of using Tewson for my own purposes or even of seeing him again. They'd briefed him to question me before they put any kind of pressure on because you couldn't feel suspicious of a chap born under the same flag and all that, and I was expected to be relaxed and make a slip or decide to give him my confidence. I'd pushed this one as far as I could and the only thing that worried me was that he'd seemed to accept the fact that I'd met him sometimes at the golf club. The dossier on George Henry Tewson that Macklin had given me was exhaustive, even to the names of his acquaintances in Redhill, but I'd expected him to challenge me on this one: *what year were you there, then? I don't seem to remember you*, so forth. But in the first few minutes of talking to him I'd recognized a whopping case of homesickness and thrown him the golf-club thing: and I think he took it without question because he'd *wanted* to run into someone from his intimate past, all the way out here on this remote prison of his where he lived among strangers.

I think he'd accepted the whole of my cover story and the two Chinese had been listening attentively so that they could trip me on the second time round. They wouldn't be able to do that because I'd been speaking to their ears and not Tewson's and there wasn't anything they could trip me on, so they'd have to console themselves with the obvious ones: *what were you doing so far from land in a small rubber dinghy, why were you sworn to secrecy, who is your friend*, so forth. That was all right. Most of the cover

was pick-proof: the thing about cutting the anchor free
and then losing consciousness was to give me a base they'd
never find but couldn't prove was nonexistent. Because
they were going to check up on every word: I'd heard the
helicopter take off soon after they'd brought me aboard
and I was pretty certain they'd gone to pick up the interrogator in Hong Kong. So I didn't have long to make a
move.

I made it.

The Chinese was leading the way and the guard had followed us out of the clinic and I don't think I could have
said anything to Tewson quietly enough without their
catching some of it and even if they only caught a couple
of words they'd get the drift. But the riveter had started
up a few minutes before we'd left the clinic and it was still
hammering away on one of the lower decks, and the
sound cover was adequate.

It was a hundred to one against my getting off this missile base with a whole skin but I was going to try and if I
got clear then I was taking Tewson.

Tewson was the target for Mandarin.

He was the objective London wanted me to bring out:
Executive will withdraw objective from target zone. And if
I was going to pull off a hundred-to-one shot and get out
alive then I was going to take the objective with me because I wasn't interested in aborting the mission.

I didn't have much to lose.

Because you don't need a capsule, you know, when it
comes to the crunch. That's just the most convenient way.
You don't even need drain cleaner or exhaust gas or a
knife or a gun or a high window without bars or a rope:
you just need your nails and an artery *and their belief that
you want to stay alive.* That bit's important because if they
think you're going to try switching off they'll start
watching you and that's a bore.

I'd do it because I don't like tunnels: I'm claustrophobic. I wouldn't want to go through with the intensive interrogation phase and the increasingly restrictive incarceration and the final mind-bending sessions in Peking because
they'd break down the psyche to the point when I didn't
think the Bureau was important any more and then I'd
give them the lot. *And I wouldn't mind.*

But I minded now.

So I hadn't got much to lose if I tried to get the objective out of the target zone and failed, even if it killed me. A lot would depend on Tewson.

He was saying something but I couldn't hear.

"What?"

"Bloody noise!" he said with his quick white laugh. "They're doing repairs!"

"Just like the Strand," I said, "always got the road up!"

We laughed about this, nodding together.

The Chinese in front of us hadn't turned round so the chance was wide open and I went over the whole thing in the next two seconds to make sure I got it right.

I had to blow my cover.

But only to Tewson: not to the opposition. They'd told him, or they would later tell him, that I was an intelligence agent sent to Hong Kong to find him and take him back to London; and I'd have to say something to him that would cut right across their story. It must be something he couldn't repeat to the opposition *without endangering himself.* And it must carry the name of a sponsor to give it high credibility, but a sponsor he couldn't contact openly for confirmation. And finally it must be short, because at any next second the din of the riveter could stop and leave me without aural cover.

All I had to do was light a fuse. A short-burn fuse in his mind.

"Tewson." I waited till he'd turned his head, then pitched my voice against the background noise. "Nora says she's found out you're expendable. They're going to kill you the minute you've done this job, for their own security. She wants me to tell you to get out of this as soon as you can."

17

Cover

"When?"

"Last night."

"What time?"

"I've told you I can't remember what the time was!"

"You told me nothing!"

"Oh for Christ sake—"

"Who are your employers?"

"I'm not going to tell you!"

"Because you are lying!"

"If you say that again I'll—"

"Where are they now?"

"Who?"

"Your employers."

"They're—oh Jesus, are you off your fucking rocker? How many times have you asked me that one?"

He'd been at me for two hours without a break but he wasn't very good. Thin chap with a wide jaw and a short haircut, Mao tunic, some kind of insignia, worker's merit medal or something. He'd started sweating because of the heat of the lamp.

They'd given me the smallest cabin on the whole rig: one narrow bunk set in the wall like a niche at the crematorium where you put the urn, cheap cardtable and picnic chair, army mirror on a chain, tin washbasin, no loo. There was only one lamp and it was high on the wall and they'd put a two-hundred-watt bulb in it and he was getting as much of the glare as I was, but I suppose he thought he should do this thing like they did it in the flicks.

"What is the name of the yacht?"

"The *Isabella.* Look, wouldn't it be better if you played that thing back a few times?"

"Where is the yacht now?"

"That's the third time. What's the point of leaving that

thing running when all you can do is ask the same bloody questions like a record player?"

I'd begun looking at him sideways a bit in the last half hour: the cover demanded that I should react with increasing exasperation and finally begin to doubt his sanity. He hadn't tripped me on anything yet because he wasn't capable. This was the best interrogator they had in Hong Kong and he'd been immediately available as a member of the local cell so they'd flown him in right away in the helicopter and now he was doing his stuff but his stuff consisted of the repetition-to-attrition technique and not much else: the idea is that if you shout the same question at the subject fifty times he'll finally tell the truth. It's meant to work on the principle that every time they shout the question you feel a bit more guilty about lying, and in the end you hear your own subconscious throwing up the right answer.

It's not funny when it happens because you start thinking it's *your* sanity that's begun to slip. Then you're strictly on the skids and if they didn't find the capsule in the lining you'd better get it out and don't let them see you till you keel over. But I didn't think this man could do any good because he wasn't fully trained: he wasn't alternating with the correct mood changes that made you think he believed you and trusted you, so that the guilt mechanism produced more power the next time you lied.

"Where were you diving?"

"In the bloody sea." I wiped the sweat off my face and tried to slide back the small metal window again to make him think I'd forgotten they'd jammed it solid: the first thing an interrogator looks for is the onset of memory lapse and it'd make him feel good and when you start feeling good you've got one foot on the soap. You shouldn't feel *anything*. In first-category interrogation—no kicks, no shocks—you don't really *talk*. You question or you answer. Anything like conversation is discouraged because it decreases the tension.

"Where were you diving?" he asked me again.

His eyes were a bit pink-rimmed under the light and I wondered how long he could keep it up. Two hours is a long time.

"Listen, I'm going to tell you the whole thing again and you make sure you get it all down on that tape. Then if you ask me just one more question again I swear I'll throw you straight through that fucking door. Okay?"

I didn't expect an answer because that one's in the book. The interrogator has to keep up the theme of repetition, and anything else he says will ease the monotony and he doesn't want to do that.

"Right. My—"

"What is your name?"

He wanted it his way: if I told him "the whole thing again" the ball was going to stop in my court. It had to be question, answer, question, answer, wearing you down.

"Harry Cox."

"Why did you come to Hong Kong?"

"To do some diving."

"Why?"

"Some people gave me a job."

"What job?"

"Look for a wreck."

"What wreck?"

"Now don't start asking me that one again. I've told you, a boat went down with a private collection of gold coins on board, and my present employers—"

"Who are your employers?"

Question 9.

"I gave them my word I wouldn't reveal their names. Listen, you let a thing like this get around and you'll have the whole of the Hong Kong fishing fleet out here looking for that boat, it stands to reason."

"What is the boat's position?"

What depth, did it blow up, was there a collision, so forth. I gave him the answers again, there wasn't any problem. But now and then I told him he was a stupid clot and asked him if he'd gone off his rocker, routine cover approach but helpful to relieve the tension in me. He could throw me this stuff till he had to bring in a relief and it wouldn't worry me but it was what they were doing outside this cabin that was starting to give me the shakes because I was a bit farther inside the tunnel at this stage and going deeper and I didn't want to go on.

The man they were going to give me in Peking would be different from this one. For the first few days I'd respect his skill and admire his techniques and then he'd start getting close and I'd have to fight back till he blew

me and when he'd blown me he'd begin on the real stuff:
the Bureau.

He would be a top professional. A brain surgeon.

"Where is the yacht?"

"Which one?" Just a gag: this was the thirtieth time.

"The one that dropped you over the wreck."

"Somewhere in the South China Sea. They didn't say
where they were going. Now listen, I've given you the
whole thing again, as I said I would. Now if you ask me
one more question I'm going to smash you up and you'll
wish to Christ you'd never set eyes on me. Now do you
understand that?"

I put a lot of spleen into it but he went on staring into
my face with his pink-rimmed eyes while he thought out
the next question. His feet were still in the stance he'd
taken up when I'd talked about throwing him through the
door: he'd quietly slid them there and I hadn't looked
down but I didn't have to because he was a belt and it
would be the first defensive position. You can't interrogate
anyone alone in a small room unless you can stop him
when he comes at you: intensive questioning can drive a
man into a psychic trap and an explosion on the subconscious level can be murderous.

"You are lying," he said and slapped down my photograph.

Phase two.

He'd taken my cover story and gone over it exhaustively
and couldn't break it so now he was going to watch my
eyes while he threw facts at me. Facts like the photograph.

"Christ," I said, "if I thought I looked like that I'd go
and shoot myself!"

"This is your photograph. We know it is."

"Bloody insulting!"

It was the same one.

"One of our agents managed to swim clear," he said,
"from the car in the harbour."

Frown. Three-second pause. Then: "What the hell are
you—"

"He says this is your photograph."

Prolong mystification. "*Car* in the *harbour?* What on
earth," so forth, till he cut in again.

Your photograph.

Your photograph.

Your photograph.

Till I blew up and began shouting, I tell you you're making a stupid mistake, I demand to phone the governor of Hong Kong, you can't do this to a subject of the United Kingdom, storming up and down, could've been an actor if I didn't have a face like a hyena's arse.

Your photograph.

I let him go on.

Very hot in here now.

Damned if I'm going to ask him to open the door.

Photograph.

Told him to screw himself, then he pulled the towel off the thing on the bed and watched my eyes closely.

"Hell's that?"

"Your radio. We found it."

Feeble laugh. "Listen, if I had a radio like that I'd get a bomb for it in Kowloon! What is it—Hammerlund?" I looked at it, very keen radio man.

"This is your radio."

"Well I must say that's very generous of you."

I timed it at fifteen minutes: he gave it all he knew how.

Your radio.

Your radio.

Your radio.

Told him he was out of his cotton-pickin' mind, told him to belt up. Bloody light was in my eyes, starting to worry me. I still wasn't completely out of the narcosis thing and I hadn't slept since eight o'clock last night and it was now six-thirty and he was still pitching it at me.

"Where was your base? The Hong Kong Cathay?"

"I don't know what you're—"

"The Maruitius? You stayed at both those places."

"Will you bloody well listen to me a minute? I tell you—"

You're mistaken.

Where was your base.

He threw me the other places on my travel pattern, watching my eyes, trying to pick his way in, the Orient Club, the Golden Sands Hotel, telling me he knew I'd been there, telling me he knew so much about me that there wasn't any point in my denying his accusations.

"You were there when Flower died."

"What flower?"

"The man Flower. You were there when he died."

"What the hell's a man flower?"

I looked at him obliquely again, worried about his mental state.

"Flower was an agent. He was *your* agent."

"Oh Jesus wept, are you back on that agent thing?"

Flower.

Flower.

Hot and the light blinding.

Flower.

One stage I thought all right we'll have a go, he's in the first defensive position but that doesn't matter, I'll start with a full *yoharka*, give him no time.

Have to watch it. No emotions. Start emoting and you'll end up right in his hands because the gut-think'll get in the way of the brain-think. Steady.

Tired, that's all. Went down too deep, too long.

"You were there when he—"

"Go and shit."

"You were—"

"Shuddup."

"You went to Jade Imperial Mansion."

"Someone else. Bloke in the snap."

"Shall we tell Mr. Tewson about your woman friend?"

"Moira? What's she got to do with—"

"Not Moira. Nora."

"I haven't got a woman called Nora. She any good?"

"You went to Jade Imperial Mansion."

Six times in six minutes.

Poor old Tewson, wonder what he's thinking now. Bit of a shaker for him. But it was pick-proof, that was all I cared. Just her name alone had given it credibility and he couldn't phone her to ask about it because her line was bugged and they'd monitor his call this end and he'd know that. And he couldn't tell his Chinese fellow workers because they'd shove him in shackles in case he believed me and tried to dive overboard. There wasn't anything he could do except worry, while the fuse went on burning in his head.

"So you have been lying!"

"I have *not* been lying!"

"With every word you have lied!"

"I've told you the truth!"

Yelling at each other.

Heat of the lamp, his face coming and going.

"Lies! Lies! Lies!"

"I've told you the truth, sod you!"

Face and the lamp, swinging.

Look out, perk up.

Tired.

"I am sorry, Mr. Cox."

"What?"

"I am sorry." Smile on his face. "Of course I believe your story, but you must understand that we have to pay close attention if persons approach this oil drill. We have very expensive machinery here. I hope you will accept my apologies."

Movement of air as he passed me.

"Listen," I said. "Can I go out and take some air on deck?"

"But of course, Mr. Cox. It is a delightful evening."

I leaned on the rail.

Below me the sea was amethyst, its haze reaching to the ochre line of the horizon where the sun had gone down. All was still, except where a sea bird wheeled in silence overhead.

"What's this stuff?"

"It's a kind of millet gruel."

I thought it looked rather wet.

There was a dish of *man-t'ou.*

"What about this?" In public I was keeping the cover.

"Millet," he said, "corn, squash, potatoes. Not bad." The line shuffled along and we shuffled with it.

"Think they've got anything except millet?"

He gave his quick white laugh but it was just habit: his nerves were pretty bad. "There's some Peking duck along there."

"Thank Christ for that."

The canteen was very clean and everything shone under the bright lights. Music tinkled soothingly from the speakers. Someone dropped his tin plate and there was immediate silence and then the clatter started up again. I didn't notice any smell of actual food: I suppose they kept it down with Airwick or something hygienic like that.

I shovelled some duck on my plate for the sake of the protein and Tewson had some too. Then we went along the deck to his cabin, carrying our trays.

"Sorry there's no wine."

As we put our trays on each side of the table I noticed his hands were shaking. His brick-red colouring had yellowed since I saw him last.

"This is very welcome."

"Is it?" He seemed pathetically pleased. "It doesn't taste too bad. I expect I've got used to it."

"I mean the whole thing's welcome. The idea of being invited to dine on board with a fellow guest. If that's quite the word."

He looked down.

"They suggested it."

"Civil of them."

"I would have asked you myself, of course, if—"

"Of course—"

"I'm glad of a chance to talk to you."

He took a sip of water.

"Cheers."

"Cheers."

We began eating.

I didn't look at him except when he made the odd remark, and he found it difficult to meet my eyes. September was a beautiful month in Hong Kong, he said: the evenings were always like this, very calm.

I said I hadn't been in this part of the globe for some years.

He asked me how the food was.

"Very good."

He seemed pleased again and I couldn't think why. Some exaggerated sense of hostmanship? His eyes went down to his plate, and the light flashed across his thick-lensed glasses.

"They treat me well. Very well."

"I'm sure they do."

"Nothing to complain of."

"That's good."

He ate rather hungrily, but I imagined they wouldn't be rationed on board a first-line missile site. Possibly he was hoping to get to the flavour.

He put his knife and fork down.

"Did you come here to take me back?"

I had to think for a couple of seconds.

"That was the idea."

"What will they do with you now?" he asked me, and looked up.

"The same as they'll do with you."

He pushed his plate away and folded his arms on the table and leaned towards me.

"I don't believe it, you know. What you said."

"Don't you?"

I left it at that, wanting to know how much he'd need convincing. He stood it for five seconds or so.

"You can't prove anything."

He wouldn't need much convincing.

"Anyway," I said, "It's up to you."

He let that go because he had to: he knew we couldn't talk.

"How—how well do you know Nora?"

Check and recheck.

I wouldn't normally have to, but that bloody light had bored holes in my eyes and I was longing for sleep and couldn't think as fast as I should.

Situation: I'd blown my cover to him. They hadn't broken me down but that didn't mean anything: they knew they were going to, if they kept on long enough. So I could talk to *him* about anything I chose but *not* about my warning to him *now*. He might not realize this and I was ready in case he let a word slip so that I could try covering it.

It was academic anyway.

They'd got us both.

"I don't know her very well," I said. "Done a bit of shopping with her, you know—House of Shen, Constellation '144' and places like that. Few evenings together at the Orient and Gaddi's—she's fun, isn't she? Loves expensive things. Of course I didn't know she was married, or—well—"

"That's all right," he said with his head going down.

I don't often see people suffering—I don't mean self-pity, I mean suffering. Maybe I don't recognize it too easily, because in my opinion it's always their own bloody fault and that's why I don't seem to have too many friends.

But I recognized it now.

I suppose she'd gone and shoehorned him into this thing.

Be a pushover in a place like Hong Kong.

My husband works for the Ministry of Defence.

How interesting.

It's interesting for him all right, but the money's not much.

I'm sure the prestige is a compensation.

You can't have a fling on prestige.

Hong Kong is certainly a little expensive.

So's everywhere, I find! Excuse me, but are you sort of—I mean fully Chinese?

I was born here. That makes me a British subject.

Oh isn't that nice!

Pushover.

He was staying at this hotel too, and knew London quite well. She ought to look up his brother when she got back, he must give her the address. The Chinese Embassy—just a temporary post.

She'd found his brother charming, and discreet, and extraordinarily generous. Because of his love for the British.

Then Hong Kong again for their next vacation and this time a prearranged contact and a blazing row in their hotel, what did she think she was doing, she wasn't doing anything except wasting the best years of her life tied to a man who couldn't even do it more than once a month and couldn't give her any money so she could at least buy a few new dresses and try to look like a woman somebody loved, but this would be *treason*, oh don't be so bloody dramatic, the Chinks haven't got anything against us, it's India they're scared of now it's got the bomb, he told me, they're a poor country and this thing you're working on would cut their costs of defence down to a tenth, oh all right, we've talked quite a lot together, so what, and listen, will you, do you know how much they'd pay us for a few months' work, just as a tehnical adviser? Better get ready for it, George. A hundred thousand pounds.

He sat with his head down, toying with some kind of fruit mush in a waxed hygienic cup.

"I haven't had time to think," he said quietly.

He meant he hadn't had time to think about what I'd

told him out there on deck with the riveter hammering
away.

I haven't had time to think.

You'd have to give me longer than that.

How much longer?

I don't know. I'd have to think.

Egerton sitting there on the edge of the table by the
voice spectrograph, telling them to do the whole series
again and double check.

Tewson's voice.

I wondered where they'd bugged him. Somewhere in
Hong Kong.

They'd been getting serious about George Henry
Tewson, maybe a long time before they'd sent for me and
put me down the hole. They wouldn't be too worried
about the Chinese Republic setting up a cheap missile system: the U.K. was a small island at the wrong end of the
telescope and the first targets in any kind of pre-emptive
nuclear showdown would be the Soviet Union and India.
But Tewson didn't have to stop at China. He'd got goods
for sale and there were other potential buyers and some of
them were in Europe and he could go from door to door
at a hundred thousand a knock and she'd think he was the
most wonderful man in the world and that was what he
wanted, all he wanted.

He didn't want money. None of us do. We want what it
can buy.

He wanted his wife.

They didn't know about that in London or maybe they
did and maybe that was why they wanted him back there
to put away and lose the key. He was a bacillus at large: a
one-man do-it-yourself bubonic plague.

He hadn't spoken for five minutes.

"That was very nice," I said, and pushed my plate away
and got up and took my knife and prised the second wall-
plug cover off and dragged out the wires and pulled down
the portrait of Mao and neutralized that one too and got
the fire extinguisher off the wall and shot foam into the
ceiling ventilator grille that didn't have any dust accumu-
lated around the vanes and threw the extinguisher on the
bunk and said:

"Listen, they don't want anyone to know they've got
this thing because people are going to feel pressed into de-

veloping their own systems in retaliation, particularly India, and if you're let loose across the frontiers everybody *will* know. They'll even know if you're caught and sent back to London and shoved in clink, because of the trial proceedings."

He was watching me from his chair and the light wasn't across his thick-lensed glasses and I could see his eyes and I could see they were looking at something he'd known would happen to him one day. So he didn't look surprised and he didn't look afraid. He looked destroyed.

"There's only one way they can make sure you keep your mouth shut about the work you've done for them. They're going to do it for real this time, Tewson: they're going to take you to Tai Tam Bay and leave you long enough for the fish to pick you clean so they can show you've been there since your fishing accident and they're going to take a leg off to show it was a shark but they'll leave your head on so the dentist can prove it's you. And don't tell me I'm giving you a load of cobblers—work it out for yourself."

No one had come to the cabin yet.

Maybe no one would.

It depended on their thinking: they knew the three mikes were dead and they knew I'd done it and they knew why. But they also knew they could break this poor bastard open and play the whole thing back. They wanted to know what we were talking about and they couldn't do that if they came along here because we'd shut up. The only thing they could do by coming in here would be to show themselves up as a bunch of lemons, and there's this face thing they're all so fussy about.

"How much longer is this job going to take, Tewson?"

He stared at me through the lenses.

"What did you say?"

I'd dragged his thoughts back, God knew from what particular hell.

"This job you're doing for them. How long's it going to take?"

He tried to concentrate.

"About two weeks."

"All right. You've got two weeks to live. Thought I should tell you."

18

Objective

His silhouette came into the window again.

This was a different one: they'd changed the guard at midnight. His ears stuck out from a rather thin neck. I couldn't see his eyes. The window was narrow and I'd taken a lot of time measuring it to see if my body could pass through it. In the end I gave it up.

That was before he'd started again. Not this one, the one with the red-rimmed eyes.

Why did you destroy the listening devices?

I've told you.

Why did you destroy the listening devices?

Gave me three hours.

Three hours can be a long time. I could still see the lamp.

What did you say to him?

Leave me alone you bastard!

What did you say to him?

Screw yourself.

One hundred and eighty minutes and five repetitions every minute and the light making pools at the back of my empty skull, blazing its way right through the sockets. One hundred and eighty temptations to tell him.

The light was still in my eyes.

They were shut but it was still there.

I would like to sleep. I would like to sleep. I would like to see the light go out and hear the dark and feel the silhouette turning slowly, the tape running through the bright metal dishes, anything else but millet? Of course if I'd known you were married, she laughed and opened her legs and the blood was there in a long red smear down the road, a man flower, what is a man—

Watch it.

Mouth dry and the breath pumping, happened, what happened?

Bloody well wake up.

Window was blank, he wasn't at the window.

Check.

00:55.

Don't do again. It again. Tired that's all, haven't had any sleep since eight o'clock last night, last no, night before, yes, a long time.

I raised my head off the pillow and waited.

He came again.

Very regular. Every five minutes. Assumption was that he paced the width of the deck and took station at the rail and surveyed and paced back. The door was locked from the outside and he'd remain within earshot and I couldn't do anything with the door and if I tried the window it'd make a noise.

What did you say to him?

Oh Christ, don't you start.

Very well. In the morning you will be escorted to Peking.

Down the long narrowing tunnel.

The silhouette left the window and I got off the bunk again and picked up the twist of newspaper and lit the end and held it to the air extractor. The grille was getting sooty: this was the fourth time and there didn't seem to be much reaction. I shut my eyes, standing there with my arm raised. My eyes wouldn't stand the light of the flame.

The night was quiet. I listened but the night was quiet.

Don't you face it, hope in hell.

The heat of the flame on my fingers.

I blew it out but didn't take it away till the last of the smoke was drawn through the grille. There was another twist of paper ready because I'd found I could light two within the five-minute period when the guard was absent. I lit the second one and the light of the flame pushed into my skull through the eye sockets. I could smell the paintwork burning around the grille.

Oh Jesus Christ you're in a locked room and the guard's armed and there are four others out there, at least four others, you saw them last night and you'd get fifty yards in the sea if the drop didn't kill you, fifty yards before they started firing and you wouldn't even float because of all the lead so what are you doing here lighting bits of bloody paper, off your rocker or something?

Heat on my fingers.

Sleep.

Bells.

Quite loud bells, don't you go to sleep on your feet, I'm warning you. Bit of action to wake you up. Whole place full of bells, more noise out there than a fleet of fire engines. They must have smelt smoke somewhere.

I hadn't really expected it to work and it took a second or two to get the brain-think going again. The ball of newspaper was in the corner with the cheap cardtable over it, three-ply, go up a treat.

I lit the newspaper.

There were voices outside. A lot of shouting. Time I went.

It wasn't really a refinement. The thing had to be credible and if I'd just started a fire in here and banged on the door they'd see what I was doing, trying to get out. But if the alarm system went off they'd take it seriously. So I broke the window and shouted and went to the door and started hammering and the place filled up with smoke and the heat was on my back and I began wondering if he'd get here and open up before the fumes knocked me out. I didn't want to try the window till there was nothing else for it, because it was so bloody narrow that I might get stuck halfway and the whole thing would turn into a barbecue.

Eyes running and the fumes burning in my throat, table was crackling, some sparks flying off. I kept on hammering but I couldn't shout any more, couldn't breathe. Everything red behind me now and roaring.

Then the door fell down and I went on top of it and the flames came blowing in the air rush as he got me by the wrists and dragged me across the deck. Hands beating at my back, slapping my shoulders, got me there I suppose, the flames had got me there. Bells.

Bells and feet running and the clang of a fire bucket.

Shouting.

They dropped me against the bulkhead below the derrick and I let my head sag. One of them had got the hose from the nearest point and they were in business now and I watched them *but you haven't got time to watch them,* couldn't see too well because eyes streaming and every-thing blurred but *come on for Christ sake come on!*

They were forming a group, watching the blaze, some of them bringing another hose, and I crawled as far as the iron ladder and got on my feet and knew I couldn't do it and then did it, still there where I'd left it but sweet Jesus be careful, *be careful*.

Thing weighed a ton.

One of them was coming now and when he saw I was on my feet he pulled his gun and I brought my arms up high, lifting the thing above my head, ready to throw it.

He stopped.

And the man behind him stopped.

The man behind him was naked to the waist, just out of bed.

He was my interrogator.

"Tell the guard," I said, "to drop his gun."

He stood still, staring above my head.

The thing weighed a ton but only because I was so bloody tired. Normally it wouldn't take a lot of lifting, a lot of holding up.

"Tell him—" but my throat was too sore.

So I brought it forward suddenly and he made a shrill sound to the guard and repeated it and the guard dropped his gun. I raised my arms again to make it easier to hold there. The big deck lamp was behind me and I could see the shadow, enormous, with the horns sticking out from its sphere. They'd be gleaming quietly in the light above my head, copper-coloured, copper red. I couldn't see them.

The shouting had died away.

It sounded as if they'd got the fire under control: there wasn't much in there that'd burn. The walls and ceiling and floor were iron. This whole thing was iron. The deck here was iron, and the gun had made a dull ringing when it fell. Even if I couldn't make it, even if it got too heavy, even if my legs just crumpled and I fell forward, the thing would detonate on the iron deck.

He knew that. And he didn't want to die.

"Bring Colonel T'ang here," I told him. *"No!"* as he moved. "I want him *brought* here. Send someone. And be quick because I don't know how long I can hold this."

He didn't do anything right away so I let one leg buckle at the knee and the big round shadow moved on the deck,

the horns swinging. He spoke sharply to the guard and the
guard began running.

I'd asked Tewson who was in charge on the rig. T'ang,
he'd told me. I wanted to know about him. Army colonel,
honorary rank, actually a physicist, their top missile man,
big in Peking. He'd do. That was what had changed my
mind. I'd unscrewed this thing from the turnbuckle and
brought it up here last night in case I could use it for a
last-ditch get-out, chuck it at the fuel tanks and drop overboard while everyone was busy, swim to the island and
make the rendezvous. But Tewson might not have been
game, didn't look like a swimmer.

With a man like T'ang on the hook we could do it with
a bit more style provided I didn't drop this bloody mine
and someone didn't shoot me.

Back on fire. I could swear those bastards hadn't got the
flames out. They were just standing there gawping, stink of
wet charred bedclothes coming out of the cabin, water all
over the place. I could hear the rest of the crew coming on
deck, some of them asking what was going on, three fast
shots banging into the girders behind me and a shrill voice
but not in time to stop the fourth one and it bit into my
ribs and I staggered and the voice of the interrogator
shrilled out again and they started dropping their guns
where they stood.

Then he was staring above me again.

I think he was praying.

Been a shock and I brought the mine down, holding it
against my chest like a medicine ball, ready to throw, I
suppose some stupid prick had panicked, well this wasn't
the most stable situation, anything could happen.

"Listen," I said, *"get T'ang here!"*

Could feel the blood under my tunic, warm on the skin.
No particular pain and nothing coming into my mouth,
smashed a rib with any luck but oh Jesus Christ I was
tired, I was tired.

The colonel was a short man, very straight-backed,
epaulettes on his white tunic, pyjama pants, comic opera if
it hadn't been so bloody deadly. I said what I wanted him
to do.

He looked at me for a long time.

It was incredibly quiet. Thirty or forty men on deck in
a semicircle and the big lamp throwing shadows.

The bells had stopped and the hydrants were shut off and all I could hear was someone whispering and someone telling him to shut up.

Colonel T'ang stood in front of me.

He hadn't said anything yet.

My eyes were still watering and he looked blurred. I couldn't see what he was thinking and I didn't really care because I was going to tell him what to think and if he didn't like it I was going to lob this bloody lollipop right in his face, getting fed up with holding—

Come on, get a grip.

Drifting away again.

"Colonel." He was like a statue. "I'm ready to die for my beliefs. You have five seconds."

If I could stay on my feet another five seconds.

One.

He didn't move.

I'd spoken in English: he was an educated man and more likely to know English than Cantonese.

Two.

I thought my hand was bleeding. My left hand. Must take great care of it, little Chih-chi had said. Fat lot of chance.

The interrogator was standing next to the colonel, a step to the rear. He was watching the mine, fascinated. Conceivably he was thinking in terms of a flying leap, catch it before it hit the deck. I'd stop that lark.

Three.

Thing of course was that nobody could really do anything without this man getting killed, and if they let that happen Peking would have their balls off.

Four.

Possibly he was wondering if he could talk me out of it but I'd pre-empted that one: tell these people you're ready to die for your beliefs and they won't question it, terribly keen on ideology, there's a species of ant that fights fires, they throw themselves bodily onto the flames till the sheer weight of numbers puts them out, I suppose it takes all sorts.

Five.

He was still watching me and I got the thing above my head and lurched forward with it and an enormous hiss went up from the crowd of men and T'ang threw his hands out but I managed to keep my balance in time when he just said:

"No!"

After that it was okay.

I told him to go first down the iron ladders and I followed him and the seaman fell in behind. He was going to pilot the launch.

"Hello," I said when we got there. "Coming along?"

He was standing by the launch, his thick-lensed glasses catching the light. I'd told him to wait for us here at 01:10 hours if he was interested. I'd expected he would be: he didn't like the bit about Tai Tam Bay.

I began thinking she wasn't there.

The break-off rendezvous was for 01:29 hours, Hengkang Chou Island, rotating sectors beginning with the north coast. So she ought to be standing off by now and I'd been using the signalling lamp on our way in.

Mandarin. Mandarin. Mandarin.

No acknowledgement but I changed it to instructions.

Surface. Surface. Surface.

Felt rotten, all this trouble and they couldn't even get here in time to—

There she was.

The sea broke ahead of us in a long dark wave and the water streamed off her hull as she came up, black and shining under the moon.

Swordfish.

The launch slowed and I had to grip the rail as the weight of the mine started swinging me round. I'd got it in the crook of my left arm and Tewson made a move to steady it but I warned him off because I didn't know how sensitive these detonators were. He was watching me, obviously worried: I suppose I looked a bit far gone because the blood had soaked into the tunic below my ribs and my back was in a mess and my eyes wouldn't quite focus, kept blurring, use some sleep that was all, but he was waiting for me to keel over and blast the whole lot of us into Kingdom Come.

Colonel T'ang stood erect in the stern, hadn't looked at us once since we'd left the rig. Shocking loss of face and all that; well I couldn't help it, got my job to do.

We pulled alongside and started wallowing in the waves

the sub had put out when she'd surfaced, our fenders squawking against her plates as a seaman swung a boat hook across. Lot of people in the conning tower: Ferris and Ackroyd, couple of officers, all with drawn revolvers as if they were expecting some sort of trouble. I told Tewson to go aboard first.

"These two men are going back to the rig," I told Ackroyd.

"All right."

"Can someone take this thing for me? But go easy."

"Oh my oath," one of the officers said, and reached down.

"Christ sake don't drop it."

I could hardly lift it now, but we managed. Most of them looked as if they'd stopped breathing for a bit. Then they helped me aboard and I nearly fell over and someone had to put out a hand, bloody embarrassing. Braced myself against the rail.

"Ferris," I said, "this is Tewson."

The objective.